More books by Earl Emerson

Thomas Black series:
    The Rainy City
    Poverty Bay
    Nervous Laughter
    Fat Tuesday
    Deviant Behavior
    Yellow Dog Party
    The Portland Laugher
    The Vanishing Smile
    The Million-Dollar Tattoo
    Deception Pass
    Catfish Café
    Cape Disappointment
    Monica's Sister

Mac Fontana series:
    Black Hearts and Slow Dancing
    Help Wanted: Orphans Preferred
    Morons and Madmen
    Going Crazy in Public
    The Dead Horse Paint Company

Fire Department thrillers:
    Vertical Burn
    Into the Inferno
    Pyro
    The Smoke Room
    Firetrap
    Primal Threat

TWO MILES OF DARKNESS

TWO MILES OF DARKNESS

by

Earl Emerson

Two Miles of Darkness is a work of fiction. Names, characters, places, and incidents are the products of the author's imagination or are used fictitiously. Any resemblance to actual events, locales, or persons, living or dead, is entirely coincidental.

TWO MILES OF DARKNESS
Earl Emerson

Published by Lost Dog Press
Copyright © 2015 by Earl Emerson
All rights reserved under International and Pan-American Copyright Conventions.
ISBN-13: 978-1516949724

ISBN-10: 1516949722

Some people count and some don't.
-- Robbie/*Dirty Dancing*

Fill your bowl to the brim and it will spill. Keep sharpening your knife and it will blunt. Chase after money and security and your heart will never unclench. Care about people's approval and you will be their prisoner. Do your work, then step back. The only path to serenity.
-- Tao Te Ching

For a few moments after I open my eyes I believe I am inside a large black box, perhaps a coffin, but then I hear the road noise and the sound of a radio behind me. I am riding in an automobile, packed into the trunk like a sack of garbage.

From the front of the car I hear the crystalline voice of Emmylou Harris singing a plaintive tune, but the volume is turned so loud the sheet metal on the fenders and trunk lid trembles. I can make out only parts of a conversation between at least two yokels in the front of the car. They're yukking it up, talking trash, some of it about me.

I am woozy and trying hard to come fully awake, but it is a struggle and my brain is saturated with memories of murder. For the last few weeks each time I awaken I think about the recent deaths I've been a part of, even if only in a small way. I know Alex Kraft's last moments were protracted. I know she was shot in two different locations of her house before receiving the coup de grâce near the front window. What I am never going to know is what was said while it was happening, whether she was begging for her life or screaming in terror or just taking it. The haunting images course through my brain as I strain to wake up.

What wakes me fully is a steady ba-bump ba-bump ba-bump. At first I cannot figure out what the sound is because it comes at me like the rhythmic heaving of a large piston motor. Ba-bump. Ba-bump. After a few moments of struggling with it, I realize the sound is entirely in my head.

It is my heartbeat.

I am hogtied, my hands bound, legs knotted together with duct tape. I can barely move, and as I come more fully awake, I am uncomfortable almost to the point of delirium. Pain clouds the cognitive portions of my brain with the same hazy, scrambling interference one gets when standing alongside a roaring jet engine.

Until the pain subsides, I will be a slave to it. Rational thought is impossible. I feel the vibration of the roadway whirring beneath me as my head throbs in rhythm with my heartbeat.

I remain very still, trying to figure out what is going on. I need to regain full clarity so I can figure out how I arrived at this juncture and what this has to do with the demise of Alex Kraft, because if I know nothing else, I know my current plight is inextricably linked to her death.

Earl Emerson

In spite of my best efforts, I slide into a slow panic. I am as helpless as a mouse in a steel trap. Panic is my only option. I focus on the voices of the men talking in the passenger section of the car. They are now conducting a casual conversation about baseball and steroid use. For a moment it occurs to me to shout at them, but I come to my senses and remain mute. Certainly they know I am locked in their trunk. And of course they are good with it.

As I struggle with my bonds, I realize with a start that I am bumping up against another warm body, also bound and struggling. I go perfectly motionless, then whisper, "That you, Snake?"

"Thomas? You awake?"

"I guess."

"You were so still I thought maybe they killed you."

"What the hell is going on?"

"They conked you on the head pretty good. Sounded like an overripe melon splitting open. Near as I can tell, they're the last dance on our card."

"What does that mean?"

"It means they're taking us out into the boonies to do us."

My trunk-mate is Elmer "call me Snake" Slezak, my longtime associate and co-conspirator. The raw fear in his hoarse, growling voice burns through what little is left of my composure. Snake is normally impervious to fear. Like most blind panic, his is contagious, and I feel myself catching the infection so that I am more panicky than ever. If that is possible.

On a typical day my traveling companion wears cowboy boots, stove-pipe jeans, and a large world championship belt buckle, all of which makes him look like what he is: a late-middle-aged, weather-beaten former bull riding champion. These days he concentrates his attentions on booze, hair-trigger pistols, and easy women. Generally in reverse order. We are an unlikely duo and we both know it.

"I'm sorry, Thomas."

"For what?"

"For getting us into this fix."

"How'd we get here?"

"I guess they got fed up with us poking into their business."

"Their business was murder."

"Right."

You'd think if you were sealed in the trunk of an automobile it

Two Miles of Darkness

would be dark as midnight, but the taillights are glowing orange and yellow and it's brighter than a Hawaiian Christmas.

1

Six weeks earlier.

As the Krafts collapsed into mismatched chairs on the opposite side of my desk, I realized I'd never seen two people more profoundly depressed. Seattle was in the midst of the balmiest summer in memory, but these two sad sacks looked as if it were the dead of winter and they'd just been informed Aunt Milly was moving in with eighteen cats.

My office was in the six-story Mutual Life Building at First and Yesler in Pioneer Square. The abbreviated park across the street included a totem pole and a pergola and today was filled with summer tourists snapping pictures. Fast-talking entrepreneurs conducted underground guided tours that zigzagged through our area, bringing the curious through what was left of old Seattle before the fire of 1889 ushered in an all-new city built atop the ruins. Several times a day the tour groups meandered past our late Victorian sandstone building in rapt but awkward and meandering clusters. I liked wading through the sightseers when I entered or exited the building. It gave me the feeling we were in the hub of something significant.

Upstairs in the Mutual Life Building, I subleased a small part of a larger office occupied by my wife, Kathy, who helmed a one-woman law firm.

Sitting across from my desk now, Alex Kraft was all angles and litheness. Her husband, Mick, was stockier and had the muscular look of an athlete who might start going to seed sometime soon. They were both under thirty. Alex appeared to be of Mediterranean extraction, with olive skin and long black hair, fit-looking and pretty in a delicate way. She was well dressed and spoke with confidence, one of those people you liked on sight. Her husband had the sandy-blond hair of a former redhead, along with bags under his eyes and a pugnacious way of moving that didn't mesh with his gloom. It was as if he couldn't decide whether he was depressed or angry.

Alex said, "We were referred to you by Charlene McIntyre. We told her we were looking for a private investigator."

"Charlene . . . ?"

"She works for Doda Woods. She said you would remember them both."

It took a moment for the gears to engage, and when they did I realized I hadn't heard from Charlene since I was a kid. She had to be in her sixties by now, maybe her seventies. I was surprised she even remembered me. "Charlene. Yes. What can I do for you?"

"We've had some things happen . . ."

"We're losing everything," Mick interjected. "We've lost our jobs. We're going to lose the house. Our bank accounts are drained. The worst part is somebody's doing this to us."

Alex waited for Mick to continue, but when he did not she filled the silence compulsively. "We've borrowed everything we can borrow. Our friends and relatives are tapped out. Our savings account is down to nine dollars. Every time we try something new it seems like there's a wall slammed up in front of us."

"There are a lot of people in the same boat."

"Yes," said Mick. "But we were singled out."

"Everybody feels singled out," I said. "The banks. Wall Street. They're doing it to everybody."

"No. You don't understand. We've been targeted specifically."

"I don't understand what you're getting at."

"Somebody's choreographing our bad luck," said Mick Kraft. "There are too many things that couldn't have happened by accident. No way they were accidental.

Somebody's following us."

"Somebody caused you to lose your jobs?"

"Yes."

"Why would anyone do that?"

"We have no idea."

"Okay. Who, then?"

"No idea."

They didn't look like nut cases, neither one of them, but a lot of my most crack-brained clients did not. "Tell me exactly what you think is going on. Some specifics."

"There were accidents where Mick works," said Alex, as if bringing up a particularly distasteful subject. "That's how he lost his job."

"And these accidents weren't your fault?" I asked.

"Of course not," Mick said. "People were following me and running into me."

"Precipitating the accidents?"

"Yes, of course. I know people follow us. I'm sure we were followed here. That's why we need you to look into it. It's all coordinated."

"Have you seen anyone? Can you give me a license plate of a car that might have been following you?"

Mick didn't reply but instead stared sullenly at the edge of my battered desk like a boy in the principal's office who'd just been asked why he did whatever he did to get himself there, a question for which, of course, boys never have a good answer. When I glanced at her, Alex shook her head. They had no tangible evidence, only suspicions and a general distrust of the bad luck and inopportune events that had swallowed their lives.

"It would take more than somebody following you to cause the loss of both your jobs," I said.

"Obviously," said Mick, slumping in his chair. "That's why we need you to investigate."

I turned to Alex and said, not unkindly I hoped, "Since the downturn in the economy, a lot of people have found themselves in positions they never anticipated."

It was clear she didn't want to contradict her husband, but after looking at him she said, "We know times are tough, but this is different."

I got the rest of their story from Alex. She'd been an architect with a Seattle firm. Mick had worked as a driver for UPS. Since they lost their jobs, neither had been able to find work. In Mick's case, he landed a second job but quickly lost it under what the couple termed suspicious circumstances, and now the bank was threatening to initiate foreclosure paperwork on their home. Like a lot of Americans with a house, a big-screen TV, and two new vehicles in the driveway, they had been struggling along hand-to-mouth, with only enough savings to tide them over for a few weeks. It never occurred to them they could both lose their jobs at the same time. Several successive months with zero income had ruined them.

Dunning letters and phone calls arrived daily. Alex owed enormous amounts on student loans. They were backlogged on utility bills. To make matters worse, using money borrowed on their house while they still had the ability to borrow, Mick got swamped in a complex business deal that just might have rescued them with room to spare but went sour instead, sucking away the last of their resources and all of their hope.

They'd been living the American dream; now they were part of the slow-motion financial train wreck engulfing too many Americans.

I mulled it over. I believed Mick was personalizing what seemed to be a nationwide phenomenon. Neither of them could name any enemies who might have reason to ruin them, but they seemed earnest enough and were both nervous and frightened, as if their situation were maybe the scariest thing that had ever happened to them. Perhaps if I could tamp their delusions down to the possible and reasonable, they might be able to handle the rest of their troubles with a degree of clarity.

"Tell you what. I'll do some checking. I don't find something right away, I won't bill you."

"And if you do?" Mick asked.

"How about we cross that bridge when we come to it?"

After they left, I put on my baseball cap with the built-in ponytail, huge sunglasses, and a purple and gold Huskies windbreaker. I followed them out of the building to their parked car and then all the way to West Seattle, where they ran errands before going home. Nobody else was tailing them, and they didn't spot me in Kathy's nondescript Prius. Nobody was watching their house either.

I spent the afternoon on the phone talking to people about the Krafts and the next morning visited their house in West Seattle. I wanted a look at their property before giving them a verdict. It was ten-thirty on a weekday morning and they were both home. Mick and I were alone in his back yard when I confronted him. His wife was in the house watching us out the window while she scrubbed the kitchen counters, which, as far as I could ascertain, were already immaculate. I could see she knew from my body language I wasn't there to hand out blue ribbons and good cheer. Mick didn't have a clue. I had a feeling bad news customarily hit him without any warning.

After he offered me coffee and I declined, I said, "One of your employers tells me you failed a drug test."

We were in front of a massive old apple tree in the back yard. "Please don't tell Alex."

"She doesn't know?"

"I was afraid to tell her."

"But you did fail a drug test after one of your accidents?"

"A few years back, I wrestled with a little problem. It didn't last long, but when it happened, Alex almost left me. I can't let her know I failed a urine test. I lied to her before, and she would think I was lying again. But I swear to God I wasn't using." He wasn't kidding about not wanting me to tell Alex. Even though the morning was mild, he was suddenly sweating bullets.

"The tests have been known to produce false positives. Did you challenge it?"

"I was going to, but something came up."

"What was that?"

"It's too complicated to go into."

"Your employer said drug-use fit a pattern of accidents

you were having."

"I can tell you're blaming me for this just like they did, but I swear I didn't have anything in my system."

"Okay. But there's more. I don't think anybody is following you."

"How can you know that?"

"I followed you home yesterday."

"You did?"

"There wasn't anybody else around."

"But why . . . ?"

"I was trying to get a feel for whether you had a shadow. Or whether you would know if you had one. You didn't see me, did you?"

"No."

"You went to the Safeway at The Junction. Then you stopped at the library on Thirty-fifth. Alex checked out some gardening magazines. You browsed the mysteries and the car repair manuals but didn't check out a book."

"And you didn't see anybody else following us?"

"There wasn't anybody."

"Maybe they spotted you and went away."

"There wasn't anybody."

After a long silence, Mick looked at me with a level of hurt in his hazel eyes I hadn't anticipated. "You must think I'm some sort of paranoid nut job."

"When bad things happen, it's only natural to scratch around for an explanation. I don't think anybody's watching you. And I'm not sure how you both lost your jobs, but an awful lot of other families are in the same boat."

"So that's it?"

"Spending any more time on this would be a waste of your money. Take my advice. Accept what's happened and move on with your life."

Mick pretended to take in what I'd said as casually as if I were giving him an estimate for a new kitchen floor. I could tell my report had wounded him, although he was trying his best not to show it. "How much do we owe you?"

"Just take care of yourself."

"Thank you, Mr. Black. And please don't say anything

to Alex about the drug test?"

"Of course not."

I looked around the yard. A year or two from now, some other family would be living in this house. Or it would be vacant. I couldn't help thinking the new family would have no idea of the heartache these two went through in losing it.

Before I left, I glanced at the tree dominating their back yard. I wanted to ask what kind of apples it produced, whether they were sweet apples or pie apples. Kathy and I had a crab apple tree in our yard, but the only thing the fruit was good for was crab apple wars every autumn with my nephews, who were both Little League pitchers, compelling me to wear two pairs of pants, two coats, and protective headgear just to survive our skirmishes.

Not wanting to face Alex again or to be put in the position of having to deliver bad news twice, I circled around the house instead of going back through the interior, but my elusive behavior didn't work. Alex caught me at my car. The June sun glistened on her hair, and her dark eyes were jeweled with longing for an answer I wasn't going to give her. "I take it you're not going to help us?"

"I did all I could. You need to talk to your husband."

"He's just so down about everything."

"I'm sorry for your predicament, but there's nothing I can do."

"What if you're wrong?"

"What if I'm not?" Two questions, but neither one of us had an answer. I wanted to tell her their lives were going to turn around, that things always turned around, but she didn't want to hear clichés from me, stale or otherwise.

2

A couple of weeks later, Kathy came home late from the office carrying a container of salad she'd picked up at the market. I'd left her dinner warming in the oven.

Having taken the afternoon off to squeeze in a sixty-mile bike ride with friends, I'd showered, and then cooked and eaten dinner before falling asleep on the couch in the living room in front of *Dirty Dancing*. From the top of the couch, Kathy leaned over me, our heads upside down from each other, and kissed me, her long, dark hair cloaking our faces. "Hello, my name is Kathy. I'm your wife. Remember me?"

"Vaguely."

"Need another reminder?"

"That might help."

She kissed me again. "Does that do it?"

"Reminders are good. Keep going."

"You might get more reminders later, but only if you're very, very good."

"I'm always very, very good."

"Except when you're not."

"Well, there is that," I said, rolling off the couch to follow her into the kitchen. "The lasagne's in the oven."

"You're never going to admit that's a bad movie, are you?"

"Of course I'm not going to admit it's a bad movie. Because it's not. As far as dance movies go, it's second only to *Top Hat* with Fred and Ginger. Did you know Val Kilmer turned down the Patrick Swayze part?"

"Batman dancing in the Catskills with teenage girls? Every time I catch you home by yourself you're watching a chick flick. My question is: Do you cry when you watch them?"

"Never."

"Come on. Never?"

"Well. Almost never. That last dance sequence where her parents realize how grown up she is usually gets to me."

"You going to keep watching it over and over all summer?"

"Gimme a break here. I watch a few minutes and then I fall asleep. Then the next time I have to go back and review the parts I missed."

"But you've seen it a hundred times. By now you must have the whole thing memorized."

"All I can say is, if Jennifer Grey hadn't had the nose job she'd be a big star now."

We were bumbling around the kitchen together, dishing up lasagne and salad for Kathy's dinner. Although I'd already eaten, had been starving after my bike ride, I spooned some salad onto a small plate for myself while she sat down.

"Have a productive day?" I asked. Although we worked out of the same office, Kathy had been at the courthouse all morning and I'd been gone since noon.

"The new DPA we drew is a little difficult to work with. She might even force this one into court."

"Sorry to hear that."

I could tell something was troubling her and had been since she walked through the door, but I didn't push her. After we'd been eating quietly for a while, she said, "Didn't you meet a couple named Kraft a few weeks ago?"

"I did."

"Alex and Mick?"

"Yeah. Why?"

"They're dead. Along with her mother."

"Dead? What happened?"

"First reports say it was a shooting."

I abandoned my salad and went to the computer in the living room, checking the most obvious local news sources. The reports were brief and in fact remained brief throughout the life of the story. Three people were dead:

Alex and Mick Kraft and her mother, Talia Celik. All of them gunned down in the Kraft home. As I stared at the computer screen, I tried to remember every nuance of my interaction with the couple. In the weeks since speaking with them, I'd often wished I could have done more for them, but at the time I had believed there was nothing I could do to help them pull their lives out of the doldrums. Now I wondered if I couldn't have done something, anything, maybe even somehow prevented this.

"You okay, Thomas?"

"It's a shock, that's all. Do they know who did it?"

"Not yet."

"I kind of thought they'd be living with relatives for a while, then they'd get jobs that didn't pay as well as the ones they lost, service jobs. That's what other people are doing. I figured they'd plug along and make do. But this?"

"I'm sorry. Did you see anything like this coming when you met them?"

"The only odd thing was that they were referred to me by Charlene McIntyre, who used to work for Doda Woods, neither one of whom I've seen in twenty years."

"*The* Doda Woods?"

"I told you I knew her when I was a kid. Of course, Charlene's probably long retired by now."

"Doesn't it seem weird that you spoke to the Krafts just two weeks ago?"

"It just seems so sad."

3

My next involvement with the Kraft story came in an unlikely manner four weeks later in August, and oddly enough, it involved my father, who'd arranged a business meeting between me and a longtime family friend.

Helen "Doda" Woods was probably the wealthiest centenarian in the state and was still living in the Medina mansion on Lake Washington where she'd sponsored more than one fund-raising dinner with a per-plate price tag that would have paid off the mortgage on my house. Over twenty years had passed since I'd visited her there, and while her house remained colossal, it also looked slightly smaller to my adult eyes.

"This place is almost as ritzy as mine," joked my partner, Elmer Slezak.

"Opulent I think is the word you're looking for."

"I know, but I like ritzy."

At the grand piano, which if I remembered correctly was once played by Artur Schnabel, I stopped to view my reflection in the burnished lid, and as always, saw myself making faces. Kathy said I couldn't help myself when I did stuff like that, but I knew I could; I just didn't want to. Beside me, Snake smoothed down his sideburns and whispered, "Pretty boy" to his own reflection, even though he was anything but, looking as if he'd just come off a ten-day drunk on a tramp steamer.

Known to one and all as Doda, Helen Woods came from old money, the bulk of it piled up over a century ago by her grandfather, who'd been in railroads, and then by her father, in oil and munitions, and later, newspapers and magazines. During my childhood, my father, who sometimes worked as a local handyman, was called to install a screen door on her gazebo. Thanks to his gift for gab, a cagey ability to con just about anybody, and Doda's genuine concern for anyone working on her estate, he became personally acquainted with her. It probably helped that my father sincerely believed he rightfully belonged to the upper class, even though there was no material evidence or family history to buttress such a notion.

My father kept about him a certain manner of phrasing that the ingenuous often confused with the ingenious. Taken in by his line of patter, Doda had hired him again and again for minor construction jobs around her estate, and over the years our family managed to carve out a small niche in a cobwebbed corner of her social repertoire.

Doubtless, anyone familiar with the relationship thought Doda had taken on our family as a "project" and that my father was an opportunistic fortune hunter. The last part may have been true, but I always believed Doda's friendship was genuine. Helping to seal the bond was a religious affiliation Doda shared with my mother, who was a strong adherent of the now rapidly vanishing religion known as Christian Science.

The last time I'd seen Doda, I was thirteen. She had been in her eighties then and was now, according to my father, a hundred and four. I could barely imagine what she'd lived through or what she thought of the vast societal and scientific changes she'd witnessed.

Doda's longtime factotum, Charlene McIntyre, was no spring chicken herself, and now led us through the multi-winged house past a ballroom and up a wide, sweeping staircase to the luxurious second floor. I wanted to ask her about having referred the Krafts to me earlier in the summer, but something in her brusque manner made me hold back.

The interior of the house was as quiet as a library on Sunday morning, and as far as I could tell, little had changed in the twenty years since my last social call. Through open windows at the rear of the house, we heard cheery voices, speedboats on Lake Washington, a jet scratching the blue sky overhead, black-capped chickadees twittering in the wisteria.

Charlene had been working for Doda since I was a youngster, functioning as an assistant, personal maid, business advisor, nurse, enema giver, diarist, and general all-around sycophant. As a kid, I overheard my father tell somebody she was only sticking it out until the old woman died to see how much she would get out of the will. There was probably considerable projection in this harsh judgment, since that was what he would have done.

I guessed Charlene was now in her mid to late sixties, her figure thickened, a stylish scarf twisted around her neck to conceal the contours of what I, as a child, would have called a turkey gobble. In the old days I had been terrified of Charlene's whip-sharp, lion-tamer manner, but now it seemed almost amusing.

Doda, on the other hand, had always been like a fairy godmother to me.

"Thomas!" barked Doda from behind the same immense mahogany desk she'd been seated at the last time I saw her twenty years earlier. I could see she was still "in Science" because on one side of the desk were laid out her Christian Science study materials: a *Bible, Science and Health*, and a quarterly, along with the blue chalk she used to mark the books anew for each week's study lesson. "It's so wonderful to see you. Absolutely delightful. I should never have let so much time go by."

"Time has a way of doing that," I said. "It's wonderful to see you, too." I noticed she didn't move from her chair, so I went around and kissed her cold cheek and then held her bony hands for a few moments. Her fingers felt like a small bundle of chilled sticks. Her voice was creakier than I remembered.

"My goodness. You're all grown up."

"So are you, Doda. All grown up." She laughed a gentle laugh, but my joke was lame, as were most of my jokes. Her head looked small even for her tiny body, almost as if shrunken by aborigines. I hadn't heard anything about her in years and was in awe that she was still here. Despite everything, she seemed almost robust and certainly alert.

"Who is the gentleman with you?"

"Doda, this is Elmer Slezak. We sometimes work together." Because he was still hung over from his adventures the night before with a woman he'd met in a south side tavern, by rights I should have left Snake in the car, but I figured he would get a kick out of Doda, and I knew she would get a kick out of him. She'd always had a fondness for characters.

She was still the same spry little woman with the same rheumy blue eyes and endearing sense of humor. It was clear from the photos on the walls downstairs that she'd been a lissome beauty in her youth. She'd had more than her share of suitors and husbands over the last century: five husbands, if I remembered correctly, all of whom she'd outlived.

After she sized up Snake, she turned her gaze on me. "You've turned into a handsome young man. Your father tells me you're a private eye."

"Licensed private investigator. Elmer's one, too."

She glanced at Elmer, who said, "Call me Snake, ma'am. Sorry if I'm a little under the weather today."

"Snake? I like that." Winking at Snake, then turning back to me, Doda said, "Your father claims you're a fair hand at this gumshoe business."

"I've been told so."

"Good. Because I've got a job for you. I've had some other people working on it, but they've proved incompetent."

"What is the job?"

"I want you to find a dog."

I should have known. Despite what he'd told Doda, my father made it clear to me, every time he had the opportunity, that he thought my profession was a farce and a general waste of time, but this took the cake. It also threw me into a high dudgeon. It was nice to see Doda again—there was a time when she'd meant a lot to me—but asking me to retrieve a lost dog was like asking Rembrandt to paint a garage. Not that I was claiming to be in the same ball park with Rembrandt.

"The dog was mine at one time, but we were forced to

give her to Charlene's former tenants, and now they've managed to misplace her."

"I'm sorry Doda, but finding stray animals is not something I do."

"I'll pay whatever you think is fair."

"Money isn't the point."

"Nonsense, Tommy. Money is *always* the point."

When I didn't respond, Doda turned to Snake and asked about the World Rodeo Championship belt buckle he was wearing, as if changing the subject for a few moments might induce me to change my mind. Perhaps it would. I'd answered instinctively and without thinking about what I owed her or how much this meant to her. While they chatted, I edged over to the window.

Climatologists said the Northwest offered the best late-summer weather in the nation, and so far August was living up to it. While other parts of the country baked and suffered droughts, Seattle was basking in clear, sunny weather, mild shirt-sleeve temperatures and light breezes, the plant life still verdant from June rains.

From Doda's office window overlooking the backyard, I observed a large rectangular swimming pool, the choppy surface glistening. It was a different pool from the old-fashioned kidney-shaped one she'd had when I was a kid. Beyond the terrace, an immaculate lawn sloped toward the eastern shore of Lake Washington, where the property had a private moorage and up against which was docked a cabin cruiser bigger than my house.

Five young bikini-clad women lounged around the pool, as two men in baggy swimming shorts splashed in the water and three more hurled lawn darts at each others' feet. As I watched, one of the men with the darts walked to the pool, doffed his shirt, and made a production of leaping in feet-first. He didn't surface for well over a minute. I quickly realized the others were timing him. He finally broke the surface and clung to the lip of the pool with brawny arms, while another man jumped in and remained under long enough for the water to grow calm.

After the second man bobbed up into the August

warmth, he swam to the side of the pool, climbed out, and collected a fistful of cash from the first. As he turned toward the house, I recognized him, even though it had been over twenty years since we'd seen each other.

I waited for Doda and Snake to run out of conversational grist and said, "Is that Joshua down there?"

"Why, yes, it is. He's staying with me until the remodel on his house is finished. You don't know how good it feels to have some life pumped back into this old hovel."

"What's he doing these days?"

"Oh, I don't keep up with everything Binky does, but I know he took over his father's oil holdings. He's quite the business mastermind. Binky's been retired for some time now."

"So people still call him Binky?"

"Everybody does. Why don't you go down and see him on your way out? Charlene will escort you to her office first. She can get you started with a contract. And Tommy? The dog means a lot to me, and I'm sure the money will help you out at this point in your life."

I'd already decided to look for the dog as a favor to her, but her last comment took me by surprise. I didn't have to think too hard to figure out who told her I needed money. It wasn't the first time my father had belittled me to mutual friends and acquaintances.

"By the way, Thomas?" Doda said as we reached the doorway. "Are you still riding that wheel?"

As a kid, I'd been enthralled with the world of bicycle racing, and Doda had always referred to my road bike as a wheel. It was a term from around the start of the last century. "Yes, I am."

"You were always crazy for the wheel."

"I guess I was, wasn't I?"

"And your father tells me you're married."

"Her name is Kathy. She practices law in Seattle."

"I'll have to invite the two of you over for supper, give my chef something to do. That would be nice for me, too. These days I find myself drinking more Ensure and eating less crème brûlée."

"We'd like that."

"You're not going to like Ensure at all," Snake muttered on the way down the wide staircase. "I had a friend was on the stuff. I drank it with her twice a day until she stopped putting out."

"Well, I doubt Doda's chef is going to serve Ensure, and I'm surprised you would forego your porterhouse steaks, even for sex."

"When you're married a little longer, you'll understand."

"I sure as hell hope not."

4

"She's a hundred four," I said defensively, even though Snake hadn't protested. "She's an old family friend. And you don't have to help."

"Oh, I want to help. Goldarn it, I need the hours. Plus there's going to be some money in it. I bet these people use hundred-dollar bills for toilet paper."

"Don't count on a bonus. She's pretty tight with a penny."

Out of earshot, Charlene had been leading us through the house on a long leash and now showed us into her office at the rear of the mansion. I couldn't see the kitchen, but I could smell a luscious broth simmering nearby. She said, "I'll show you the flyer the first people distributed. We've been thinking about upping the reward. It was originally five hundred, but we might make it five thousand. What do you think?"

"Doda really wants this dog back, doesn't she?"

"The first people we hired to search were a disappointment. It's been almost three weeks, and we're afraid we'll never see Pickles again."

"Who did you hire originally?"

"The Auckland Group." Snake and I exchanged looks. Neither of us recognized the name, which was odd because the community of investigators in the Northwest was small enough we should have heard of them.

"How long did you say they worked on it?"

"The entire three weeks from the time of the murders."

"Whoa," Snake said. "What's this about murders?"

"Surely you read about Mick and Alex Kraft." Charlene said.

"What do Mick and Alex Kraft have to do with this

dog?" I asked.

"Why, they adopted Pickles after Doda developed her allergy. They're the ones who lost the dog."

"But they're dead," I said. Since their deaths, the Seattle police had come out with a statement saying it had been a murder-suicide. Mick Kraft had shot and killed his wife, his mother-in-law, and then himself.

"And the dog hasn't been seen since the day it happened."

I remembered seeing a dog at the Kraft house, a dachshund mix sleeping on the sofa as Alex ushered me through their house to the back yard, where Mick had been waiting.

"How did you and Doda know the Krafts?" I asked.

"At one time, years ago, they were my renters over in Magnolia. When Doda was ailing with her broken hip, we got her Pickles. But it didn't work out, so six months ago we adopted her out to Alex and Mick."

"Who you knew because they had been your renters?"

"Right."

"Who you referred to me six weeks ago?"

"Why, yes. I'd forgotten all about that. Mick mentioned he needed somebody in your line of work, and your father had been bragging you up. I'm sure you know how proud of you he is. So, naturally, I sent them to you. Did you ever meet them?"

"Briefly."

"And now they're dead?" said Snake.

"It was bad," I said, glumly. Their request for my help and subsequent deaths were the black cloud over my summer. I couldn't help thinking if I'd been friendlier, if I'd been more help to them, if . . .

Pickles was a dachshund mix, with floppy ears that probably dragged on the ground from time to time and big brown eyes, just the sort of critter people might adore on first sight and adopt off the street if she wandered into their yard, which made me wonder if she hadn't already found a home. "How did she come up missing?" I asked.

"We have no idea. The day after the murders, I sent a

maid over for her but she was gone. The police couldn't tell us anything."

"Maybe one of their friends is keeping her," I said. "Or a neighbor."

"The first people we hired would have found her if that were the case. I don't know why we ever gave the dog to Mick and Alex."

"He probably wasn't shooting his wife the day you gave them the dog," I said, despite myself.

My incipient sarcasm did not escape Charlene, who gave me the same sharp look I remembered receiving from her as a boy. I'd always had a mouth on me and Charlene detested comments that didn't religiously toe the party line, whatever that line was.

The Kraft murder-suicide was one of those tragedies no one seemed able to comprehend, even though the same kind of gun crime occurred on a daily, if not a weekly, basis in our cowboy culture. Nearly half of all murdered women in this country are killed by a partner or a former partner, but we're always surprised when it happens, always surprised to find out love and murder could be separated by such a thin membrane.

"How long ago were they your renters?" I asked Charlene.

"Years ago. By the way, Tommy. Doda doesn't know about the Krafts, and I would appreciate it if you didn't tell her they've passed on."

"What *does* she know?"

"Only that the dog ran away."

Charlene had been guarding Doda's fragility for as long as I could remember. Centenarians didn't usually play touch football on the lawn with the rest of the family or eat popcorn with their own teeth, but as far as I could tell, Doda was as hardy as a lumberjack sitting down to a pancake breakfast, which made me wonder if there was an ulterior motive for Charlene holding this back from Doda.

After Charlene cut me a check and gave me free rein in her office, I mocked up a flyer for the lost dog, incorporating two photos of the mutt and including one of our office phone numbers, which we could use to collect messages. I put the file and photos on a thumb drive and printed out two hundred flyers. The whole operation took less than an hour.

On the way out of the mansion, we ran into the crowd I'd seen outside Doda's office window, their bare feet slapping chlorinated pool water across the polished hardwood floors. A beleaguered maid dropped to her hands and knees behind them and sponged up the puddles.

"Thomas, my man!" It was Joshua Compton, heir to the Compton empire—and probably the Woods fortune as well—and Doda's grandnephew, or great grandnephew. I never did have it straight. It had been twenty years since I'd spoken to him, but for one glorious summer when I was twelve and he was eleven we'd been best pals, plotting our futures together in the naive belief we would remain best friends into an idyllic adulthood where we would become professional scuba divers or maybe astronauts. We would each have a gorgeous girlfriend who looked exactly like the current teen singing sensation of our choice, and we would always carry folding knives with at least ten blades. Like all kids that age, we were innocuous morons, trying on the world to see which parts fit.

"Binky? Doda says she still calls you that."

"Everybody does." He laughed. It was a generous laugh, but raucous, too, and I remembered it from our childhood. "It's good to see you, old pal. Who's this? Your personal cattle wrangler?"

I watched Snake unbutton his jacket, which he did whenever he got close to this much testosterone. It was a little warm to wear a jacket, but it did the job of concealing the pistols he shoe-horned into shoulder holsters under each arm. With the jacket unbuttoned, he showed off the butts of the pistols the way an ingénue in a tight prom dress might show off cleavage. One of the young women took a step back in the face of the munitions display. Snake always managed to look dangerous when he wanted to, though never quite as dangerous as he actually was.

"Binky, Snake. Snake, Binky." The day had turned into

a parade of ridiculous nicknames.

"So you're a professional dog hunter now?" Binky asked in a tone that hinted at derision.

"Private investigator. This is the first time I've ever looked for a dog."

"Nobody else has been able to find her," said one of the other men, who introduced himself. "Chad. Chad Baumgarden."

"Sure," I said. "I remember you from the ranch."

He was another specter from my boyhood. I'd only known him a few days, but the memory stuck with me like a faded scar. I could tell he didn't remember me any more than he remembered what he'd been served for lunch the previous day.

"Nobody else has been able to find the dog," Baumgarden repeated.

"We'll find her," said Snake.

"Care to bet on it?" Binky asked, grinning.

Snake stared at Binky, his eyes growing cold, his whiskers quivering. The crack about him being a cowpoke had been just a little too low for his taste, and now this challenge. "How much?"

"Say . . . a thousand dollars?"

"I ain't got a thousand on me," Snake said. "How 'bout a hundred?"

"You're on. A hundred says you won't find the dog inside of . . . say . . . two weeks?"

Binky widened his eyes theatrically, which turned two of the three women in the room into gigglers, not including the maid, who was still on her knees mopping. As a youngster, Binky had been a natural clown and he apparently still was, which made it difficult not to like him. His father died the year I was introduced to him, and he'd been motherless since his toddler days, yet he'd always been able to spur laughter in children and adults both.

Binky was taller than any of us and heavier but less muscular than Chad, who I was guessing had a personal trainer. Binky's coppery eyes matched his baby-smooth skin, which he'd tanned to the hue of maple syrup. When I knew him, Binky had two major proclivities: clowning and wagering. Following his sojourn into the business world, he'd apparently reverted to those childhood hobbies.

Binky followed us out the front door and through the massive parking area past the garages. As we drew close to a pair of low-slung Maseratis in lollipop yellow and purple, he said, "You should tag along on one of our rallies. We drive these babies all over the state. Do a circuit over the Cascades and through Eastern Washington and then stop for lunch in Winthrop. Last month we had three troopers chasing us, but they never even got close. It was a blast."

"I'll have to pass. My Maserati's in the shop."

It took Binky a split second to realize I was being sarcastic. "Jesus, Tommy. I was planning to outfit you with one of my spare cars. You should think about coming with us."

"Must be nice," Snake said, as we walked toward my weathered Ford. "To have an extra seven hundred horsepower you can loan out to any Tom, Dick, or Harry who wants to grind the gears. To be able to take off whenever you want. To have no responsibilities or worries."

"I wouldn't grind the gears."

"You would if you were in *his* Maserati."

"No, I wouldn't."

"I think you would. In fact, I *know* you would. You hate rich people. Think about these guys. The rest of the world works for a living, but these guys have nothing to do all day but drink Mai Tais and sit around the pool waiting for their dividend checks to arrive in the mail. It burns you up. I know it does."

"No, it doesn't. Why would I hate rich people?" My protest prompted more laughter from Snake. "I don't . . . do I?"

5

As I drove back across the lake to Seattle, Snake slouched in the passenger seat perusing news reports on Mick and Alex Kraft, reading aloud snippets that caught his eye. I knew the story of their deaths by heart. In the days after it happened, I studied the articles like a catechism and now, three weeks later, it was still fresh in my mind and I was still carrying around a folder of news stories I'd clipped from the local paper.

I felt part of the blame was on my shoulders, having essentially told Mick Kraft he was imagining things. Perhaps he was, but if so, he'd imagined himself into an early grave. My glance into their problems had been cursory, almost glib, and I regretted my haste even before I knew about their deaths. I couldn't help thinking about Alex's question as I left their house that morning, *What if you're wrong?* and my harebrained reply, *What if I'm not?* If only they'd gotten just a little bit of endorsement from somebody, anybody, perhaps they wouldn't both be sitting in urns on a mantel.

Snake interrupted my mordant reveries. "You're okay sharing this job with me?"

"Sure. I need the help."

"Split the fee?"

"Forty percent for you. I've got overhead."

"Sounds fair."

Snake and I had a close but complicated relationship. In the early days, I'd done business with him out of necessity, but he was a canny player and I'd grown to trust him. The previous year, he'd been instrumental in helping me find Kathy, who'd gone missing and was feared dead. Kathy didn't take her debts lightly, so despite her disapproval of Snake's lifestyle and misgivings about his more extreme personality quirks, she would have his back until the end of time. As would I.

Earlier that morning when I'd picked him up outside the city limits on MLK South, he admitted he had another pissed-off husband on his tail. Pursuing married women was a point of pride with him, as if seducing a female away from another man was a more valuable game than winning over a woman who was actually available and unencumbered. Ironically, his brother had the same proclivity, having wooed and stolen two wives from Snake.

Snake said, "What exactly is your history with these people, Doda and them?"

"For years now, Doda has given odd jobs on her estate to my father, who managed to worm his way into her good graces. When I was twelve, she invited me to stay for a summer on her ranch in Wyoming. I was more or less a charity case, and she was scrounging around for a companion for Binky, who'd recently lost his dad. He'd thrown a series of tantrums, which got him booted out of his private school. We got along, which was important at that moment in his life. We rode horses at the ranch, and when we weren't on horseback, we were in the pool with swim fins and snorkels. We fished for rainbow trout in the river. I came home as brown as a nut."

"And then you lost touch?"

"I was invited again the next summer. After that I lost touch."

"I noticed you were using your cellphone to snap pictures of all those people. You have a sneaky way of pretending you're screening a call when you're actually taking a photo."

"I do it on every case."

"You get those girls in bikinis?"

"Some of them."

"Can I have copies?"

"No."

"I didn't think so. So what's going on with you and Binky? You got some history I should know about?"

"What makes you say that?"

"The way he was looking at you, I figured maybe you used to light firecrackers under his bed to wake him up."

"Really? He was looking at me like that?"

"I think so."

"I never did anything like that."

"So, what can you tell me about the Krafts? Gimme some details."

I told him about Mick Kraft's suspicion that they were being watched and followed, about how Mick was unwilling to accept that things in his life had gone sour on their own, and about his desire to keep the failed drug test from his wife, Alex. I kept it brief. My association with the Krafts wasn't anything I cared to review at length. In fact, I'd told no one but Kathy and the police when they questioned me after finding my name in Alex's appointment calendar.

"You meet them and then a few weeks later we get hired by somebody to find their dog? Jesus, it's a small world."

"Charlene recommended me to them. She's the locus in all this."

"I thought Doda called us."

"Charlene runs that household."

"I've got their pictures right here. Alex was twenty-eight and Mick was thirty. They were a handsome couple. What I don't get is why people pull shit like this. Killing his wife? I mean, if he wanted to commit suicide, why not leave everyone else out of it?"

"I've never been able to understand it either."

"You have any idea it was going to happen?"

"Hell, no. They were in financial trouble, but they seemed like they were devoted to each other."

"Except he didn't want to tell her about his failed drug test. Maybe she found out. They had a fight . . . . Hey, I just thought of something. If he was doing the whole fandamily, maybe he shot the dog?"

"That occurred to me, too, but where's the body? The police didn't find it."

"Maybe the dog was wounded and crawled under the house. Be easy for a wiener dog to crawl into a hole and die there."

"If that's what happened, we'll know from the smell when we get there."

We drove across the lake and under the monorail line past the Seattle Center, drove past the Space Needle and the EMP Museum, and went north on 15th Avenue West. Just beyond the Whole Foods, we pulled into the animal shelter parking lot, where we went in and asked about Pickles. If anybody had picked up the dachshund, they hadn't taken her to the pound, nor, as near as we could tell, had The Auckland Group contacted the shelter. I found that last almost as strange as Charlene asking us not to tell Doda the Krafts were dead.

6

We crossed the bridge over the Duwamish Waterway into West Seattle and took the Delridge Way exit, followed Delridge slightly uphill for a couple of miles and then hooked a left on Croft Place, which took us up yet another hill at a diagonal until it merged with Twenty-first Avenue Southwest. This was the low-rent part of West Seattle, a suburb of Seattle proper.

The home of Alex and Mick Kraft, now occupied only by ghosts, was on the east side of Twenty-first. The neighborhood was a hodgepodge of small single-family residences, most of which abutted narrow green belts on either side of the street. Twenty-first had a small-town look, cars and trucks parked along the street, only a few driveways and no sidewalks, just a sprinkling of gravel along the edges of the bullet-straight road which ran north and south almost as far as the eye could see on the spine of a hill.

As we pulled up, three boys on bicycles scuttled away from the front of the Kraft house. They'd been loitering like crabs around a dead mollusk. A house where a murder-suicide occurred was bound to be an attraction for kids in the neighborhood. Halloween in August.

There was no crime-scene tape, nothing to signal the house was the location of recent infamy, and nothing to indicate there was a missing dog. As far as we could tell, the first team hadn't even put up fliers in front of the house.

"That's it?" said Snake, squinting at the house. "That's where the bastard did it?"

"This is where they lived."

"Wouldn't you just love to have caught him in the act? Blow his brains out?"

"I wouldn't want to blow anyone's brains out."

Two Miles of Darkness

"It's not a matter of *wanting* to. It would be simple justice."

"It'd certainly be an excuse to pull out one of those useless guns you carry everywhere."

"Useless?"

"You heard me."

"They're useless until you need them."

"You want them to be useful, tie them into a sack and use them for an anchor on that boat you're housesitting."

"Funny."

Even though I started it, I didn't want to get into a discussion of gun justice with Snake, who was never without his armory and who had grown up steeped in cowboy lore, thought it was real life. I'd been a police officer and a gunman myself until I got cured of it, so I could argue both sides of the debate with equal facility, if not equal fervor.

The house was a nondescript bungalow the color of a ripe banana. I knew Alex and Mick Kraft had taken out a large second mortgage on it in order for Mick to invest the money in an Internet business venture with a friend, a venture in which he lost everything in a matter of weeks.

The grass was unkempt and a month tall.

Like gawkers who didn't have enough money to get into the freak show, we traipsed around the perimeter of the house peeping through cracks in the blinds and looking for bullet holes in the walls. Our sightseeing probably looked ghoulish to the neighbors, but I wanted to get a better feel for the place than I'd gotten on my first visit, and Snake, who maintained a morbid fascination with all crime scenes, was going to peek in the windows whether I accompanied him or not.

The house sat on a large lot, the property tailing off down a slight embankment into a thicket of blackberries, brush, and saplings. Each of the neighboring yards oozed downslope into the brambles in the same manner.

The yard to the north held a large maple tree in which some enterprising spirit had cobbled together a lopsided tree house, definitely a kid's handiwork, bent nails, smears of mismatched paint, everything out of plumb. It occurred to me that if there were kids next door they might have the dog.

Like gophers tunneling through a cemetery, we had no idea what we were going to run into by poking around the Kraft place. We tacked lost-dog flyers to both sides of the telephone pole in front of the house, then Snake took the west side of the street while I canvassed the east side. At the house just south of the Krafts', I found a woman napping in a large lime-colored recliner.

Appearing to be in her late eighties, Pearl Boulanger answered the door drowsily, but after she planted her wide derriere back into her easy chair by the front window, she was happy to talk about the neighbors and even happier to talk about the murders, as if they were the highlight of her long life. She had permed white hair, wore sturdy black lace-up shoes she'd probably owned for fifty years, and from her front window had a clear view of the street, though not, I noticed, the driveway next door.

"Mick was the best neighbor an old woman could ask for. I still can't believe he did it. He used to come over and take out my garbage every Thursday evening. Anytime my son-in-law couldn't get over to mow the lawn, why Mick would do it. I just can't imagine whatever got into that young man to make him do such a thing to his pretty little wife and her mother. And then kill himself, too. Just like something on the TV."

"You ever see any signs of drug use over there?"

"Drugs? Why, no. Why would you ask such a thing?"

"No particular reason. We're actually looking for their dog."

"That little bitty thing? Pickles, they called her. What a silly name for a dog."

"Yes, ma'am."

"Why, I thought Pickles' former owner sent her maid or someone over to pick it up."

"She couldn't find her."

"That dog was funny. Mick would chase her all over the yard and then he would scoop her up and roll around with her like she was a baby doll, laughing the whole time." Pearl had tears in her eyes now.

"Have you seen the dog since the murders?"

"Not that I recall."

"Anybody else come around asking about Pickles?"

"Just that maid."

As I was leaving, it occurred to me that Mick might have taken the dog somewhere and disposed of her before killing his wife and himself. If so, we were never going to find her. Pearl Boulanger interrupted my ruminations. "There was a truck up the street that day."

"Pardon?"

"The day they died. There was a truck parked up the street. A big white truck. I never saw it before and I haven't seen it since."

"You see anybody with the truck?"

"No, but I know it was there."

"You get a license number, by any chance?"

"I used to write down the numbers of strange cars in the neighborhood on a pad here. Years ago—oh, sixty years ago now, before it was paved—we had a little neighbor boy snatched right off this street . . . . They never did find him. But my eyes aren't so sharp anymore."

"Did you tell the police about the truck?"

"Why, yes, I did."

"And?"

"Oh, you know how it is. Nobody pays attention to an old woman."

It was probably just a FedEx truck.

I spoke to three more neighbors while Snake worked his way along the other side of the street. Nobody seemed to realize the dog was missing, and nobody remembered a white truck on the day of the murders.

We slapped up more flyers before we met back at the car.

"You get anything?" I asked.

Snake said, "Nothing on the dog. They say the murdered wife was in training to be a manager at McDonald's. Before that she was an architect."

"I know. I met them, remember?"

"Sounds to me like two people sliding down the ladder of the American dream about as fast as a body can slide without getting their ass greased. Nobody knows a thing about the mutt."

"Doesn't seem like the other people who were hired to look for the dog lost any sleep over it."

"No, it doesn't, does it? Charlene told us she paid them close to ten grand. Which gives me an idea. Maybe if we find the dog right away, we could let it go on for a couple of weeks, run up the bill?"

"I'm not going to rip off a friend of the family. Or anybody else, for that matter."

"You said yourself she's got more money than God."

"Did I say that?"

"Something along those lines. Forget it. It was just a thought. What about that Auckland Group? Think there's a chance they found the dog but didn't produce her so they could up the price? Maybe they've got the dog right now and they're waiting for the reward to get bigger?"

"If that's the case, we'll hear about it soon enough."

While we mulled over what to do next, a ramshackle Chevrolet pulled up to the residence on the north side of the Kraft place. Complete with a blue tarp on the roof to keep out rainwater, this wreck of a house stood in sharp contrast to Pearl Boulanger's immaculate home. A woman in her late fifties climbed out of the Chevy laboriously and manhandled a little girl out of a car seat in back, the two of them tottering into the house alongside three boys, each toting a sack of groceries. The oldest boy was ten or twelve. The youngest, maybe six or seven, was hauling a sack almost as big as he was.

"Who are you?" the woman asked, clasping her dress together at the neck as she stood behind her broken screen door after I knocked a few minutes later.

"Name is Thomas Black. I've been hired to locate the dog the Krafts used to own."

"Don't know nuthin' about no dog."

She had the door almost closed when I said, "There's a reward."

"What?"

"There's a five-thousand-dollar reward for the dog." I handed her one of the flyers, which she examined through bifocals before folding and tucking it down the collar of her dress.

"Come in. Come in."

It was a small house, stuffy and humid, full of broken toys and frayed furniture, a house drenched in poverty, smelling of animal cookies, BENGAY, and desperation. The primary heat source was a free-standing gas stove in the living room, though it wouldn't be needed in this August weather. The wallpaper was stained and peeling in spots, and the furniture was of the sort you might find dumped in the woods.

After she got the children situated on a broken-down sofa in front of the television with their dinner of hamburgers from the same fast-food chain where Alex had been training, she said, "So, how do I get my hands on that reward?"

7

Edith Kennedy was taking care of four children for a single mother who worked at Sea-Tac Airport. To save money, the mother of the children lived with her parents, sharing a bedroom with a younger sister who was still at home, while the children stayed at Edith's, wooden-spoon spankings thrown in gratis. In the short time I'd been there, I'd already heard her twice threaten them with a whipping, though the children seemed docile and well-behaved.

Kennedy bent my ear, telling me how twenty-five years earlier she and her husband lost everything in a house fire, including the bulk of their savings, which they'd kept hidden inside a wall because her husband never trusted banks. She was a widow now and saddled with four kids who weren't even related to her, her own health deteriorating. Despite her troubles, my sympathies fell with the kids, whom she treated like intruders.

"Will there be tax on the reward money?"

"I'm not with the IRS. I'm just looking for the dog."

"My boys used to play with that mutt. If they knew something, I suppose I would get the cash?"

"Whoever finds the dog gets the reward."

"Charlie, get over here." The oldest boy quickly stood alongside Mrs. Kennedy. "You help this man locate that mongrel from next door. You find it, I'll buy you and your brothers an electric train set. And don't dawdle."

Charlie Hatcher followed me outside. He was rail thin and had enormous gray eyes, his hands and feet and skull growing faster than the rest of him. He had an intelligent look about him, as if he would someday transcend his humble circumstances to become the dean of a law school or the president of an international banking conglomeration, someone important. When I asked how old he was, he told me he was almost thirteen. I had to smile at the way he puffed up when he announced it. I remembered doing the same thing at that age.

"What can you tell me about the dog? When did you last see her?"

"Three or four days ago."

"Really? Where?"

"Up the street by Sanislo Elementary."

"Think she's still in the area?"

"I don't know. She was hurt. I think that's why she ran from me."

"Hurt how?"

"I couldn't get close enough to inspect her, but I saw it that first day."

"You mean the day the people died?"

His voice became almost inaudible. "Yes."

Clearly the tragedy next door had affected him. I wondered how much cachet Charlie was going to get next month when school kicked off and the other kids found out he lived next door to the Kraft murder house. News that Charlie had been their next-door neighbor would blow through a middle-school rumor mill in a matter of hours, draping a certain type of fame over Charlie. "You were here the day it happened?"

"Yes, sir. I was in the back yard when Pickles came running into our yard. I thought she got into an accident, because she had blood on her. I was going to take her back over to Mick, but when I went to pick her up she just kinda gave me this look and shot off into the blackberries. That was the last I saw of her until a few days ago."

"Did the police talk to you?"

"One of them did. He asked if I saw anything next door."

"Did you?"

"No, sir."

"You tell him about the dog?"

"He didn't ask about the dog. He didn't ask if I heard gunshots, either."

"Did you?"

"Right before Pickles came over. I thought they were firecrackers."

"Can you take me to where you last saw Pickles?"

"Sure."

We headed south on foot. A block away, we ran into Snake, who was again canvassing neighbors. I introduced the two of them, after which Snake told me his bones felt impending rain and he was going to wait in the car, which I took to mean he was still hung over from his drunk the night before. I knew he was wrong about the rain, just as I knew he would make up for it later.

"Who was that?" Charlie asked.

"Elmer Slezak, former world champion bull rider."

"No kidding?"

"No kidding."

Twenty-first Southwest ran along a ridge that flowed north-south. Running parallel with Twenty-first to the west just down the hillside lay Delridge Way, one of West Seattle's main arterials. In several spots the woodsy hillside between the two roads was bisected by a flight of concrete stairs. Charlie took me up and down the stairs, where he'd last seen the dog. As we chatted, I learned he was well read for a twelve-year-old and that he wanted to be a pilot but "without going through the military."

"What do you have against the military?"

"I don't want to be part of the military-industrial complex. I think dropping bombs on civilians in cities is immoral. As far as I can see, it's a war crime." He looked at me nervously, as if I might tell him he was too big for his britches, a phrase I'd heard Mrs. Kennedy apply to his brother.

"You've done some reading on this."

"And watched videos on the Internet."

"For what it's worth, I agree with you. Dropping bombs on civilians is a bad thing."

As we hiked through the neighborhood and clomped up and down each set of stairs, Charlie called out to Pickles. Knowing the dog was more apt to respond to a voice she

Two Miles of Darkness

recognized, I kept quiet. Closed for the summer, Sanislo Elementary School sat just beyond a dip in the road at the south end of the street. We searched the school grounds without success.

Charlie hadn't seen his father since he was five, and I had the feeling the hours we spent together were something of an audition that might place me in a father-figure role. It made me feel a little bit self-important in a way that subsequently makes you feel stupid later when you think about it.

"About that reward?" he said, as we walked back to his house. "If I find the dog, the reward doesn't go to Mrs. Kennedy, does it? I mean, if *I* find Pickles?"

"You find the dog, I'll make sure you get the dough."

"Thank you. There is one other thing I should tell you."

"What's that?"

"There's a camera in the tree over there."

"Pardon?"

"In Mick's backyard. There's a camera in his apple tree."

"What do you mean? Like somebody threw it up there? Or it fell out of a plane or something?"

"Heck, no. It's all set up and aimed at the house."

"Are you sure?"

"Yes."

"Did you tell the police?"

"They didn't ask, and I didn't think about it until later."

For a moment, I felt as if a giant trapdoor had opened beneath me and, like the coyote in roadrunner cartoons, I was just standing there with egg on my face waiting to fall a million miles through space. I'd been in the backyard twice now and hadn't noticed anything in the apple tree.

"You sure about this?"

"Yes, sir."

If this was true, Mick had been right and I had been wrong. People *were* watching him.

"Let's go check it out."

8

Under the apple tree in the Kraft's back yard, Charlie looked up and said, "Shoot. It was right there."

"Show me."

"That branch near the top. I swear there was a camera aimed at the back of their house."

When I scaled the tree, the limbs were springy but held my weight, the leaves rustling like paper money, the branches laden with hard, green apples. There was no camera, but I found what appeared to be a small mounting plate zip-tied to the limb Charlie had pointed out. The plate was black and shiny and new-looking and faced the backside of the house in such a manner that a camera mounted on it would have had a clear view of the house's rear windows. Maybe there hadn't been a camera, but there'd been something. I took a photo of the plate with my cellphone and added it to the file I was keeping.

"When did you last see this camera?"

"Yesterday. Maybe the day before."

"You sure?"

"Positive."

"You didn't see the police up here removing anything, did you?"

"No, sir."

"Have they been back at all?"

He looked up at me with his large, gray eyes that resembled smoky glass. "Not that I saw."

Of course the police hadn't asked about the camera. Why would they ask if he'd seen a camera in the upper branches of a tree? Why would anybody even think to ask such a thing? The only person who should have asked that question would have been me. Six weeks ago, I might have asked the neighbors if they thought anybody was spying on the Krafts. Had I posed the query, things might have turned out differently. The thought began to nag at me like stomach acid.

If I'd found the camera, it would have corroborated Mick's suspicions and maybe he wouldn't have been so frustrated later on, maybe gunshots wouldn't have sounded out on that quiet summer day. Maybe three people wouldn't be dead and maybe the dog wouldn't be missing. Maybe I wouldn't be here now.

The question now was, who had been spying on them and why?

I remained in the tree for a while. The neighborhood looked different from this bird's-eye view. Peering over the roof of the Kraft house, I could see domiciles down the street, including one neighbor we hadn't yet interviewed who was standing boldly in an upstairs window staring at me through binoculars. I must have presented an odd picture, a grown man balancing in the branches of an apple tree in the back yard of his dead neighbors.

From my perch in the apple tree, I surveyed the backside of the Kraft place as well as their driveway. A camera would have had a direct view into their bedroom window and, because the rear of their house faced their own back yard and the green belt beyond, my guess was they probably did not routinely close their blinds. At night their bedroom and the family room would look like a backlit TV screen. Any camera in this tree would have gotten an eyeful.

I had Charlie go back out front to fetch Snake, who came around the house and, after I came down, climbed the tree as eagerly as a squirrel. "I'm pretty sure this is a piece from a Tecktrixonic Remote Camera," he said, after examining the mounting plate. "I had me one of these. Takes great pictures. You can remote it to wherever you want. You want me to bring it down?"

"Leave it there. It's part of a crime scene."

"You think this had something to do with the murder-suicide?"

"I'm beginning to wonder about the suicide part of it."

"It does give one pause. That's a dandy little camera. Judging from where it was placed, somebody got some spankin' pictures."

Because her name had been associated with the case, I phoned Carol Cooper, who worked Homicide for the Seattle Police Department. I'd recently cooperated with her on another case and felt that if we hadn't established a rapport, she at least knew who I was. My idea was to tell her about the tree and the missing camera; sound her out to see if SPD was holding back any pertinent information regarding the case.

"Mick Kraft?" she said, after I'd introduced myself and told her my story. "I handled that one. You're not going to try to reverse this on me like you did on that thing last year?"

"I'm just asking questions. We've been hired to look for their dog."

"And you were looking in a tree in their back yard? I got news for you: Dogs can't climb trees."

"Thanks. I'll keep that in mind. We're pretty sure the mounting plate belongs to a camera setup. The kid next door says there was a camera there until a few days ago. Like maybe whoever left it was waiting for things to cool down before they came over and retrieved it."

"You there now?"

"Yep."

"I'm in Rat City interviewing a wit. Wait right there. I'll see you in ten minutes."

Though I hadn't heard it called that for a while, Rat City was a local nickname for White Center, which was only a mile or so to the south. On the phone, Carole Cooper sounded brash, but I knew she used a brazen, in-your-face attitude to cloak what I could only guess was uncertainty. Less than a year earlier, she'd signed off on the case of a woman who hurtled to her death off a three-story building, labeling it a suicide, only to have me prove her wrong. At the time, she seemed good with it, but now that I was in touch with her again, I sensed it had all been an act. I could tell she was more than a little irritated to be hearing from me again.

Screwing with that case could not have endeared me to Cooper, especially after it made national headlines when it morphed into a multimillion-dollar financial fiasco people eventually compared to the Bernie Madoff Ponzi scheme. I couldn't tell now whether she respected me, was afraid of me, or merely regarded me as a trifling irritant.

Eighteen minutes later, Carole Cooper arrived in a city car and, after dispensing with the pleasantries, said, "Where is the camera?"

The three of us walked her around the house to the back yard, where I pointed out the mounting plate, which one could just barely see if you knew exactly where to look. I could tell from her posture she had no intention of climbing the tree. "That's not a camera," she said, bluntly.

"Like I said, the camera is missing. But the mounting plate's there. Snake had a camera just like it. He says it's a Tecktrixonic Remote. He recognized the plate."

Turning to Snake, she said, "Who were *you* spying on?"

"Your mother," said Snake.

"You people want my help, or what?"

"We want your help," I said, giving Snake a dark look. He shrugged. He didn't know Cooper, but she was a cop, so he was more than willing to regard her as the enemy.

Ignoring his jibe, she turned to Charlie. "But it was there? A camera?"

"Till a couple of days ago. Yes, ma'am."

"What happened to it?"

"I don't know," said Charlie.

"I don't know what to make of this," she said, thinking aloud.

"They tried to hire Thomas two weeks before they died," volunteered Snake.

"What?"

"They thought they were being watched," I said. "They thought somebody was screwing with their lives."

"Typical paranoid," said Cooper. "He shot everybody he could shoot."

We all thought about that for a few moments. Then,

without explaining why, she took me and Snake on a guided tour of the house, while Charlie dutifully waited in the yard.

"I figured you wanted to see this," she said, meaning she wanted to go over the scene one last time herself before making up her mind about what we were telling her. There was a key hidden under a planter near the front door and she used it to unlock the house, the police lockbox long gone.

Carole Cooper was a short, mop-haired woman with stout limbs and an enthusiasm for her job that rarely flagged. If you tried her patience, she got snippy, but she was fair, or at least she had been with me. The Glock she carried in a belt holster under her light civilian jacket was more conspicuous than the four weapons Snake carried, but I had the feeling she made sure it was conspicuous in the same way certain small dogs make sure you know they have teeth.

As one might expect of a house that had been closed up in August, the interior was stuffy. I thought I could smell the metallic tang of blood, but that was probably my imagination. The air seemed heavy and thick with the odors of dust and old toast and the sweet smell of a ten-dollar bill in somebody's purse.

There was dried blood where each of the bodies had been found, the first swatch inside the entranceway on the flagstones. The second was in the living room on the hardwood floor near the front window. The third was around the easy chair, which was squared up in front of the television in the family room just off the kitchen. Other than the dark splotches and a hole in the front door, where police technicians pulled a slug out of the wood, it was a well-appointed house, decorated with care, almost exactly the same as when I visited earlier in the summer. One would think a double-income couple with no children could have easily afforded this place, but Seattle real estate had been appreciating at phenomenal rates until the crash, so there was no telling how much they'd overpaid for the home. Clearly, they'd put a fair amount of money into renovation, too.

Two Miles of Darkness

"Turkish extraction," said Cooper. "The wife. In fact, they spoke Turkish at home when she was growing up." I remembered Alex as wearing her black hair long and straight, parted in the middle. She had a strong chin but otherwise delicate, patrician features with olive-complected skin that would have tanned nicely and the sort of slim figure other women envied.

Mick had been stocky and played football in high school. Judging by the photos around the house, he enjoyed hoisting a brew with the gang at the local pub.

We were in the living room in front of the house when Cooper said, "We figured the wife and husband got into it back in the kitchen. She ran out here to get away from him. He shot her once in the back as she was running away. She then turned around and he shot her once more. The second round penetrated both hands and her stomach. Defensive wounds. She collapsed over there by the front windows.

"After that he stood over her and fired a third slug into her skull. Some time after but in close proximity to the first shooting, the mother arrived. We never did figure out if she heard the shots from outside or just walked in blind. Either way, she stepped inside and closed the door before he shot her. Bullet went through her throat and into the door. As far as we could tell, she never moved from the spot where she went down."

"From how far away was she shot?"

"The empty shell casings put it at twenty feet. That's why we figured she came in on her own. If he'd opened the door, he would have been closer."

"The weapon?"

"Forty-five caliber handgun. Springfield. Some guy at the tavern loaned it to him for shooting practice."

"You're sure he did this?"

"We found the gun in his right fist. There wasn't anything here to suggest anything but a double murder capped off with a suicide."

"A forty-five? You say he shot his wife three times. Was he running target loads?"

"Hardball ammunition. Silver Bear, if I remember. An

off brand."

"The wife must have been made out of Teflon. That or she had an extremely strong desire to live."

"Don't we all?"

"What about the guy who gave him the pistol?"

"We haven't located him. You run into him, tell him we need to talk."

"So Kraft shot the two women, and then what?"

"Sat in front of the TV for maybe five minutes, long enough to drain a beer, then shot himself in the temple. There was blood from the mother-in-law on the beer bottle. Beer in his stomach contents. It all fits."

"He went over and checked out the mother-in-law, got blood on his hands?"

"Appears that way. He was right handed. Gun was in his right hand. Residue on his right hand. No wits. We didn't find anything here that didn't point to his murdering these two women and then doing himself."

"Was there a note?"

"No, but he'd talked suicide to his friends. The ideation was there. Everybody thought he was joking. Shortly after it happened, one of the wife's co-workers stopped by to pick her up for a training session at Mickey Dees and found the bodies. We figured he got here within half an hour, give or take. He said the husband was still alive but unconscious when he got here. He was dead by the time the first uniform walked through the door. The medics told me the witness might have mistaken agonal breathing for signs of life."

"So you guys got here right away?"

"Within a half hour of the shooting, confirmed by the medical examiner. The kid outside? He was the only one with any information."

"Charlie Hatcher."

Cooper looked around the house as if the human part of her work had just now struck her. "All murders are bad, but this was one of the worst."

"No doubt about it. They're all bad." I walked to where the wife's body had been found near the front windows. "So, over here?"

"Right where you're standing. One in the back. One in front which passed through both hands before entering her torso about here." Cooper pointed to her solar plexus. She was wearing a brilliant magenta blouse under her jacket. "Then one to her forehead as she lay on her back. The coroner said she might have survived if it hadn't been for the last one."

"Where was she running to?" Snake asked, following me to the front of the house. "This alcove? She wasn't going to get out of the house through these windows. They don't open. You think she was running over to warn her mother? Was she outside about then?"

"Way I figure it, she was headed for the front door when the first bullet hit her from behind and twisted her around, changed her path. It probably knocked her down, too. Maybe he was stunned by what he'd done, because he didn't shoot again right away. He didn't shoot again until she got up, turned around and faced him. Or, maybe you're right and she heard her mother pull up and wanted to warn her through the window. The second bullet severed her spinal cord. If she'd lived she would have been a paraplegic."

"I'm surprised she lasted as long as she did."

"So were we."

Being in this house where three people had died violently, standing amidst their belongings, gave me a palpable feeling of loss. I could almost feel Alex Kraft and her mother in the room with me.

Cooper added, "God only knows what the mother-in-law was thinking when she came through the door. You hear gunshots in your daughter's house, what do you do? Barge in? Run? Freeze? She barged in. She had any sense, she would have run."

"If she heard shots. She either came through that front door completely unaware of what was taking place, or she came in despite what she thought was taking place."

"From where we found her, she couldn't see her daughter's body, so she didn't know her daughter was dead when she got it, probably didn't have any idea why the husband was pointing a gun at her. The way these houses are all set back from the road, none of the neighbors heard anything."

"Charlie said he heard shots."

"He never told us."

"You found no open windows that day?"

"It was before the heat wave. Nothing was open. Wasn't much above sixty degrees."

"What about the dog?"

"What dog? We never saw a dog."

"There was a dog. Mind if Snake and I look around?"

"Don't touch anything," she said, eyeballing Snake the way a store detective eyeballed a suspected shoplifter. I knew she was only allowing this because of our recent association and because, as far as she was concerned, she had cleared the case. As near as I could tell, she had already discounted our information about a camera. She hadn't taken any notes, hadn't taken a picture, and hadn't called for a tech.

Snake and I paced the rooms and in the bedroom glanced at each other as if making a silent pact. We'd started the day looking for a dog, and now here we were standing among a dead couple's belongings. It bothered us both, a lot.

Everything was tidy. No signs of cigarettes or drugs. Almost no booze in the house, just two beers in the fridge. A dog dish just inside the back door. A small doggie passageway cut into the back door in the kitchen, now blocked with a slide-down panel, so even if Pickles tried to come back, her accustomed route was barred. Cooper told me they put the panel in to keep raccoons and other varmints from getting inside a house that had become a crime scene. Despite claiming no knowledge of a dog, she knew all about the dog door. I wondered what else she was playing coy about. Then again, she didn't have to tell us anything. She didn't have to let us inside. She didn't have to be here.

There were no gun collections, no book collections, no video collections, just a large-screen TV in the family room off the kitchen, with a small video-game console next to it.

Two Miles of Darkness

His games were mostly sports related, no slaughter or army role-playing shoot-em-ups. The wife subscribed to photography and architecture magazines. From everything we could see, they appeared to be a normal couple who'd led a relatively quiet life.

After we were finished in the house, Carole Cooper left and Snake went back to sleep in my car. Charlie said, "What did she say?"

"Said it was a double murder-suicide."

"Mick wouldn't do that."

"One would hope nobody would. But sometimes people do."

"He wouldn't. I know he wouldn't. You have to believe he would never do that."

"The police are convinced he did."

"But he didn't." There were tears in Charlie's eyes.

I had no business poking around a crime scene on a murder the police had already cleared, but even if Cooper was determined to ignore it, the camera plate in the tree put a new wrinkle on things. There was something else, too, something that shouldn't have influenced me in the least but did anyway—Charlie Hatcher's faith in his neighbor's probity. There was something about his willingness to push this point with a relative stranger that made me want to believe him.

If she was smart, Carole Cooper would come back with a ladder and inspect the tree, have a tech remove the metal plate and place it into evidence, maybe glance through her casebook to see if the Krafts had bought surveillance cameras or similar equipment before their deaths, yet she'd signaled no such intention.

"Tell me about that day again," I said to Charlie. "Did you see any strangers in the neighborhood?"

"Just the guy from McDonald's out in the front yard talking to a woman cop. I could tell it was something serious."

"How could you tell?"

"Because he was crying. I don't see adults crying very often. Do you?"

"Not often. How'd you know he was from McDonald's?"

"He was wearing the uniform."

"What about earlier? You see anybody at the house? Notice anything unusual?"

"Just those bangs I heard. But I'm still not sure if that was the real thing or firecrackers."

"Let's assume it was the real thing."

9

After driving Snake to the lot where he'd abandoned his truck the night before—Snake loudly thanking the baby Jesus the angry husband hadn't located it—I stopped at a hardware store and picked up some articles we would need the following day.

Once I was settled into our living room with Kathy, I phoned Snake and heard grease sizzling in the background. I could almost smell his daily sirloin over the phone. "How about bringing your truck over in the morning?" I said. "I think we're going to need two vehicles."

"I'm assuming you've come up with a plan?"

"Thought we'd go over to The Millionair Club and get some help. Eightish?"

"The Millionair Club. I love the smell of money in the morning." I was pretty sure he was confused about what the Millionair Club was, but I didn't bother to set him straight.

Before I could hang up, Snake added, "Had a friend in Arizona killed himself, his wife, his dog, and two horses. It makes you feel hopeless right down to your wet socks. I don't know if I'm going to be able to sleep tonight without a woman to distract me."

"You can't sleep any night without a woman to distract you."

"True."

"You think it's creepy for you, think about the kids who live next door."

"You spent a lot of time with Charlie. I could tell he likes you."

"He's a good kid. He told me he thinks carpet bombing is a war crime."

"Where'd that come from?"

"He reads a lot."

"I guess so. Well, you think about it, you can murder a hundred thousand civilians from three miles up and get a medal for it, but you line up two soldiers against a firing wall and you'll be hanged as a war criminal sure as shit."

I phoned Brad Munch, my telecommunications expert and a perennial grad student at the University of Washington. Brad lived in Greenwood near the zoo in a cramped apartment and was a wizard at anything having to do with computers or the Internet. Or electricity. When he didn't pick up, I left a message.

"Brad. Your assignment, should you choose to accept it, is to help us find a lost dog named Pickles. Your job will be to use every available means on the Internet to help locate this animal. I'm sending you our hotline phone number, a photo of the dog, information on last seen, etcetera. I'll pay your normal scale. Call me if you can't do it. This tape will self-destruct in ten seconds."

After I hung up, Kathy, who was across the room on the sofa, looked up leisurely from the *Harvard Law Review* and said, "You're funny."

"Brad likes that stuff."

"Not as much as you."

"No. He really likes it."

"Right."

"When you say I'm funny, do you mean funny in the head, or ha ha funny?"

"Don't worry. I think it's cute."

"You didn't answer the question."

My wife was a defense attorney and was currently representing a battered wife who'd been accused of murdering her husband, probably the highest profile case she'd ever handled. Before her client punched an ice pick into the back of his skull—a fact not disputed by either side—her client's husband worked as a kick-off-return specialist for the Seahawks, and because of his standing in the community, the media had been bombarding the house and office for quotes. The trial wasn't scheduled for a couple of months, but even so, I needed to dispose of this lost-dog business so I could help her.

Now I had the added complication that perhaps my erstwhile clients, the Krafts, had been murdered–not just the wife and mother-in-law, but all three of them. They had almost certainly been spied on. Maybe Cooper could walk away from the fact that there'd been a camera in their apple tree. I could not.

Ten minutes later, Kathy glanced across the room at me and started laughing. "Thomas, are you holding your breath?" I shook my head, which only made her laugh harder. "If you're not holding your breath, why is your face all red? And why aren't you talking? You *are* holding your breath." I shook my head again, but she was right, as usual. When I reached the point of near agony, I decided I could suffer for another five seconds. Funny how that works. You can always cram in another few seconds. And then another few. And another. I began letting air out slowly, which gave me fifteen more seconds.

"New record?" she asked.

"I can do better."

"Planning to take up pearl diving?"

"It's just something I used to do as a kid. I was wondering if I could still do it."

"You practice holding your breath all the time."

"No, I don't."

"A month ago when we were waiting for Bill and Marsha at Jhanjay's, I caught you holding your breath."

"I wasn't holding my breath."

"Then what were you doing?"

"I was balancing on one foot." Kathy was my wife, my lover, my confessor, and my best friend. Even though lately we had not done much business together, I worked out of her law offices downtown, where she was establishing a reputation as a dependable, bright, hard-working, criminal defense attorney who had a knack for getting the best deal for her clients. And of course I thought she was by far the most beautiful attorney in town, maybe on the whole planet.

"How was your visit with the old woman?"

"A hundred and four and still kicking. But that's not the

half of it. This dog she's got us looking for? Know who the dog belonged to?"

"Paul Allen?"

"Mick and Alex Kraft."

"The names ring a bell, but . . ."

"The couple I told to get lost right before he shot her and then killed himself. Except I'm not sure that's what happened."

"I thought it was open and shut. Murder-suicide."

"Today we found evidence there might have been a surveillance camera in their back yard."

"You think somebody really was watching them?"

"The trouble is we don't have a whole lot of proof. Just a mounting plate in a tree and a kid next door who says the camera was there yesterday or the day before. It's gone now."

"You think whoever put it there knew you were coming?"

"I don't know. Six weeks ago, I was fifteen feet away and didn't see it."

"Maybe it wasn't there six weeks ago."

"Oh, I think it was there."

"So why does this old woman care about the dog?"

"Doda? It was hers before Mick and Alex Kraft adopted it."

"And she's willing to pay thousands of dollars to find it?"

"Yes."

"The infamous Doda Woods. They say she was a spy for the Allies during Doublya Doublya Two."

"They say a lot of things when her name comes up. She probably *was* a spy."

"Didn't you tell me once that when you were a kid she had you out to her ranch in the summers?"

"Two summers. The second one lasted about a week."

"Tell me about it."

I walked across the room and sat beside her on the couch. "You really want to hear this?"

Kathy turned sideways and planted her legs on top of

mine. "Doda Hunt is practically world famous, and little ol' you have known her all your life. Of course I want to hear it."

"Doda and my mother both happened to be two of the handful of Christian Scientists left in the universe, so they saw quite a bit of each other because of that. Doda also gave my father carpentry work around her various estates, so he got to know her, too. I think she thought by giving my father work she was helping all of us, that some of the money would trickle down, but by then he was estranged from us and he always flew under the radar where tax records and child support were concerned. I realize now my mother could have taken him to court and made him pay, but for some reason she chose not to. I think she felt sorry for him."

"Or was afraid of him."

"Maybe. Joshua, who everyone calls Binky for reasons known only to the rich and famous, was the son of Doda's deceased nephew and a year younger than me. She became his guardian when his father died. He may be her only heir now. Not that he needs her money. According to the photos I saw in her house, he's wealthy enough to hire Sting for a birthday party. Anyway, back in the day, Doda had this ranch in Wyoming where she kept horses. There were mountain bikes for us and a swimming pool, and she invited me out there one summer to keep Joshua company. For a twelve-year-old, it was heaven.

"The next summer I was invited again. I'd been there on my own for two days when Binky arrived with some friends from his posh private school in Vermont, and as soon as they arrived I sensed my position in his universe had dropped a couple of rungs. Maybe a whole lot of rungs."

"How so?"

"He just didn't seem to have time for me, and his friends purposely left me out of all their activities. I ended up spending most of my time alone in the library. Then one evening Doda called me into her office and said my plane ticket was ready, told me they were flying me back to Tacoma. Joshua and the others made like it was a big deal that I was leaving, said they were going to miss me, but we all knew that was bogus."

"Seems like he'd made new friends."

"One of them, Chad, is still pals with him."

"So why did Doda send you home?"

"I never found out the reason."

"And you were never invited back?"

"Nope."

"It still bothers you, doesn't it?"

"I guess. One of those childhood mysteries that was never solved."

"It would bother anybody. You got blackballed."

"I haven't thought about it in a long while. My father said he asked Charlene why I was being sent back two months early, but she claimed she didn't know."

"And Charlene is?"

"Doda's flunky. Still works for her. Later that same year my mother drove me over to the Medina estate, where she and Doda had a long chat about my mother's problems while I waited in the hall. Then Doda called me into her office and gave me a Christmas present. I didn't see her again until today."

"And you didn't say anything about that summer?"

"No."

"Just out of curiosity, what does a woman with that much money give a twelve-year-old for Christmas?"

"Same thing she gave me every year. An embossed copy of the *Science and Health*."

"The handbook for her religion?"

"I had a stack of them by then."

"Were you ever in the religion?"

"She knew I wasn't interested, but she thought the book had some sort of magic, that if I had it in my possession I would somehow be converted."

"Didn't work, obviously."

"No, it didn't."

10

    Before we headed out for the day, I performed a cursory inspection of the interior of Snake's truck, policing it for brass knuckles, empty Cracker Jack boxes, half-smoked cigars, and used condoms, which he insisted on calling loaded conundrums. Snake wasn't the tidiest housekeeper when he was organized, and from what I could see, he was never organized. I found fast-food wrappers on the back seat, empty Hennessy VS bottles, and a stray brassiere that prompted wonder. Snake had never been biased against large-breasted women.
    "So there's that little rascal," Snake said, snatching the brassiere out of my hands.
    "Nothing little about it."
    "Svetlana used to play rugby. On a men's team. You don't want to cross her."
    "I hope I never do."
    Founded in 1921, The Millionair Club was located just north of the central core of downtown Seattle. It was a charity that dispensed hot meals, counseling, and beds, also serving as a job exchange and resource center. It was a valuable community resource for employers looking for day laborers and for the homeless and unemployed seeking temporary work.
    Before I could come to a complete stop, one of the men standing in front of the building strode purposefully over to my car window. I was supposed to go inside and fill out a form before hiring anyone, but like everybody else, I was all for cutting corners.
    Garrulous and friendly, the man seemed a good fit for our task. "Worked on the docks, ran a construction crew," he said, smiling crookedly. He was scarred up, probably

from fierce battles with the bottle, but he was sober now and looked as if he had been for a while. He helped us round up seven other men looking for work, then we split them between Snake's crew-cab and my Ford.

Anthony Throckmorton was the name of the man who approached me, a moniker better suited for silent film stardom than for 21st century day labor. During the drive to West Seattle, Throckmorton regaled the rest of us with stories about his elderly parents, who were apparently a couple of characters. If he could be believed, they had both recently been arrested for fist fighting at the Tacoma Mall.

When we got to the Kraft house in West Seattle, Snake and I gave each man a clipboard with a stack of fliers, a staple gun, and a name tag which we hoped would provide a veneer of officialdom. We parked near the house and briefed them about the dog but didn't go into detail about the killings.

We split into two groups, me leading one, Snake the other, and headed in different directions. The air had warmed significantly. I took my team north toward Pigeon Point, with the intention of making a large loop back to the community college. Snake and his team went south toward the elementary school.

Just before noon, Snake called and told me they were running into kids who'd seen our flyers, posses of boys on bicycles using dog whistles and cold hotdogs for bait, scouting the neighborhood in the hope of seizing the dog and taking the reward, which could make any boy's summer the best ever. Snake said they'd already brought him three dogs, all the wrong breed.

After I felt they had the routine down, I left Throckmorton in charge of my group and used the key Cooper had shown us, sneaking back into the Kraft house, where I conducted a search for hidden cameras, nanny cams, you name it.

I found nothing that would hint anybody else had been in the house without the Kraft's knowledge. The pickup truck Mick had driven the day I followed them to West Seattle from my office was still parked in front of the house.

Two Miles of Darkness

I knew Alex had a small Toyota, but it wasn't on the premises. I found the truck keys on the kitchen counter and searched inside and out for a GPS tracker or anything else that could substantiate Mick's claims of being followed and watched, all the while thinking I should have gone over his truck six weeks before, when his claims were fresh and he and his family still among the living. I found nothing.

Later, I climbed the apple tree again and received a shock when I discovered the mounting plate was missing. For a few moments, I scanned the tree and the limbs nearby, thinking I'd forgotten the exact location, but it was gone. I found nothing but zip-tie marks on the branch.

Carole Cooper answered on the third ring. "Detective Cooper," I said. "Thomas Black. I'm in the back yard of the Kraft place again, and that mounting plate is gone. Did you send someone out here to retrieve it?"

"I'm sorry. I can't talk. We're heavy into a gang shooting at Twenty-third and Union. Is this important?"

"The mounting plate in the tree at the Kraft's place. It's gone. Did you take it?"

"Tell you the truth, I haven't had time to think about it. Listen. I've got stuff going on here. I'll get back to you."

Except she wasn't going to get back to me. I could tell from her tone she was blowing me off in the same way I'd blown off Mick and Alex Kraft. She'd cleared the case and was through with it. Once again, Mick and Alex were being dismissed. Nothing I could tell her about them or about a camera in a tree in their back yard was going to change what she thought about the case. We had only the testimony of a twelve-year-old boy and a dubious—Cooper would think it dubious—confirmation from Snake that the mounting plate belonged to a camera.

By two o'clock, my group was hungry, so we packed everybody into Snake's truck and he drove them to a taco shop across the street from the fire station on Holden, while I remained at the murder scene. It was strange to compare Mick Kraft to these men. Obviously, Mick found himself at the end of his rope. But the rope ended in different places for different people. Throckmorton and the others had all slept on the streets last night, yet as far as I could tell, none of them had given up hope or murdered anyone.

Throckmorton in particular was as jocular and upbeat as anybody I'd ever met. It made me wonder about happiness, whether people bought it, earned it, or were born with it, and how some managed to hold on to it through adversity while others did not.

I was leaning against my car in front of the house, letting the summer sun warm my face and arms, when Charlie Hatcher pedaled up on his mountain bike. He seemed to be reading my mind when he said, "It's sad, isn't it?"

"Doesn't get any sadder."

"Mick was such a nice guy. And I really liked Alex."

"How long was that camera in the apple tree?"

"I don't know."

"A couple of weeks before they died?"

"I guess. I always thought it was Mick's."

"And they didn't know about it?" I was asking a question I already knew the answer to. If either of them had known about the camera they would have told me when they attempted to hire me.

"I see you brought some people," the boy said. "You find Pickles?"

"Not yet."

"I got up at five this morning and went out to the tree house. I saw some raccoons and a rat, but not Pickles. I'm going to find her, and when I do I'm going to use this for a leash." Charlie pulled out a cruddy piece of twine. I hadn't thought about securing the dog after we found her, which showed how many dog roundups I'd conducted. Outflanked by a twelve-year-old.

"After we left yesterday, did you see anybody in the Kraft's back yard?"

"No. Was somebody over there?"

"That mounting plate for the camera is missing."

"Wow."

Charlie was still with me when Snake called from the taco joint. "Throckmorton just got a lead from one of the customers here who said she saw our dog running across the street a half hour ago on Highland Park Way. That's less than a mile from where we're standing. We're headed there now. Going to fan out and comb the woods. Thomas, my boy, I believe we're closing in on the little rat."

"We know the dog's skittish, so don't be running her into traffic and getting her killed. The last thing I want is to take Pickles back to Doda in a shoe box. And give the guys another chance at lunch when you're through out there."

"Will do. Don't worry about the dog. Nothing is going to happen to her, and if it does, we'll wrap her up in newspaper and stick some dandelions in her teeth for the old lady."

"Glad you've thought it through."

I spent the next couple of hours canvassing the neighborhood once more, only this time I wasn't asking about the dog but whether anybody had seen anything unusual on the day of the murders. If they'd seen anybody climbing the apple tree last evening. Several neighbors reported two men in the tree the previous day, but they were talking about Snake and me. Nobody had seen anything else.

11

A few hours later, Snake and I were at a coffee shop near the marina where Snake was housesitting. We'd paid off our helpers and taken them back to the Millionair Club. They'd searched the woods near Highland Park Way for over two hours without success.

The dog was still missing. The Krafts and her mother were still dead. Having thought through the situation from every conceivable angle without coming up with a plan, I found myself disheartened.

"Shame to be punching bullets into a woman looks that good," Snake said, staring at a photo of Alex Kraft on his cellphone.

"It would have been okay if she hadn't been good-looking?"

"Don't be parsing my words like that."

"I'm just reacting to what you're saying."

"Well, she was damn pretty. And I still say it was a shame he shot her up like that."

We were in a hole-in-the-wall coffee shop hunched over a small table, just me and Snake and the .44 Magnum pistols tucked under each of his arms in shoulder holsters, a Glock behind his back, and of course the two-shot Derringer he was never without, which moved from pocket to pocket, depending on whim. Last year one of his paramours inadvertently triggered the Derringer under his pillow, firing a bullet into the headboard, and as a consequence, he was now partially deaf in one ear. He was lucky she hadn't shot him in the head, but he refused to acknowledge that possibility.

"You in love with her, Thomas?"

"Pickles?"

Two Miles of Darkness

"Alex Kraft. The dead woman."

"Am I in love with her?"

"That's the question."

"In love with a dead woman? I'm in love with Kathy."

"Being in love with a dead woman is nothing to be ashamed of, especially a looker like this here Alex. I fall in love with dead women all the time. A counselor at the jail in Arapaho County told me I do it because it's safe. A dead woman is never going to change, and she's never going to challenge me. Hell, the whole country's been in love with Marilyn Monroe for decades."

"Snake, you're in love with every woman you come across, dead or alive."

"I do like my women. Only difference is I wouldn't sleep with a dead one."

"Not again. You did once."

"I did, didn't I?"

"But that was because you thought she was from space."

"Please don't remind me."

"The deaths next door really slammed Charlie," I said. "Thing like that's going to impact his life forever."

"Maybe if he locates the dog and gets that reward money something good will come of it."

"Maybe."

"You like the kid, don't ya?"

"He reminds me of me when I was his age."

"I been thinking about that missing mounting plate. Could be the neighborhood pervert put it and a camera up there to take pictures of Alex. I lived next door to someone like her, I'd be tempted to do the same thing."

"You saying if you lived in that neighborhood you'd be the pervert?"

"I don't live in her neighborhood."

"But you *would* be a pervert?"

"Now you're parsing my words again."

"Maybe you're right. We should be looking for the neighborhood pervert here. If there is one."

"There's *always* a pervert."

"If that's so, and it was his camera, he might have gotten some pictures on the day it happened."

"On the other hand, here's an alternate theory on their deaths. Suppose they were having marital problems. You said he was afraid she'd find out about his failed drug test. Maybe she found out. She's driving to work with this other guy each evening, training to be a manager at Mickey Dees. Maybe she's complaining about the hubby, and the carpool guy starts making time with her. Hubby walks in on them and threatens him. Loverboy grabs the first weapon at hand, which happens to be the borrowed pistola, shoots them all, and stages it as a murder-suicide, calls the cops and claims he got there after it was all over."

"That's a lot of maybes."

"Or maybe he made a play for her and she turned him down and he got his nose out of joint. Could be she kicks him in the balls. He picks up the gun and shoots her. The hubby walks in before he can make good his escape, so he plugs him, too. While he's doing this, the mother-in-law shows up."

"So let's talk to this dude found the bodies, see what he has to say."

Snake found the man's name in a KOMO-TV online article, then tracked him on Facebook and several other social media sites. Judging by the photos, Marvin Huntzinger was a young, portly gentleman with a goatee, full-faced, pleasant looking, nothing like the rake Snake had posited earlier while he was cooking up alternate theories of the crime. Snake found his phone number and used my phone to call him.

"Mr. Huntzinger. My name is Elmer Slezak. I'm a detective here in our downtown office, and I have another detective here who would like to speak to you about the Kraft case." Having listened to Snake's introduction, I was aware Huntzinger probably believed I was with SPD, a card Snake played often and willingly, even though an overt impersonation of a police officer could bring jail time. Even so, I saw no reason to disabuse Huntzinger of the false impression he must have.

Two Miles of Darkness

"Mr. Huntzinger?" I said.

"Yes, sir?" He had a washed-out southern drawl and came across as friendly but cautious, if not actually timid. While we spoke, Snake turned on his phone and displayed more photos of the man I was talking to, along with photos of Huntzinger's Facebook friends. His girlfriend looked and was built similar to him, could have passed for his sister. The couple liked to spend time at the ocean, where he flew gas engine model airplanes he built in a basement workshop.

"I know you've already told this story, but I'd like to hear what happened the day you found the bodies at the Kraft home."

He told the tale slowly, haltingly. It was a narrative he'd undoubtedly spun many times already. He and Alex were both taking the McDonald's management course in Bellevue. On the day of the murders, he'd known Alex less than a week and had never met Mick. It was the second time they'd carpooled.

When he knocked on the front door at the Kraft house, the door was unlatched and popped open an inch before it bumped against what turned out to be the body of Alex's dead mother, although Huntzinger didn't realize it at the time. At that point, he went around to the front windows, where he glimpsed Alex on the floor, a pool of crimson giving her a bizarre halo. It was, he said, so clean and neat it looked like artwork.

"I returned to the front door and forced it open. When I saw everyone in the house was beyond help, I called the police. Then, I started thinking the killer might still be inside, so I went out to the front yard to wait for the first patrol car."

"You didn't think the husband was the killer at that point?"

"I didn't know what to think. I was kinda wigged out."

"But you saw the gun in his hand?"

"Oh, yeah."

"Why'd you go inside?"

"I guess I seen too many cop shows. I thought somebody might need medical assistance. I had to take a first aid course for this McDonald's job, and they stressed how fast people can bleed out. I thought maybe somebody needed me to put pressure on the wound. That's how you stop bleeding. You put pressure on the wound."

"Was anybody still alive?"

"I think the husband might have been, but I didn't want to touch him. I was afraid he was going to wake up and shoot me."

"And the women?"

"I'm pretty sure both women were dead."

"So Mick died while you were waiting for the police?"

"Talk to the medics. They worked on him. They worked on him for half an hour. Then they left him there on the floor."

"I thought he was in a chair."

"They placed him on the floor when they were doing the CPR."

"You touch anything?"

"The TV. I turned it down. It was too loud."

"Just out of curiosity, what was on?"

"Twenty-four hours of ultimate fighting."

I believed his story. Snake did not. Snake wanted to interview him in person, wanted to look into his eyes so he could personally verify he was lying. But then, Snake was overly suspicious of just about everyone except women he planned on having sex with.

12

The next morning, I phoned Carole Cooper again. Almost two days had passed since I began looking into her call on the deaths. "You going to work this case again?" I asked.

"Tell the truth, I haven't thought about it. We picked up a gang-related shooting last night. Two dead. Two critical in the hospital. You gave me some things to think about, but I don't have time to re-open the investigation right now. Maybe that mounting plate you keep talking about . . . coulda been kids. Kids have been all over that property." She was right about the kids. It could easily be that some of the neighborhood youngsters saw us in the tree yesterday and took the mounting plate as a souvenir.

"One other thing. I read where Kraft did a lot of drinking towards the end."

"You want to follow up on this, you're on your own. You're not going to piggyback on my work." I'd seen matchbooks in the house with the name of a tavern printed on them. It was called The Dregs. I knew it was up the hill on California Avenue. "He *was* doing a lot of drinking. It all fits, Thomas. It was a murder-suicide. I know what you're trying to do. You got lucky last time, so you think you're going to get lucky again, but your days as a Monday morning quarterback are finished. You're going to end up looking like a fool, and you're going to piss me off doing it."

"I think you're wrong on the call."

"Because you think there was a camera in that tree?"

"I know there was."

There was a pause. "You're not going to leave it alone, are you?"

"No."

"You feel guilty because you didn't help that couple when they asked. Is that it?"

"That's part of it."

"Okay. Fine. I'm sorry I let you in the house now. I thought it would put a halt to your nonsense. Give me a buzz if you turn up anything real. Otherwise, I'll take another look at it when my schedule frees up."

We both knew Cooper should have had a tech remove the plate as soon as I told her about it.

We'd received over eighty calls since we put up the number, our Internet listings sucking in swindlers from as far away as the Ukraine and Nigeria. While I tried to track the missing camera, Snake was running through any callbacks that had even a hint of legitimacy, driving from one reported sighting to another, X-ing them on a map, ruling out pictures of dogs e-mailed to us. Most of the pictures were not the correct breed, but the few dachshund photos we got were quickly and easily ruled out. Pickles had a distinctive blond patch running over her left ear, which wasn't evident in any of the photos we'd published.

When I confronted Charlie, he was wearing the same jeans and T-shirt he'd had on the day before, reminding me of my own boyhood summers, when I would wear a set of clothes until my mother confiscated them while I was sleeping and tossed them into the laundry. "You didn't happen to see anybody poking around in this yard at night?"

"There've been kids in front, but they're too scared to come close. Somebody spread the word we've got ghosts here at night." Charlie grinned wickedly or, about as wickedly as a twelve-year-old could.

Earlier that morning, I'd watched Mrs. Kennedy herd all four children outside before slamming the back door. The two youngest headed for a bare area of the lawn, where they began playing with battered toy cars and a grimy-looking doll. One of the boys glared at us from across the yard, seemingly at loose ends. I looked at Charlie, who was just the other side of the fence. "Your brother going to help us today?"

Two Miles of Darkness

"He doesn't think anybody will ever find Pickles. He cries whenever I bring it up. He really liked Mick."

"I can understand that."

13

The Dregs was a small tavern four doors down from a busy corner on one of the main drags in West Seattle, California Avenue Southwest, which stretched along the backbone of the peninsula. There was a large grocery store across the street, a hair salon next door, and abundant parking all around. The neighborhoods surrounding the intersection were bursting with single-family residences and modest apartment buildings.

I heard somebody rumbling around in the back and walked to the rear of the building. I could feel the August sun radiating off the walls. The morning warmth hadn't come close to peaking, but it would soon. Today was supposed to get hotter than yesterday, which had been hotter than the day before. In Eastern Washington, wildfires were spreading. Here, on California Avenue convertible tops were down and car windows open. Pedestrians on the street wore shorts and flip-flops.

An Asian man, possibly Korean, was in the rear of the tavern mopping the floor from a soapy bucket.

"We don't open until ten-thirty," he said, without missing a stroke. He was short, had jet black hair that needed a trim and stuck out on the sides like toothbrush bristles. His round face revealed no expression.

"Did you ever have a regular customer named Mick Kraft?"

"You a reporter?"

"Private investigator. I'm working for friends of the family." I didn't bother to tell him I'd been hired to find their dog. The whole dog gig made me feel like a once-famous-rock star reduced to delivering singing telegrams to nursing homes and sororities. Not that I'd ever been famous, or could sing, but the come-down I felt when thinking about the assignment was almost as ruinous. I was still annoyed at my father for giving my name to Doda. Maybe that was the real reason I couldn't let the murders alone; maybe I needed something to make myself feel more important. Maybe this whole thing was just my own cognitive dissonance.

"What can I do for you?"

"You work here at night, too?"

"I'm here twenty-four/seven. I own the place."

"Tell me about Mick Kraft."

"I talked to the cops. I'll talk to you, too, if you want. Come on in." He continued mopping, forcing me to step lightly across the wet floors. It was a dark tavern with a lot of unlit neon, the most complex of which depicted a cartoonish pirate. At night the lights would produce a carnival of colors, making the customers faces look garish.

On the walls were hundreds of photos of men and women astride or leaning on their motorcycles, most taken outside on California Avenue with the building in the background, obscene gestures, tattoos, and topless women in abundance. We were a long way from the Marlon Brando days of "What are you rebelling against?"—"What have you got?" but these people were all taking on an attitude for anyone who cared to notice.

"Who'd he hang out with?"

"Hung out with this one guy named Manny. They had some sort of business deal cooking. They were pretty excited about it for a while there."

"You don't know what the business deal concerned, do you?"

"Hell, no. They weren't letting anyone else in on it."

"What do you know about Manny?"

"Just a guy used to come in. I haven't seen him in a while."

"Know where I can find him?"

"The cops asked the same thing. Tell you the truth, I think he mighta had a warrant out for him. Lot of the guys in here do. I got my joe-six-pack customers, and then I got a few who got warrants chasing them. Couple of arrests made right here. Tell you the truth, my wife doesn't like it, but believe it or not, it's good for business."

"Manny was a longtime customer?"

"Mick was. Mick started spending a lot of time here after he lost his job. Sometimes he'd be here waiting when I opened."

"Was he an alcoholic?"

"I wouldn't call him that, not exactly. Heavy drinker, maybe."

"Manny ever use a credit card?"

"Strictly cash."

"He ever borrow your phone?"

"Not that I recall."

I glanced at the pictures on the wall behind the bar. "Is Manny in any of these pictures?"

"The police already looked. He wasn't there. He was camera shy. But I have one of Mick here." He showed it to me, Mick sitting at a table with a couple of beer steins in front of him, the shoulder of another patron showing at the edge of the frame.

"He's drinking with somebody in this picture. Do you know who?"

"I'm pretty sure that's Manny. He rarely drank with anybody else."

"And you haven't seen Manny since Mick's death?"

"Nope."

"What's he look like?"

"Manny? Regular guy."

"White, black, Hispanic? Five hundred pounds? Give me something here."

"Two bills, maybe a little more. About your size."

"I'm one eighty."

"Okay. He was a little bulkier than you. Maybe not as tall. Caucasian. Just an ordinary guy."

"Long hair? Short hair? Beard?"

"I don't think he had a beard or mustache or anything. And he always wore a cap, so I don't know if he even had hair."

"How old was he?"

"Somewhere between thirty and fifty. I'm not good with ages. Nice guy. You'd like him. Everybody liked him."

"He have a last name?"

"Not that I heard."

"Or was Manny his last name?"

"I couldn't tell you."

"Anybody else comes in who might know where he is?"

"I doubt it. It was mostly just him and Mick."

I had covertly snapped a picture of the proprietor and was on my way out, traversing the half-dry floor when he called after me, "You know, it freaked out a lot of people that he killed his wife and mother-in-law. He coulda just as easily come in here and wiped out the place. I got a pistol behind the counter that holds eighteen rounds, but there's no guarantee I'd get to it in time. You read about these massacres, but you don't expect it to be anybody you actually know."

"No. You don't." I handed him a couple of the wanted posters for the dog and added, "You don't happen to know where she is, do you?"

"Nope. One thing I don't allow in here is dogs."

I was lingering in the doorway trying to think of questions I might have missed when the barman said, "You might try talking to Johnny."

"Who's Johnny?"

"I always thought he was Mick's brother-in-law. I'm not sure how I got that idea. I don't see him much, but I believe he lives somewhere close, because I run into him at the grocery across the street sometimes."

"Johnny? You know his last name?"

"Wish I did."

Sitting in my car while the morning sun streamed through my open driver's window, I used the King County Parcel Viewer to look up the names of nearby homeowners, scanning the records for combinations of "John" or "Jonathon," or "Kraft," in case the bar owner was wrong and he was a brother, not a brother-in-law. Working my way slowly through the computer records, moving west from the intersection, I struck gold when I came up with a John Stacey and Angela Celik. They owned a house six blocks away.

Talia Celik had been shot in the entranceway of the Kraft home while her daughter lay dead only a few paces away. Her other daughter lived six blocks from The Dregs and had a husband named John, and fortunately for me had not changed her last name when she married, which now that I thought it through, was awfully independent for a young woman raised in a family where they still spoke Turkish at home. But then, her sister had been her own woman, too.

14

Angela Celik's two toddlers were adorable, with huge, dark gumdrop eyes and black hair so thick and mop-like it was amusing. Angela, herself, bore the same Mediterranean complexion and flawless features as her dead sister, looking eerily similar to Alex, except that she appeared to be about seven months pregnant.

Exuding a calm demeanor, she invited me into the back yard, the two toddlers spinning around us in the grass, laughing and tumbling. "If you're investigating the deaths of my mother and sister, I'd be happy to help any way I can. I still can't wrap my brain around it."

"I've come across some disturbing anomalies and I want to chase them down."

Her dark eyes were wet now, not tears really, but portents of tears to come. I had to remind myself it had only been three weeks since her sister and mother were murdered, and murder in the family isn't something people get over quickly, if they get over it at all.

I told her about the camera Charlie Hatcher had spotted in the apple tree. I told her about Manny, Mick's friend nobody seemed able to locate, and asked if she knew him. She did not. She thought about it and then, distracted, called out something to her oldest, Sean, told him to be more careful with his little sister, who had clearly learned to walk less than a year before and was glorying in the freedom of it, though not as much as she gloried in the attentions of her older brother. I could tell Celik was worried I might think her kids were out of control, but I thought they were delightful and told her so, watching her glow in light of my compliments, as I knew she would. It was hard to go wrong praising a woman's children, but I meant it.

We were seated in lawn chairs, using the shade from the table umbrella to avoid the morning sun. Although I don't normally drink coffee, I accepted the mug she offered me and nursed it, hoping the ritual might extend our conversation. Most interviews were like panning for gold in that the longer you kept at it the more likelihood you would see a glimmer that would interest you. Aside from which, there was something tranquilizing about this back yard and this family, something I didn't want to leave.

"Alex never said anything about a surveillance camera. If they'd installed one, I'm sure she would have told me."

"If she knew."

"You think Mick did it without telling her? I don't know. Maybe so. That whole business deal he had going with Manny was behind her back. She warned him not to invest with somebody he barely knew, but he wouldn't listen. There was a time when they were so close I was envious. Then he lost his job and started drinking, and things started unraveling."

"Maybe he was worried about break-ins?" When she didn't respond, I added, "They ever say anything about prowlers on Twenty-first?"

"Alex would have told me if there had been burglaries nearby. But if Mick didn't put up the camera, who did?"

"That's what I want to find out. Your husband used to visit The Dregs with Mick?"

"John's not a big drinker. He was trying to be supportive of Mick, but all Mick and his friend, Manny, talked about were guns and that hush-hush business deal they were cooking up. They wouldn't share details on the business plans, and John wasn't interested in guns. When John was ten, his cousin was accidentally killed by a neighbor kid, who found a loaded World War II pistol in a drawer. John was in the room when it happened. He told Mick the likelihood of a gun stopping a crime was minimal compared to the odds of the same gun injuring someone in the family either by accident or suicide. I guess Mick didn't believe him. The pity is if Mick hadn't had a gun at hand . . . they might all still be alive.

"According to the police, Manny lent the murder weapon to Mick."

She was quiet for a few moments, sipping her coffee and studying me. "Mr. Black. Do you think we'll ever know why Mick did what he did?"

"I'm not sure he did it."

I'd just said something she wasn't ready to hear. It was too big a jump for her to transition to. She fanned herself with a section of newspaper from the table. "I always feel too hot these days. They say it's going to be ninety."

"That's the claim."

She smoothed her long summer dress across her thighs, her bare feet tanned from time in the yard with the kids. I noticed her toenails had been painted and pedicured, but the crimson was chipping. She continued as if speaking from a dream. Clearly my questions had dredged up dark thoughts she'd been struggling with. "Mick worked at UPS for years, and then he lost that job and another one in a matter of weeks. It went from bad to worse when Alex's company laid her off.

"I suppose they extended themselves buying that house, what with her student loans and old medical bills. They couldn't really afford the payments on the house even when they were both working, but they managed to make do. Alex told me they were going to lose everything, even their furniture, which they still owed on. We wanted to loan them money, but I haven't been teaching since before Sean was born and we're on a budget. And now Sean keeps asking where Mick is. How do you tell a four-year-old his uncle shot his aunt and his grandmother and then himself? How do you explain any of that to a child?"

I glanced across the yard at the two toddlers frolicking in the sunshine and said, "I don't even know how to explain it to an adult."

"Sean used to love it when Mick came over and tumbled around with him. John has a bad hip from a Jeep accident in high school, so he can't roughhouse too much. But Sean just loved it. It was so funny to watch them together, like a bear with her cub. He would pick Sean up and roll around with him. Let him jump on his chest. Pretend Sean was beating him up. We used to laugh so hard we would end up crying."

"Mick doesn't sound like the kind of guy who would murder anybody."

"That's why we've been having such a hard time coming to grips with this."

"Was it possible Alex was thinking about leaving him?"

"She would have told me. Besides, she never would have left Mick."

"He was depressed, wasn't he?"

"Depressed and bitter. Alex and I talked about it on the phone almost every day. It was bad enough Alex lost her job, but while she was going through her own problems she had to play nursemaid to Mick, who was really taking it badly. Especially after he lost all that money in that crazy investment."

"How much did he lose?"

"I think about twenty grand, but it was twenty grand they didn't really have."

"Did you talk to your sister the day she died?"

"We talked about our father. Mom wanted to get a part-time job so she could help Alex and Mick with their bills, but our father wouldn't hear of it. Now, he thinks the whole thing was his fault, that if he'd let mom get a job Mick wouldn't have been so desperate."

"And how did Mick feel about his mother-in-law helping out?"

"He didn't know. Alex never told him. You have to understand it was a nice gesture, but it was only a gesture. Mother never could have earned enough to get them out of the financial sinkhole they were in. They *were* going to lose the house. Their savings were down to nothing. The fact is, they were days or maybe weeks away from camping out in their car or moving into our garage."

"How did she lose her job?"

"She worked for Vereecken and Sons, an architecture firm in Seattle, but they got bought out. When the new management came in, they decided to streamline. Alex just happened to be in the wrong place at the wrong time."

I liked sitting in the sun in their postage stamp back yard. I liked talking to Angela Celik. There was something familiar about her, as if we were distant cousins who hadn't been in touch in a while. Maybe it was the way she reminded me of her sister, or her name, Angela, which was the name of a friend of Kathy's, who'd died recently.

"How did Mick lose his job?"

"He was a driver for UPS. Had a spotless record. Then all of a sudden he started having one fender-bender after another. They told him one more and he would get suspended. I don't know all the details except that one night the maintenance people found some damage to his truck and claimed he'd had another accident and failed to report it.

"Mick swore he didn't know anything about it. But now, since the shooting, I'm thinking maybe there was a dark side to Mick we didn't know about. He was able to get another job driving a delivery truck for a grocery chain, but within a week he'd wrecked their van. Even after all of that, he swore the accidents weren't his fault."

"Was he volatile? He have a temper at all?"

"Heck no! They had a wonderful marriage. Six years. Then, just like that!" She snapped her fingers, making a whip-like sound. "Everything went sour." Across the yard her boy stopped what he was doing, stared hard at his mother and attempted to snap his fingers, perplexed when he couldn't make the same noise his mother had. "You know what I think? I think he was going to kill himself and she tried to stop him, that he shot her by accident."

I thought back to the scenario Carole Cooper had painted for me, Alex taking a bullet in the back as she ran away, fired on again after she turned around, and then the coup de grâce as she lay paralyzed on the floor. I said, "It was no accident."

"I guess he didn't shoot both Alex and Mom by accident, did he?"

"No. But I'm not sure he was the one who did it."

"I do know this. God has a plan. We might not know what it is, but he has a plan. God loves each and every one of us, and right now He's loving Mom and Alex. I know they're in God's arms."

After I left Angela Celik's house, I called Snake, who was running around West Seattle contacting all the people who claimed to have spotted the dog. "What's up, Thomas?"

"I'm thinking we should get inside that house again and see if there was anything I didn't spot. Electronic eavesdropping or whatever. I've got gear, but it's not like yours. I'd also like to look around for any evidence about that investment scheme where Kraft lost so much money."

"My gear's in storage in Tacoma. I could drive down and pick it up and come back. But that's two hours I won't be looking for the dog. You sure?"

"Call me when you're on your way back," I said. "Seems to me these folks got into a downward spiral about six months ago. It was almost as if somebody flipped a switch. Everything was okay before that. Then everything turned to shit. The question is, what happened six months ago?"

"Six months ago they got that dog."

"It *did* start about that time, didn't it? It started *exactly* at that time."

15

Snake and I are about as helpless as two overturned beetles on a hot sidewalk. We're trussed up tighter than a pair of inmates in the same straitjacket, can't scratch our heads or move more than a few inches in any direction. Yards of sticky tape bind our wrists and ankles.

Even if Snake hasn't, I've noticed from the tone of our voices that neither of us actually believes we're going to emerge from this plight intact, that we're each thinking this is our last hour on earth.

I've had that thought in the past, and so far, obviously it's been wrong. This time we're most certainly headed for an anonymous grave in the dirt, and we can struggle all we want, but we're not going to push the plan even a millimeter off course.

Bound but not gagged, we are in the trunk of a moving automobile. Had Snake been his normal voluble self, he would probably be gagged, but they hooded him, taped his hands and legs together and manhandled him into the trunk of the car so quickly Elmer didn't have a chance to protest. He'd been stunned by the vicious quickness of it all and by the guilty knowledge that he'd made a phone call that was going to suck me into the same sticky vortex.

The taillights in the trunk are glowing orange and white. We discuss kicking out the taillights, perhaps with the thought of promoting a traffic stop by an alert officer of the law, which might put a halt to this journey, but it is a slim gamble, and odds are, these people would shoot the patrolman in the face and leave him by the side of the roadway. More than likely they would drive away scot-free and we will remain in the trunk. A single officer on what he thinks is a routine traffic stop will be no match for the killers sitting up front.

In all likelihood, we're all five of us traveling in a stolen vehicle. After we're dead and buried, the only remaining evidence will be what we manage to leave in the trunk, which isn't going to be much more than a few stray hairs from Snake's hirsute chest and some specks of blood from my head wound. If the police ever retrieve the stolen car, it's doubtful they'll vacuum the trunk for trace evidence of kidnap victims.

As I think about all this, I wonder if our kidnappers are planning to set it on fire to eliminate evidence, perhaps to eliminate us as well. The idea makes my blood curdle. I put it out of my head as soon as it occurs to me. Funny how you can avoid thinking about certain horrifying but very real possibilities right up until the moment they slap you in the face: cancer, divorce, tooth decay, getting burned to death in the trunk of a car.

For a while, I entertain the foolish hope that some random civilian has witnessed our abduction and called in the license plate of the car, that every law officer in the state is scouting for us right now; but it is the middle of the night, most cops are at home in their beds, and the marina on Lake Washington, where all this fuss began, was deserted. The Blue Water Bistro next door was closed, no homes nearby, all the boats in the marina dark.

The only certainty is that we're going to vanish.

The Emmylou Harris song is loud enough that I don't believe the men in front can eavesdrop on us, though we easily listen in on them. What we hear doesn't help. They are braying over recent baseball scores, arguing over which is the best imported beer, seemingly oblivious to what they're transporting in the trunk. From time to time, I sense one of the men moving around, his body shifting against the springs in the seat which forms one wall of our prison.

"Who are these guys?" I whisper to Elmer.

"It was dark."

"You didn't get a look?"

"First thing I knew they had a sack over my head."

"And what's that stench?" I whisper.

"Sorry."

"Was that you?"

"Sorry."

"Jesus!"

"Was it a bad one?"

"Are there any good ones? That's the foulest odor I ever smelled."

"I get nervous when I'm about to die."

"You do that again, they won't have to kill us. We'll be asphyxiated."

After a while, Snake said, "They sure are taking their sweet

Two Miles of Darkness

time. We been driving almost an hour. I've been trying to get my hands loose the whole time. It ain't happening. How about you?"

"Me? I'm taped up like a mummy in a museum."

16

Once again, we used the hidden key Cooper showed us that first day. We worked our way through the Kraft house slowly and methodically, using several electronic scanning devices Snake owned. We found no sign of cameras, bugs, or spying devices of any nature.

I saw things I hadn't noticed before, unpaid bills under a phone book on the kitchen table—lots of them—food moldering in the refrigerator, stale laundry waiting in a hamper outside the bedroom for owners who would never return to wash it. The bed in the master bedroom showed signs that somebody had napped on it that last day.

Try as I might, I found no evidence of Manny or the financial scheme that had taken so much of their money. Was it possible Manny had done this? The camera? All of it?

It was a humble abode, more humble even than my own house, where Kathy's clothes and shoe collection filled two small closets to bursting.

"I'd give my left nut to get a look at their computers," Snake said.

"Me too, but the police have them."

"That would be funny, the two of us walking around with only one nut each."

I ignored his attempt at humor. As we were locking up, Snake gave me a look I knew well. It meant he wanted me to violate my moral code in some way. He wanted to do something he felt required my stamp of approval. "You think it would be sick if I took some of her underwear?"

"Jesus! Yes, it would be sick. Of course it would be sick!"

"I was just kidding. Bad joke."

"Underwear? Christ."

"I told you I was kidding."

In an attempt to deflect my anger, he said, "You see those pictures in the house? You can learn a lot if you study a photograph long enough. These two were happy with each other. From beginning to end, they were happy with each other."

"I agree."

"On the other hand, hard times can put a torque wrench on a relationship. When we were in South America, my brother and I went at it tooth and nail."

"Given your history, I'd expect nothing less."

"I had a girlfriend down there he tried to take away from me."

"That's standard operating procedure for him, isn't it? Didn't he steal your second wife?"

"Second wife. First wife. Stole 'em both. Since we were whelps, he's gone after all my girlfriends. It doesn't help that we're identical twins. He wears my clothes, talks my talk, makes my moves until they think they're in love with *him*. He's been after my women since we were on the tit. I didn't figure out why until recently."

"I'll bite. Why?"

"We were breast-fed, but our mother only had one boob."

I laughed, but I could see from Snake's face my mirth hurt. He was serious. "You expect me to believe that?"

"Don't you get it? We're twins. We had to fight for one nipple. She let us fight. That's how she was."

"This sounds like one of your tall tales."

"It's true."

"I don't believe it."

"Mother claimed she got bit in the tit by a jackass she was trying to geld, but then again, maybe that was her tall tale. Maybe she lost it some other way. She used to tell us some real whoppers. But I do know a jackass has a bite like a bear trap. You know what else happened with my brother in South America?"

Snake unbuttoned his rumpled Hawaiian shirt and exposed his chest. I'd seen most of his tattoos, but this one was fresh. In the center of his sternum the blue ink read: *In Case of emergency, do not resusitake.*

"You were drunk?" I said.

"You think I did this? This was payback. I got *him* drunk and paid a tattooist to ink *Wife Stealer* across his chest. Figured I'd get even for all the wrongs he done me."

"This isn't even spelled right."

"He misspelled it to make me look stupid."

"It worked."

"Thanks."

For the rest of the day I was haunted by the image of Snake thieving from Alex Kraft's underwear drawer. There were times when I wondered if I really needed a friend like Snake, someone with a dicey moral code who told fantastic lies and expected me to take them on faith, but on the other hand, when he came through for you, he came through like nobody else could. In tough situations, he was about as perfect a backup as one might hope for. He was afraid of nothing and stood behind you like an iron backstop.

The rest of the day was spent tracking phone calls, searching for the dog, following leads, and conferring with Brad Munch on the phone. Snake managed to get hold of an ex-girlfriend—now married to someone other than the man she'd cheated on to be with Snake—who wrote for *The Seattle Times*. She was one of his few paramours who had not at some point been sidetracked by his brother, and she promised she would place an article about the dog in the next morning's paper. He was able to convince her to incorporate a photo, too, and even wrote his own caption—*Have You Seen Me?*—to be placed in a sidebar alongside a larger article about people abandoning their family pets during the economic downturn, a dismaying cultural phenomenon of late.

I received two phone messages from Anthony Throckmorton asking if I had more work for him and whether I thought he should take a Greyhound to Ohio to meet with a woman he only knew through the Internet. He'd been showing her semi-nude photo to one and all the day we met him, a photo Snake told me he recognized as commercial porn from his own Internet wanderings.

I told him it was a scam, that he was corresponding with a teenage boy pulling a prank or a Ukrainian mobster trying to siphon money from him. He'd already sent thirty dollars. She claimed to be broke, which belied another of her claims, that an estate she was about to inherit was worth five million dollars. "Throckmorton. Does she know you're homeless?" I asked.

"I'm not homeless. Okay. I'm sleeping in the church basement on a temporary basis, but I've got irons in the fire."

"You're not sending this person more money, are you?"

"I sent another envelope with ninety bucks in it."

The high August sun continued to bake the pavement as it had all week. By late afternoon the air had grown hot and muggy, which didn't stop clusters of school kids on bicycles from canvassing the neighborhood for Pickles. Most of the prospects they encountered were lounging on porches, under cars, or in the shade of yard trees, and all of them had current owners.

On the way home, Snake and I stopped at a coffee shop on Lakeside Avenue, across the street from the marina where he was staying. Cyclists were whizzing past in the street. I began wondering why I wasn't on my bike mixing it up with the others.

"You're taking this too hard," Snake said.

"It's crazy, when you think about it. A man loses everything and we all stand by until he's so miserable he kills himself and everyone he loves; but a dog comes up missing and all of a sudden there's a five-thousand dollar reward."

"People love dogs."

"Yeah."

"Shake it off, Thomas. Tomorrow we'll pick up that dog, collect our paycheck, and celebrate by having dinner with Kathy and the woman of my choice. I'm thinking of askin' *her*." He gestured at one of the nearby baristas, a young woman with short hair, a half-dozen steel piercings, and a colorful tattoo running the length of one muscular shoulder.

Earl Emerson

Having overheard Snake's comment, she smiled and said, "You'll have to do better than that crappy old cowboy hat if you're going to ask me out."

Snake laughed. "Lady, if you have a daddy complex, I'm your daddy. If you don't, I ain't nearly as old as I look. And if you want an athlete, I catch bullets in my teeth and have been known to leap tall buildings at a single bound."

"Good. When my boyfriend shoots at you, I'll tell him to aim for your teeth."

Snake guffawed. Later, before I left, I thought I saw a pair of lace panties peeking out from his jacket pocket, although it might have been a handkerchief. I tried to put it out of my mind.

17

That night I spent several hours at the Dregs, nursing a root beer and scrounging around for anybody who could tell me anything about Manny. It was a long evening and I came up empty.

The next morning I parked on the road in front of the Kraft house, my mountain bike in the back. The daytime temperatures were predicted to be in the mid- to high-nineties with a mild breeze, and it was already warm.

Snake had taken the barista out to dinner the night before, and apparently things had gone in his favor. As weather-beaten and bewhiskered as he appeared on first glance, Snake was not a bad-looking man in a kind of Marlborough-cowboy way. His main strength was a built-in radar that could detect receptive women anywhere: at the beach, a coffee shop, a nunnery. He'd zeroed in on the barista with uncanny accuracy.

Once people had read our newspaper article that morning, we began getting tips hand over fist. Snake was prioritizing them in order of feasibility, while scouting some of the locations in his truck. I'd been brooding all night about Manny. It might be the case, as the bar owner had theorized, that he had a warrant out on him and didn't want to see the police. But I thought it was more than that.

I researched the various Tecktrixonic remote camera models online and found that the more advanced Tecktrixonic systems featured a battery-operated camera which could send signals to a nearby receiver up to two thousand feet away, which meant somebody living nearly a half mile away could receive signals in the comfort of their living room, sipping martinis while watching the lighted windows at the back of the Kraft house on one screen and pro basketball or *Live From the Met* on another.

I called Carole Cooper and left a message. I knew she was busy and screening my calls, but a spy camera in the Kraft's backyard should have started some wheels in motion. Manny, the missing drinking buddy, investment partner, and gun supplier only added to my quandary.

If nothing else, Manny's disappearance should have kept the case open. It occurred to me that maybe he was dead, too. It was possible Mick Kraft hadn't stopped with his family, that he'd gone after a man he thought had propelled him into a financial sinkhole.

"You okay, Mr. Black?" Charlie Hatcher was in front of my car in the same jeans, sneakers, and torn T-shirt he'd been wearing the day before, his thick hair unkempt, as if he'd slept on it wrong.

"Sure. I'm fine."

"Mister Black? I've come up with a plan. I know where people live who might be leaving food out for raccoons. I figure that's where Pickles is getting her chow. She has to be eating at night. That's why nobody can find her."

"Mrs. Kennedy's okay with you staying out late?"

"She's going to loan me an old sleeping bag. It smells like mothballs, but I guess I can stand it. And I have a flashlight. I tried to talk my brother into coming, but he likes his TV too much."

"Charlie? How about I hire you for a couple of hours? I'd like to bike around the neighborhood and have you tell me everything you know. I'll pay you the same rate I paid the homeless men who worked for me yesterday, plus fifty percent extra for your specialized knowledge of the area. Four hours minimum."

"What does that mean?"

"It means if it only takes two hours, I'll still pay you for four."

"Those guys you had with you yesterday were homeless?"

"Most of them, yeah. Want to do this? I think you might know where some skeletons are buried."

"Skeletons?"

"It's just an expression."

"Okay. I'll do it. But where do homeless guys go at night?"

"There are shelters where they can sleep out of the weather. When it's nice like this, they camp out in parks and such."

"Once we saw a guy sleeping under the freeway in a cardboard box. Mom gave him five dollars. My uncle said he was going to buy drugs with it."

"Or maybe he was going to buy rolls and coffee."

"Don't they have families? Can't they stay with somebody?"

"If they could, they probably would."

After we OK'd it with Mrs. Kennedy, Charlie and I launched off on our bikes. Before we left, I oiled the chain on the rusty mountain bike Charlie shared with his brother, raised the saddle to the proper height for his leg length, and adjusted his brakes so they didn't drag. I gave him an old set of Allen wrenches, a screwdriver, pliers, and a crescent wrench so he would have the tools to keep the bike tuned. Before we left, he cached the tools in a box in his tree house.

"What's that all about?" I said.

"Mrs. Kennedy snitches our stuff if we leave it where she can find it."

"You're kidding."

"No, sir."

Charlie knew the neighborhood like a cheating husband knew every creaky stair on his front porch. He knew the teenage girl across the street, who was pregnant by an unknown suitor, still living with her family and planning to keep the baby and raise him at home; knew it was going to be a boy and would be named Noah.

He knew the compulsive shopper across the street, who had two or three packages delivered to her door every day and had entire rooms in her house stacked to the ceiling with boxes she hadn't even opened. He knew the two guys down the block who rented a house together and regularly got drunk Saturdays and Sundays watching football games;

told me the whole neighborhood could hear them yelling through their front door, which they left open even in the winter.

We meandered through the streets on our bikes while Charlie pointed out two houses that had been burgled over the past year, each abutting public right-of-ways where concrete stairs—maybe two hundreds steps in each set—ran through the woods from Twenty-first down the hill to Delridge Way.

Charlie knew where all the aggressive dogs lived, something I would expect a boy his age to keep tabs on. At one point, two dogs came flying out of their yard and raced after us, causing Charlie to pedal for all he was worth. I turned on the dogs and directed my front wheel at them as if to collide. I didn't hit either of them, but a counterattack persuaded both animals I was the alpha in the neighborhood. Both fled.

Charlie showed me a house near the elementary school where an elderly war hero lived—he wasn't sure which war—drinking his life away, a kindly man who lived alone and tended his tidy vegetable garden when he wasn't too inebriated and who, according to Charlie, gave out the biggest candy bars of anybody on Halloween. I interviewed him, found out he was ninety-two, had poor hearing, and hadn't seen the dog. He'd fought in Korea and had a steel plate in his leg from shrapnel injuries.

Charlie told me of a neighbor who lived four houses down from the Krafts in an untidy hovel where we so far had failed to speak to any occupant. Charlie told me that he and other kids had spotted the man once in his upstairs window watching them through a pair of field glasses. I realized this was the house where I'd spied a man watching me when I was in the Kraft's tree.

According to the mailbox, their last name was Cavendish. Charlie told me he once saw Mrs. Cavendish get a speeding ticket on the street a half block from her house. The couple had two high-school-age daughters who rarely left the house when they weren't at school.

According to Charlie, Cavendish had an enormous pot

belly and one bulging eye that failed to track with the other one. "He's a one-man creep show," Charlie said. "I guess that isn't very Christian."

"This isn't Sunday school. You're doing fine. What else can you tell me about this guy?" I asked.

"His dog is fat. And mean. He tries to bite everyone."

"Anything else?"

Charlie gestured at a queue of houses that included the bungalow where he lived with Mrs. Kennedy. "He stares into the windows, especially if it's after dark and we haven't closed the blinds yet. Mrs. Kennedy thinks he's going to rape her."

"You tell your mother any of the other stuff about Mrs. Kennedy?"

"Our mother's looking to place us in another home, but she's been looking for a couple of years now. She wants to keep us together, but nobody's willing to take on four kids. She thought about quitting her job so she could go on welfare, but she said welfare sucks. It could be worse. Hey, there are kids at school who don't even remember having a home. Some of them live in their cars. One kid I know lives in a tent at a campground with his grandmother. I guess we're doing okay."

"What about your father?"

"We haven't heard from him since I was in second grade." I couldn't help thinking Charlie's relationship with his father was a lot like my relationship with mine.

I made a mental note to check Cavendish's background later. After two and a half hours, I paid Charlie in cash and we pedaled back to his house.

At the Kraft residence, I noticed a car parked in front, driver's window rolled down, the man in the driver's seat fiddling with a small electronic device in his lap. The woman next to him reclined with the easy familiarity of a wife. A quick glance told me they'd placed a cheap metal bucket filled with gladioli on the front porch of the Kraft home. It wasn't the first time someone had left flowers on the porch, for there were clumps of withered flowers all around the front of the home.

"Talk to you a minute?" I asked.

When he pulled out his earbuds, the distant, tinny sound of rock and roll spewed out. "Who are you?"

"Name is Thomas Black. I've been hired to find their missing dog."

"I didn't realize Pickles *was* missing."

"She hasn't been seen since it happened. Did you know the Krafts well?"

"I worked with Mick at UPS. He more or less got me the job."

"A guy does something like this, he usually shows some signs beforehand. Did you notice anything?"

"Heck, no. It surprised the hell out of us."

His wife remained in the car while he walked toward the house and I rode beside him on the bumpy lawn, balancing on my bike. When we were a good distance from the car, he said, "Look. Melissa's kinda pissed. She thought I was taking her to Spuds, but I detoured here. You want to talk, how 'bout we meet on Alki? That way she can get some lunch and I can give you more time. After that, I'm taking her to the doctor. We're pregnant." He grinned with the half-mad, nervous look of a first-time father. There were no infant seats in their car, so I guessed the baby would be their first.

"See you at Spuds."

I covertly snapped a photo of Gregory Rowsell and noted his license plate in case he decided to rabbit.

The peninsula that defined West Seattle was crowned at the north end by a sandy beach that ran for miles around its tip, sporting a magnificent view of downtown Seattle across the bay to the east. On hot summer days, Alki Beach was a magnet for young and old alike. Already, the line of cars cruising the avenue along the shoreline had congealed into a minor backup, stop and go, gawk and stop.

Men strutted the beach without their shirts. Volleyball games were in full swing. A young woman wearing tight cut-off jeans glided on in-line skates along the paved path above the beach with the skill of a pro ice skater.

As I crawled along in traffic, I phoned Snake to tell him where I was. "Hey, old man," Snake said. "I'm a couple of doors down from where you were parked earlier, talking to an attractive young lady who wants me to show her my medals." I heard an elderly woman tittering in the background.

"One house south? Same side? The old woman who sits in her window all day?"

"That's the one."

"You must have got up there right after I left. I talked to her, too. You get anything?"

"Nada. But I just may elope with this young lady." I heard more tittering in the background. If nothing else, Snake knew how to flatter a woman.

"You do that. I'll be back up there later, after I interview a guy I found leaving flowers on the Kraft porch."

"That could be good."

"Let's hope."

18

Gregory Rowsell and I sat on a chunk of driftwood that had been sculpted by waves to resemble a very smooth giant shoe. Thirty yards away, Rowsell's wife sulked in the car with the windows rolled up, the motor running so the air conditioner could keep her cool. I didn't think it was hot enough for air conditioning, but then I wasn't pregnant.

Rowsell was beefy and deep-voiced, like a radio announcer, moving with a quirky gait he told me was the result of a bad knee from high school football. He'd been on the same football team as Mick Kraft, who'd been a star running back. Unlike Kraft, rich food and a soft life had erased any signs of his ever having been an athlete.

He started off with a lame joke I'd heard several times in the past week. "Last summer seemed nicer. Last summer I wore flip-flops both days." When I didn't react, he continued, "Wife got kind of PO'd. She thinks I'm leaving flowers for a monster. I tell her they're for Alex, but she doesn't buy it. She thinks Alex should have left him a long time ago, that her death was somehow her own fault."

"For staying with Mick?"

"Right."

"You said you didn't see any signs that he could do it. Does your wife disagree?"

"She didn't see it coming either, but she refuses to cut either of them any slack. I think the whole thing hit her pretty hard. Her stepfather committed suicide a few years ago. I'm not sure she's ever really handled it."

"Tell me about Mick."

"Mick was the nicest guy in the world. He'd give you the shirt off his back. Always in a good mood."

"So what happened? How'd they get into their financial

bind?"

"First of all Mick lost his job at UPS. He got another job, not as good, and lost that one, too. They were always a little precarious on the house because Alex was still paying off massive student loans. I guess she owed over a hundred grand. And then with the housing problems everybody else is having, they went upside down on the mortgage. It was like a rowboat capsizing in the middle of the Atlantic.

"That was when Mick came up with this scheme to get it all back. He was so high on it, I put eight thousand dollars of *our* money in, too. Almost everything I inherited from my grandmother. That's another reason Melissa's pissed. Mick was positive we would double our money at the very least. It was a start-up company for an Internet social site that was going to be better than Facebook. Trouble is, it never even got off the ground. It was bad enough he did what he did, but he took our savings with him. I never even told Melissa I was investing until after they died. Man, she hit the ceiling. That was our money for the baby."

"Tell me about the investment."

"I wish I could. I feel so stupid now. I never did understand the whole thing. Mick was a careful guy with his money. Usually. He'd done a lot of research on this and he was sold, which was what sold me. We were going to make millions because we were getting in on the ground floor. Mick scraped together every cent he could lay his hands on. He took a big risk taking out another loan on the house. Don't ask me how, but he convinced a bank to give him a second loan.

"Some buddy of his who used to be a stockbroker was investing the money for him. I never really figured out what happened except it all went south. I know. I know. It was stupid to invest in something I didn't understand. But I was going along with Mick, who said he'd researched it, and he was just so damn positive. When you lose money on a deal like that, you're accused of being greedy. You get rich, you were smarter than everybody else. Got in on the ground floor. Some kind of genius. But me? I was greedy."

"Who was this ex-stockbroker?"

"I never met him. Name was Manny. Never even got a last name." He winced. "I know, I know. Greedy and stupid both."

"How about a phone number? An address?"

"No idea. I gave my money to Mick, and he gave it to Manny. Said we had to do it that way, that we were lucky to get in at all. It was a closed investment. Only insiders. Our money was going in under Manny's name. I don't think Melissa is ever going to get over it." He glanced back at the car and waved, but Melissa pretended not to notice.

"Tell me more about Mick's bad luck."

"It started at UPS. Mick had a perfect driving record. Then he hits a station wagon, and the driver goes to the hospital for minor stuff. Mick thought the woman was grabbing for more insurance money, because it was only a fender-bender and it was *her* fault. He said she raced around in front of him and then slammed on her brakes. Like she was trying to get into an accident. She said there was a rabbit in the road. A rabbit? It was downtown Bellevue. His supervisor judged it preventable, which meant it went against his record with the company.

"You don't want to see 'preventable' on your record. Doesn't matter who's legally at fault. Two days later, a truck slams into the side of his van. The guy driving the truck swears Mick pulled out in front of him. Mick says the guy was speeding and actually gunned it to get to the intersection before Mick cleared it. So it was Mick's word against this other driver. Again, preventable.

"Two days later he takes his truck back to the depot and they discover it's been bashed in near the fuel spout. Looked like somebody had done it with a sledge hammer or a rock, maybe while Mick was away delivering something. Mick said he didn't report it because he didn't see it. The company decided Mick was trying to hide a third accident.

"As it turned out, there'd been numerous complaints against him in the weeks prior to the accidents. Complaints about his driving. About damaged packages. Even about his hygiene."

"So his job performance was going downhill?"

"The union was going to bat for him, but then Mick got into a shouting match with his supervisor. Later that night the van he'd been driving burned to the ground in the parking lot. If that wasn't enough, it caught two other vans on fire. That's when the union washed their hands of him."

"They thought Mick torched the van?"

"By that time, everybody did."

"Even you?"

"He loved the company. I don't think he would ever do anything like that."

"He wasn't a murderer, either, was he?

"I still don't believe it. But the police are saying he did it. They usually get it right, don't they?"

"What else was going on in his life?"

"Three weeks after he got canned, he found another job driving a delivery truck for a local grocery chain. It wasn't union, but it was a job. Now, get this. In the new job he has four fender-benders in his first week. They're thinking he's on drugs. He volunteers for a drug test—*volunteers*—and he fails. The lab says his system is stinking with cocaine."

"Which would explain the vehicular accidents."

"It would if Mick did drugs. But Mick didn't do drugs."

"So it was a bad lab result?"

"Had to be."

"This is a lot of bad luck hitting one guy. All these accidents and now a faulty drug test?"

"I know it's hard to believe. Even Mick began to think there was something wrong with him, like maybe he was having blackouts. He went to his doctor and told him the whole story."

"And?"

"The doctor said he was fine. Said drug testing labs made mistakes every day and he should go in for another test with a different lab."

"And?"

"He never made it. The night he saw the doc he got arrested. Then his new employer let him go when they found out he was out on bail. His mother put up the bond money, but she had to sell her car to do that. After that, looking for another job became problematical."

"How did he come to get arrested?"

"A friend of his took him to a Mariner's game, you know, trying to cheer him up. On the way out of the stadium his buddy got into a beef with a couple of guys who were drunk. These other guys started whaling on him, so Mick jumps in to help. Then one of the guys pulls a knife. Mick gets the knife away from this dude, and when the cops show up, Mick's holding the knife, so *he* gets arrested. The others, including his buddy, escape into the crowd."

"You know the buddy's name?"

"Same guy we gave all the money to."

"Manny?"

"That's him."

19

Snake and I were on our way to Doda's when I decided to stop at my father's place first. He had known Doda Woods since before I was born, and after he and my mother separated he confided to me that he and Charlene might get married, a confidence inspired by alcohol, as were many of his confidences in those days. "What do you think of Charlene for a stepmother?" he asked one day. I wasn't sure if he actually wanted my opinion or if the question was some form of mental torture, but the thought of Charlene as a stepmother chilled me.

The marriage never took place, though not for lack of scheming on his part.

My father lived on Capitol Hill in the basement of a small house owned by an elderly widow he'd met in church. In religion, my father found a vast feeding trough filled with well-off widows, most of whom were apparently waiting for some cad to park himself in one of their spare rooms. So far, despite the fact that he was chronically out of work and had almost nothing going for him, every widow my father rented from believed he was an undiscovered genius, and they'd all told me so in no uncertain terms. In fact, the percentage of his female acquaintants who lectured me on his brilliance was so staggeringly high that he had to be coaching them.

He'd been living in this moldering basement for twelve years, sponging off an infirm woman who probably would have been better off in a nursing home. He claimed to be renting the accommodations, though I doubt any money changed hands.

We found him working a crossword puzzle in the kitchen at the back of the small paint-peeling house just off

East John and Twenty-ninth. The owner of the house was, we were quickly informed, napping, so we were to keep our voices down. In the center of the table a burned-out cigar sat in a plastic butter container like a turd, a half-finished Budweiser just out of reach beyond that. The back door was open to the morning heat, the screen door unlatched.

"Come in, stranger," said my father, who remained motionless.

He nodded at Snake. There was no love between the two of them.

"What's goin' on, kiddo?" my father asked. His feet were propped on the kitchen table. He wore an old dingy dress shirt and threadbare suit pants, playing the thrifty businessman on a cheap holiday.

"I'm working for Doda."

"I'm working over there, too. Designing and rebuilding a porch. The guy I replaced was a scam artist. If there's one thing your father's an expert at, it's design concepts."

"Looks to me like you're sitting in the kitchen, not working in Medina," Snake said.

Ignoring him, my father continued in a solemn voice, "Carpentry wasn't too humble for our Master, and it isn't too humble for me."

"Shouldn't you be over there now, Nigel?" Snake needled.

"Myrtle's car needs work."

"You doing the work yourself? 'Cause I saw it out there in the driveway."

"Thinkin' about it."

"We're on our way to Doda's," I said. "We could give you a lift."

"No thanks. I may have a dental appointment later."

Typical of my father, who could charm the pants off crooked politicians, cab drivers, attorneys, ingénues, or the dowager in the other room, who was essentially supporting him, he was nonplused when his act didn't work on me or Snake.

"I've got a couple of questions," I said.

"Fire away, kiddo." As we chatted, my father continued

to write as if he could actually work a *New York Times* puzzle while carrying on a conversation.

"What do you know about the missing dog?"

"Pickles? What makes you think I know anything?"

"You knew enough to recommend me."

"Yeah, yeah. You're welcome."

"And what's the deal with Charlene? Is she running the place?"

"She hired me to redesign that porch. Yes, I guess she does run it. Why do you ask?"

"I never really understood the dynamics over there."

"There's a lot of history. Charlene used to work for Warner Brothers. In publicity. Doda met her at some charity event Doda was running, feeding orphans in Southeast Asia or something. Hired her on the spot. Doubled her salary, which just goes to show anybody can be bought. Don't ever forget that, kid. Anybody can be bought.

"The way I understand it, Charlene keeps the books, deals with the attorneys, keeps an eye on the nurses, watches the medications—although I don't know what a Christian Scientist is doing with pills—and keeps avaricious sycophants at bay. Charlene thinks of herself more as Doda's daughter than her employee. Whatever she is, there's no denying she's the power behind the throne, especially now that Doda's crossed the century mark. She was actually pretty sharp until just recently."

"She seems sharp enough to me," said Snake.

"It was Charlene's arm I twisted to get you that job," said my father.

"I didn't want the job."

"You took it quick enough, didn't you?"

"I didn't want to disappoint Doda."

"But you took it. And you're welcome."

"Charlene had a couple living with her years ago, renting out part of her house. Did you know them?"

"She's got a mother-in-law apartment built into her place over in Magnolia. Nice place. At one point I was going to rent it myself, but she got a little persnickety over the deposit. These are the people who lost the dog, right? That who you're talking about?"

"The people who are dead. Alex and Mick Kraft."

For a moment my father looked up at a ceramic chicken hanging on the wall, part of a poultry motif that reigned throughout the kitchen, a theme the old woman who owned the place must have picked out years ago when she had more appetite for home decoration. The frayed table cloth bore the image of a faded rooster.

"It was a shame, wasn't it? A crying shame. Alex was a beautiful woman. Even made that wife of yours look like a pastrami sandwich."

"Kathy will be interested to hear you think she looks like a pastrami sandwich."

"Now don't be submarining my relationship with your gracious wife. She happens to think I'm pretty special, and I don't want you spoiling that."

"She told you she thinks you're special?"

"I can read between the lines." He'd been disappointed when Kathy hadn't warmed up to him and had been sniping at her ever since, playing out one of his favorite dramas, the myth that he'd been ousted by the family when I was ten. To say he'd deserted us was closer to the truth. Now, in spite of the fact that he'd been AWOL for almost twenty years, he was aggressively resentful that I wasn't fonder of him. On my side of it, it was hard to be close to a man who'd been missing for so long, a man I barely knew.

Years ago, he'd pulled every emotional deceit he could muster in an effort to get Charlene interested, but it hadn't worked. I was only a boy, but watching him work his ploys before he was officially divorced from my mother both angered and confused me. It was the first time I realized who my father really was, for despite all the problems he'd caused her, my mother had nary a bad word to say about him.

"Next time when you run across a missing dog, I would appreciate a heads-up before you drop my name."

"I was under the impression you needed the work," he said, mildly.

"What made you think so?"

"For starters, the cramped little house you live in. Then there's the way you dress. The stuff you eat. When was the last time you had a grade-A steak?"

"I don't eat meat. You know that. And the fact is, this dog is delaying my investigation into a manslaughter case for Kathy."

"Hey. I was only trying to help."

"And it doesn't make me happy when you're out there telling people how poorly I'm doing."

"I never told Charlene you were doing poorly."

"No? What *did* you tell her?"

"I told her . . . hmmmm . . ." His pen hovered over the crossword. "What was the name of the actress who played opposite Paul Newman in *Hud*?"

"Patricia Neal. She was in *The Day the Earth Stood Still*, too. What *did* you tell Charlene?"

He continued scribbling. "I just thought you needed the work. Sure. Castigate your old man for trying to pull you out of a jam. That's no more than I would expect."

"I wasn't in a jam."

"Maybe you aren't destitute. But you live like you are."

"Hey," Snake said, sharply. "He's not the one camped out in some old lady's basement."

My father stopped writing and mulled over Snake's insult, fixing me with his penetrating brown eyes as if I were responsible. He could stare like a stuffed owl when he wanted. When I was younger, it used to frighten me, but not any longer. "If you'd been raised under my roof, you wouldn't have friends like this. And you sure as hell wouldn't be a gumshoe."

"You never had a roof," Snake said. "To raise anybody under."

"It was your mother," my father said to me. "She was going to sic her relatives on me. They wanted to run me out of town on a rail. I had to get out." It wasn't true. It was part of the myth he'd created around himself and possibly even believed.

For months now, he'd been hinting broadly that the daylight basement apartment in my house, which we rented to students, would suit him nicely and that if I asked in just the right manner, he might agree to live there. Aside from the fact that I had no appetite for trying to collect rent from my contentious father, Kathy was even more averse to the idea than I was. I promised her I would burn the place to the ground before I let him sponge off us.

Snake and I were on our way out the door when I stopped on the small, concrete stoop that served as a back porch and turned back to my father. "By the way. The last summer I went to Wyoming. What happened?"

"Last name of the man who played opposite Ray Milland in *The River's Edge*?"

"Quinn. Anthony Quinn."

"Wyoming? That last summer you went to their ranch with Joshua Compton? What about it?"

"All I know is, I went to Doda's ranch to spend the summer with Binky. Next thing I knew I was on a plane back to Sea-Tac."

"Didn't Doda talk to you before you left?"

"All she said was that I was going home."

"Joshua . . . Binky . . . accused you of . . ."

"Of what?"

"Moral depravity."

"What?"

"Those were Doda's words."

"What sort of moral depravity?"

"I don't recall."

"Come on."

"She said you were trying to play with some kid's wiener."

"Wiener? As in penis?"

"That's right, kiddo. She said you were diddling some kid's wiener."

Nothing else he might have said could have rendered me so unequivocally speechless. I stared at him in disbelief, as he and Snake both avoided my eyes.

"I was sent home and not invited back because she thought I was a pervert? You tell her it wasn't true?"

"How could I do that? I didn't really know if it was true.

I wasn't there. I told her I'd straighten you out."

"You didn't stick up for me?"

"Welcome to the world of adults, kiddo. You need to realize there are things we grownups have to consider besides the feelings of a kid. Doda was giving me work. I didn't need your conniptions queering the deal."

"That's how you saw it? My *conniptions*?"

"That's how it was."

"How could you let them think that about me?"

"Well, you know what they say. Where there's smoke there's fire." He continued working the crossword. "Director of *Shane*?"

"George Stevens. You knew me. You knew it couldn't be true."

"I didn't know any such thing."

He didn't trust me then and he didn't trust me now, more than twenty years later. It wasn't news to learn this about my father. The shock was that for almost a quarter of a century a lie had been circulating with my name stuck to it, following me like a trail of toilet paper on my shoe, a fabrication I hadn't known about and thus could not possibly refute.

Snake and I were sitting in the hot car waiting for the air conditioner to blow the interior cool when Snake said, "That guy's so dense he could hide his own Easter eggs."

"They say he's a genius."

"You know what really pisses me off?"

"What?"

"It pisses me off when a guy can't see what a great kid he raised."

"He didn't raise me. Even before the divorce, he was barely around."

"Maybe it turned out for the best. If he'd raised you, you might have turned out like him. And then we wouldn't be friends."

"Why not?"

"I'm not usually friends with assholes."

"Thanks."

"You're welcome."

20

Realizing I needed some space to digest this new wrinkle, Snake was silent as we crossed Lake Washington on the 520 bridge.

Doda had summoned us. We had no idea what she wanted, but when a regal summons is issued, the peasants scamper to the ramparts. Besides, I wanted to talk to Doda about the Krafts.

Charlene had warned us not to mention the deaths to Doda, but it was time somebody clued her in.

Then there was the other matter. For almost twenty years, I'd been wondering why I'd been jettisoned from the Wyoming vacation that was to have extended through the whole summer, a vacation that would have been a near replica of the perfect previous summer, in which Binky and I shared our dreams and secrets and spent our days wandering the ranch, splashing about in the pool, or riding horses. I knew something or someone had moved my name to the negative side of the ledger, but in a million years I never could have guessed the mechanics of it.

At twelve I'd been about as asexual as any kid could be. My passions were riding horses, reading, playing board games, and playing mumblety-peg with my new pocket knife, a knife my mother allowed me provided I followed a list of rules she'd laid out. I collected action-hero comic books and read extensively from Doda's library. It wasn't that I didn't know about sex. Like everyone else my age, I entertained the occasional schoolboy crush on a classmate or teacher, or a friend's sister, but my fantasies unfailingly revolved around the opposite sex, not other boys; they were never precocious, and they were always, by any standards, of an innocent and naive nature, as one would expect.

Two Miles of Darkness

As far as I could remember, there had been no skinny-dipping or peeing off bridges for distance, and nothing else that might have been misinterpreted by Binky and his two pals, who arrived a few days after I did and spent almost no time with me. Then before I knew it, I found myself banished. Doda gave no reason for the ejection, and her dour demeanor when she sent me off kept me from asking questions.

Until I disembarked from the plane at Sea-Tac and saw her, I erroneously thought I was being sent home because something had happened to my mother. But there she was at the airport, as puzzled by my unexpected return as I. While she was genuinely perplexed, my father assumed an attitude of befuddlement. Looking back, I realize he wasn't befuddled so much as he was disapproving. As off-putting and depressing as it was to feel a parent's disapproval, there was nothing I could do about it. I knew from experience that confronting him was only going to make things worse.

When Snake and I arrived at Doda's mansion, we spotted Binky and Chad in the back yard, sitting at the shaded table near the pool in their swimming trunks. With them were two women and a man I hadn't seen before, all young eager-beaver business- or law-school types dressed as if for a day in court and wielding forms and briefcases. It looked as if some sort of financial meeting was in progress and that Binky and Chad hadn't been informed of the dress code.

As soon as Binky saw us, he unceremoniously abandoned the meeting along with any pretense of sobriety and jogged toward the house. "Thomas, Thomas, Thomas!" Then, addressing his companions, "Hey guys! Look who's here. It's Dogs R Us." Laughter followed from behind him in the yard. It was clear everybody at the table had heard about us.

Binky shook hands with each of us and then went back outside without breaking eye contact with me. Inexplicably, he tossed a hula hoop into the pool, where it dimpled the surface, and said, "You think I can dive through that from the board?"

In the blink of an eye he had reverted to his eleven-year-old persona. Having myself been accused of puerile behavior on more than one occasion, I was reluctant to take the bait, but Snake had no such compunction, so we followed Binky outside into the relentless sunshine.

It was a long jump and would require some athleticism, but with a running start and an energetic bounce off the the diving board, he might just make it. I wouldn't have bet either way. "You think I can't do it?" Binky asked again, staring at me.

"Hell, no," said Snake, still unhinged over the Dogs R Us remark and the laughter it had generated.

"Fifty bucks?" Binky turned his attention to Snake.

"You're on, buckaroo." They both placed their bills under a glass paperweight on one of the tables near the pool.

For my part, I couldn't look at Binky now without seeing my eleven-year-old friend and wondering what I had done to make him lie so blatantly about me. It seemed preposterous that something so trivial and so far in the past could deliver even a glancing blow to my equilibrium, but there it was.

Binky clambered up onto the diving board, moving as if he could barely walk, then performed some mugging and bouncing, which prompted laughter from his audience—the guy would have been a star in the silent movies—paced out a couple of pretend runs toward the end of the board, then did a quick turn-around and a heavy-footed launch, making a perfect, feet-first splash through the hoop while cupping his balls comically with both hands. It was hard not to laugh.

"That was a damn easy way to lose money," Snake groused as we walked alongside the maid and back into the house, up the wide staircase to Doda's office.

"From what Charlene said the other day, Binky loves to make wagers, and most of them are sure things. You shouldn't have bet."

"Those boys need some serious payback."

"Don't let your emotions run your life."

"Thanks for the advice. By the way, what happened to

you back there?"

"What do you mean?"

"It looked like you were having a stroke."

"I was thinking."

"About what they did to you all those years ago?"

"Something like that."

"Don't let your emotions run your life. A man told me that once."

"Sometimes men tell you things."

"And sometimes they're worth listening to. You're right. It was a sucker bet."

When we got to Doda's office, Charlene wasn't in evidence and the maid who'd walked us through the house retreated quietly, so it was just Snake and me and a hundred-four-year-old woman I'd once loved like my own grandmother. I stood near a window where I could observe the shenanigans in the yard, though the shenanigans had largely ceased and everybody was back at the table pushing papers around again.

"I called you here to find out how you're doing with the dog," Doda said. She was behind her desk, just as she had been on our first visit.

"We've got scouts out," said Snake. "There's maybe a hundred kids on the street trying to claim the reward. They've already turned in poodles and labs, and one kid tried to give us a cat, you name it, but so far we haven't laid eyes on Pickles."

"Sounds like you're off to a rollicking start, though," said Doda.

I stepped closer to her desk. "Something else has come up. Charlene told me not to tell you, but I'm going to take a chance."

"Ignore Charlene. She thinks because I broke my hip I'm brittle in the head. I've seen more things in this world than she can dream of. For godsakes, I had dinner with Hermann Goering. I don't need to be mollycoddled. What is it?"

"Alex and Mick Kraft are both dead. The police say he shot her, then her mother, then himself."

"Oh, I know all about that. You think I didn't know about that? I read five papers a day and have since I was fifteen. Now, what is it you want to tell me?"

"I have grave misgivings about the veracity of the official version. Before it happened, Mick ran into a spate of bad luck that defies explanation. He had a friend who seems to be a key in all this, but he's missing now."

It had already occurred to me that Mick might have killed Manny the same day he killed his wife and himself; that of all people, Manny, who'd convinced him to risk the last of his money in a losing financial scheme, might have been his first target. On the other hand, Manny might have gotten into it with Mick and done the shooting himself, making it look like a double-murder/suicide.

"Don't forget the camera," said Snake.

"What camera?" Doda asked.

"It looks like somebody set up a surveillance camera overlooking the windows at the rear of their house," I said. "It's been removed, but we have a witness who says it was there until earlier this week."

"Who would do such a thing?"

"As far as the camera goes, we have a suspect in the neighborhood, but he's only that. We haven't vetted him yet."

"I still don't understand where this is going."

"I'd like to investigate this at the same time we look for the dog."

"Because you think the answers will help you find Pickles?"

"That's a possibility, but it's more because something stinks in Denmark."

"I believe the line spoken by Marcellus in *Hamlet* goes, 'Something is rotten in the state of Denmark.'"

"Yes. I should go back and reread that," I said, although I'd never read *Hamlet* or any other Shakespeare all the way through. "I'm just saying I have to find out what happened to the Krafts and her mother. If it wasn't a murder-suicide, there's a killer running loose."

After a long silence, Snake said, "He can't stand it.

Two Miles of Darkness

Three people are dead, and he can't stand for there to be a grain of ambiguity about it. He's going to dig until he finds out what happened or until he hits oil. Besides, the Krafts were his clients once."

"Tell me what you think happened," Doda said.

"I honestly don't know."

"They seemed like such nice kids, just struggling to make a place for themselves in the world."

"You want my opinion?" Snake said. "I think they were murdered by an outside party."

"What makes you say that?" Doda asked.

"That camera. It was removed after their deaths, which means they didn't put it up themselves. Somebody was spying on them. Plus, right up until just about the end, Mick Kraft was cleaner than a Mississippi prison warden's toilet bowl. It just don't seem right that he would go off his nut like that."

"People go off their nut all the time," I quipped, arguing against our position, despite myself.

Doda thought it over for a few moments. "If you want to look into this, Thomas, then I think I'd better finance it so you can do it right."

"I need to warn you," I said. "The police have cleared the case."

"Yes, but you and I've been around long enough to know the authorities are not infallible. Go with your nose, Thomas. Bill me for the hours, and report back with whatever you come up with. Meanwhile, let's try to get that poor dog back into a good home. Anything else?"

"One thing. This is completely off topic, but twenty years ago in Wyoming, I never did anything wrong."

I had been expecting to have to refresh her memory of that summer, but she squinted over the top of her wire-rimmed spectacles and said with conviction, "I know that."

"But you sent me home."

"I could tell Joshua was lying. I can read that boy like a book. What he and his friends did was wrong, but I didn't want to give them a chance to do it again. Sending you home seemed like the best thing for everyone concerned.

Now that you're grown, you must realize family has to come first."

"Of course it does, and I appreciate everything you did for me, but sending me away without telling me why wasn't right."

She stared at me, her blue eyes watery. "I spoke at length with your father on the phone when it was going on. He said he was going to explain it all to you when you got back to Tacoma. He did explain it, didn't he?"

On the way downstairs, Snake said, "The way your father tells the story, you were guilty. Think he actually remembers it that way?"

"Hard to say what he remembers."

"Seems to me he wanted to shame you."

"Looks that way."

"Know what I think?"

"What do you think?"

"I think you should punch his lights out."

"His net worth couldn't be more than about six hundred bucks. All he's got is this elaborate fantasy world he's constructed for himself. And I suspect there are plenty of other people who would like to punch his lights out. If it's going to happen, I'll leave it to one of them."

"Sure, but if he was my father, I'd let him have it."

"Maybe that's why you've got a brother who tattoos your chest when you're drunk."

"Well, there is that. But I wouldn't get drunk around your father, I were you."

"Not planning to."

Chad was in the kitchen gathering an armful of imported beers to take out to the company. "The maid won't serve us outside," he said, grinning. "Last week Binky accidentally pushed her into the pool. You should have heard the old lady yelling at him. '*Josh*ua!' Just like when we were kids. It was hilarious. Come on out."

Snake and I glanced at each other. I knew Snake was thinking about the fifty bucks he'd lost to Binky.

I followed Snake and Chad into the yard and walked alongside the pool, where the others were gathering up their documents. The meeting was over and they were going to celebrate with a brew.

"Hey, Thomas," Binky said. "Remember all those bets we used to make as kids? Who could hold their breath underwater longer? How about it? Let's do it again."

"You're kidding, right?"

"Serious as a heart attack, man."

"I'm not really a betting man."

"Oh, come on. Of course you are."

"Yeah. Be a sport," urged Chad. The two women smiled a boys-will-be-boys smile. I could tell they could hardly wait to get out of there.

"No, thanks," I said.

"Come on. Come on," cajoled Binky. "Have some fun."

"We'll give you odds," said Chad.

Snake had been champing at the bit from the outset, and I knew he traveled with a wad of greenbacks. I tried to remember how much money I had in my wallet. "I don't have swim trunks," I said lamely.

"In the pool room," Binky said as if the deal were already concluded, pointing toward a door. "There's a pile of them on the counter, freshly laundered."

As I passed Snake, I whispered, "We go fifty-fifty on this."

"You sure you can do it?"

"Take the money you've been saving for a pacemaker, old man, and bet it all."

By the time I got back into the August sunshine, Snake had put down two hundred dollars at two-to-one odds, the woman in the beige business suit having been inveigled into refereeing the wager. I'd found the hideout bill I kept in my wallet, a lone Benjamin Franklin, and added that to the pile, so she ended up holding nine hundred dollars in cash, three of ours, six of theirs.

"We go in together," Binky said, curling his toes over the lip of the pool. "And whoever comes up first pays. Got it?" They were the same basic rules we'd used at the ranch in Wyoming, when we ran this contest almost every day. Back in those days, Binky won nine times out of nine and I could see his burgeoning confidence now.

On the count of three, Binky and I jumped into the deep end simultaneously, each of us with our arms winged out, slowly flapping our way to the bottom. I watched him clowning underwater, entertaining the people up top, although I think his primary goal was to make me expel air by laughing. In fact, it took will power not to laugh. After a while, he ceased his antics and concentrated on conserving oxygen.

Ninety seconds into our odyssey, I could see he was starting to worry; I was showing no distress. At a minute fifty, I saw him begin to struggle. A minute fifty-five, fifty-six, fifty-seven . . . With a titanic struggle, he made two minutes on the dot before he pushed off the bottom and rocketed to the surface. I waited four seconds longer, coughing and spluttering when I broke the surface, as if I was at the end of my tether, which I wasn't. As if it was a miracle I'd made it that long. Which it wasn't.

I was at the side of the pool listening to Snake brag that I could outlast a Harp Seal when Binky swam over and said, "Give us a chance to get our money back?"

"I don't—"

"Come on, man. That was pure de luck and you know it. You can't do it again. You guys just took six hundred bucks from us."

Six hundred dollars was a slow night out on the town for him, but still, I could see the loss was eating at him.

Even though I suspected he'd thrown the first heat so he could pick our pockets on a second, where the odds he'd dangled to coax me into the water in the first place would go down and the amount wagered would go up, I agreed to a rematch, doing my best to look unsure of myself. Binky argued querulously for odds in the other direction, but Snake, betting the entire nine hundred he was now holding, insisted on a straight bet, no odds either way.

I wondered how long Binky could really hold his breath.

We took several deep breaths and splashed in together,

Two Miles of Darkness

Binky breaking the surface a full two seconds after I did, taking any small advantage he could muster, this time serious as a hoot owl. After a while, I realized I should have given myself more time to recuperate from the first effort, because the first forty-five seconds proved as strenuous as the last forty-five of the earlier match.

As the surface waters of the pool calmed, I stood on the bottom and watched the distorted faces above us, listened to the sounds of people talking, heard Snake's garbled voice shouting blasphemous encouragement.

At a minute forty, I started to feel lightheaded but knew if I ignored it the feeling would diminish. At two minutes and ten seconds, we'd both eclipsed our previous efforts and my lungs were screaming for relief. Surprisingly, Binky showed no sign of discomfort, remaining as still and composed as a stone Buddha in a garden. He had definitely been faking it during our first dive.

At two fifteen, I let out some air. I felt as if I were strangling. At two twenty-five, I saw Binky let out some air. My lungs felt as if they were collapsing in on themselves. At two minutes and thirty seconds, Binky opened his eyes, looked at me and shrugged his shoulders, as if to say, 'Is that all you've got?' Feeling as if I were going to die there on the bottom of Doda's pool, I grinned. The seconds ticked by, each one noticeably slower than the last.

They say when you drown you don't actually inhale water into your lungs, that your gag reflex shuts down your throat so that you merely pass out from lack of oxygen. I had a feeling one of us was about to test that theory. At this point, I couldn't be sure I would make it to the surface once I gave up.

Still, I remained in place. If he could suffer this kind of agony, so could I. At least, that was what I told myself.

Two minutes and thirty-five seconds. Thirty-six. Thirty-seven. Thirty-eight . . .

Without warning, Binky shot off the bottom of the pool and punched through the surface, gasping loudly for oxygen. I came up a couple of seconds behind him.

Snake and I were now fifteen hundred dollars in the

black, and Binky wasn't asking for another dive. In fact, he didn't even congratulate me. He just held onto the side of the pool gasping and staring at the water splashing in the pool's gutter.

After I toweled off and was back in my street clothes, I found Snake in the parking area behind the garages talking to the younger woman from the meeting. The older of the two women was already driving away in a rental car, having flown up from California for their pool-side conference. "Thomas? This is Crystal," Snake said, then indicating the young man standing off to the side, "and her brother, Steve."

"Nice to meet you both," I said.

Crystal blurted out, "I'm just glad you two beat Binky at his own game. He'll bet on anything. It's good for him to lose once in a while. Did you see how he sulked after you beat him? He gets so mad that sometimes I wonder if there's something wrong with him."

"Something wrong with Binky?" I said, in mock surprise. He'd had a temper as a kid, but until a few minutes ago, I'd assumed he'd been suffering over the loss of his father and that he'd shed it in the way we all shed childish things. People grow up. At least most of us do. I didn't, not completely, but most of us do.

"*Is* there something wrong with Binky?" Crystal asked. She seemed to want our confirmation, as if she'd been mingling with the Binky acolytes so long she was beginning to doubt her own judgment and needed outsiders to confirm the validity of her thoughts. "He's maybe just a little off, don't you think?"

"How do you mean?" I said, scratching my chin.

"Okay. Listen to this. Binky was driving us to lunch last week when some woman stopped traffic in the Arboretum so a mother duck and her ducklings could cross the road. Everybody was stopped in both directions when Binky pulled out and gunned it. There were feathers and little bodies flying everywhere. It was horrible." Relating the story brought tears to her eyes.

"Sounds twisted," I said.

"He and Chad laughed. How could he do something like that? There's something going on with with him I just can't explain."

"You explained it just fine, girl," said Snake.

"There's more. Remember those people in the news a few weeks back? The guy murdered his wife and his mother-in-law and then killed himself? Remember all those really bad mother-in-law jokes?"

"I guess I didn't hear any of those," I said.

"You talking about Alex and Mick Kraft?" Snake asked.

"Yes. Well, Binky and Chad must have made some sort of bet about them, because they were making tasteless jokes about the murders, and then a lot of money changed hands. Is that sick?"

"How much money?" I asked, casually. Snake was working hard not to look any more interested than I was, but he was having a hard time concealing it.

"I just know it was a lot."

"Out of curiosity, who was the winner?" I asked.

"I believe Binky gave a check to Chad, but I don't know for sure. I didn't really want to know the details, and they won't talk about it now. In fact, they've gotten real quiet about the whole thing. Maybe they finally have enough sense to be embarrassed. Maybe someone had the guts to take them to task for making a game about someone's tragedy."

"Binky lost a bunch of money, he must have gotten upset," I said.

"No. They don't mind losing to each other. It's losing to anyone else that bugs them."

"Did they know Alex and Mick Kraft?"

"I don't know. Like I said, they'll make bets about anything, even about people and events they only know from the news."

"Do you know if this bet was made before or after the murders occurred?" I asked.

"I only heard about it after."

"Why are you telling us about this?" I asked.

"You're detectives, aren't you?"

"Private investigators," corrected Snake.

"Well, I just thought you should know."

"And maybe you're a little pissed at somebody?" I added.

She reddened. "Binky promised he was going to get my sister a job. Instead, he got her hammered and slept with her. And she still doesn't have a job." When the two of us didn't respond, she added, "She's seventeen."

"You maybe should get the police in on that," Snake said.

"I tried, but she won't cooperate. She says she slept with him of her own volition."

Later, when Snake was divvying up our winnings in the car, I said, "What do you think about what we just heard?"

Snake thought about it before handing me a wad of bills. "Well, in this state seventeen is above the age of consent for sex but not for drinking. So he broke at least one law. But he does sound like a royal prick. I mean, who the hell would want to be called Binky? Even if the alternative is Joshua. Why do the rich anoint themselves with names that are too saccharine for kittens?"

"The nickname's not his fault. He was handed that at birth. But this new information? We already talked about this. The Kraft's bad luck started six months ago right about when they got the dog. They must have come over here to pick up Pickles."

"Where they very well might have run into Binky and Chad."

"That's what I was thinking."

"Just like those ducks. You think Binky and Chad could have something to do with the deaths?"

"Money changed hands afterward. And the wager, whatever it was, could account for the camera in the Kraft back yard. Maybe they needed visual proof of . . . whatever . . . to win a bet."

"I can't see those two sneaking around in somebody's apple tree."

"No. But I can see them paying someone to place the camera for them."

Two Miles of Darkness

After thinking things over for a minute, Snake added, "Hey? I've never seen anybody hold their breath as long as that. How did you do that? I thought you were going to die."

"It wasn't so bad," I lied.

"Just out of curiosity, how much longer were you prepared to hold your breath?"

"Not that long."

"No, really. How long?"

"Until hell froze over."

"That's what I thought."

"One thing, though, Snake."

"What's that?"

"Do me a favor? Don't tell Kathy where all this money came from."

"What? She doesn't like you gambling?"

"It's not that exactly. It's . . . she thinks sometimes I act too . . ."

"Retarded?"

"She calls it juvenile."

"Retarded."

"Right."

"Your secret's safe with me, buddy."

21

I dropped Snake off at his truck and went back to West Seattle, where I parked in front of the Kraft house. I knew the tallest reaches of the apple tree in their back yard offered a direct line of sight to the upper floors of the Cavendish house four doors down. Not that the Tecktrixonic Remote Camera required a line of sight to send signals.

I knew Cavendish had seen me in the tree. Chances are if he'd installed and later removed the camera and then saw me in the tree where his camera had been until just days earlier, it would have made him jumpy, jumpy enough to skulk over at night and make the mounting plate disappear.

Sitting in my car in front of the Kraft house, I traced the Cavendish's property records online through the King County parcel viewer. I could tell from recent sales in the area that like a lot of people in town, he was under water, meaning his house was now valued at less than he'd paid for it. Most people didn't have the cash to get out unscathed, and I saw no reason to think he did, either.

His full name was Herbert Carl Cavendish. His wife was Helen Magdalene Cavendish. I ran his name through every criminal database I could find and learned he'd been picked up for DUI twice in the past three years, once in Puyallup near the fairgrounds and once a few blocks from his home.

In the first case, charges were dismissed for reasons I could not fathom, probably an error in police procedure; but after the second incident, he served two days in county lockup, received a fine, and had his license suspended for three months.

The real pay dirt came in the form of his California criminal records.

Two Miles of Darkness

Seven years ago in a Pasadena court, Herbert Cavendish found himself convicted of indecent liberties and voyeurism. A camera in the neighbors' back yard would qualify as voyeurism, too. He served two months in jail and moved to Seattle a few days after he was released. Cavendish was not likely to volunteer information concerning any of this, especially if he'd been spying on the Krafts, but it wasn't going to hurt to look him in the eye and ask.

If he possessed surveillance videos, the police needed to see him.

He answered the door in a robe, bare legs poking out beneath like a couple of hirsute shovel handles, a gray Denver Broncos cap pulled low on his simian brow. Under the robe, he wore a dingy, V-neck T-shirt a lot like the one I sometimes wore around the house, though mine usually had a few more food stains. "Yeah?"

He was medium height, stocky, and Charlie was right: his left eye wandered at infrequent intervals in a manner that was unnerving. A pot belly that looked hard as a rock protruded over the tight belt of his bathrobe. His dyed-black hair was over the collar and curly in back. I had the feeling he'd been a cute baby, but as it did for a lot of us, the cuteness ceased somewhere around middle school. He wouldn't look particularly pretty climbing an apple tree, but it didn't seem impossible for him to accomplish the feat, either.

I told him who I was and explained we were looking for the Krafts' missing dachshund. "I don't know nothin' 'bout no fuckin' dog," he said, attempting to slam the door, but I was moving to hand him a flyer and blocked the door with my foot and shoulder, making the whole boogie two-step look as if I'd done it inadvertently.

"There's a five-thousand-dollar reward for information leading to the dog's return," I said, grinning like an imbecile.

"Yeah?" He took the flyer and pretended to be interested. What he wanted was to get me out of his doorway.

"I was just wondering. Did you know the Krafts?"

"Nope."

"Not even to talk to?"

"Nope."

"Kind of creepy, huh? The way they died?"

"How'd they die?"

"You didn't read the papers?"

"I don't take the paper."

"It was all over the news. A double murder and suicide."

"Sounds tough." He was lying. He knew the whole story.

"I was hoping you could help me solve a problem we've come across."

Cavendish stared at me without blinking, though I couldn't tell whether he was using his good eye or the bad one.

"Seems there might have been a hidden camera in their backyard."

"What did you say?"

"A hidden camera. I thought you might know something about it."

"I don't know nothin'. You think there's a camera over there, why not just go look?"

"We were told you bought a surveillance camera."

It was an outrageous bluff, but I wanted to see how he would react. I had been listening to the huff and buzz of his breathing all along, and now I heard his breath catch. The constant hissing and whistling from his nostrils must drive people around him batty. He held his breath for a few moments.

"Who's been talkin' about me?"

"People talk. It happens. I can't reveal sources, but if you don't speak up, I'm going to be forced to pass this information along to the police."

It was interesting that he did not deny having a camera but was more interested in who might have ratted on him. We stared at each other for a few long beats. "I don't get what you're trying to say here. You accusing me of something?"

"Heck, no. I'm just wondering why somebody might

set up a surveillance camera at the Kraft house."

"You found a camera?"

"Found evidence of it."

"If you didn't find anything, why all the questions?"

"I guess I'm just wondering what kind of guy would do such a thing."

"This doesn't have anything to do with me. Now take your wondering ass off my property."

I felt a blast of fetid air as the door slammed in my face. I'd noticed earlier the house had a peculiar smell to it, like wet dogs. I'd been rude, but he'd been shifty, shiftier as we went along. I'd wanted to glean something from his behavior and attitude, but I hadn't learned anything conclusive. Snake would have said he planted the camera and removed it for sure. I wasn't ready to hang him just yet.

He was, however, the first neighbor to react negatively to my questions, but then I hadn't purposely irritated anyone else the way I'd irritated him.

Every neighborhood had a resident pervert of some sort; at least, that had been my experience. They didn't always come out and announce themselves in some way, nor were they necessarily dangerous, but people were strange creatures. Even if Cavendish had placed a camera in the Krafts' tree and spent his spare time masturbating to the videos—and that was a big *if*, because we didn't have any real proof tying him to the missing never-been-seen-except-by-a-twelve-year-old-boy camera—it didn't mean he'd done anything else. It didn't mean he was a murderer. But it could mean he had video taken on the day of the deaths. If so, that video might prove or disprove my theory about the deaths.

It was possible he'd planted the camera and then been as horrified as everyone else when Mick went off his nut with the gun. There was a large patio slider not far from the chair in which Mick had died, and it would be in full view from the spot in the tree where the camera had been.

Maybe the smart course of action would be to stake out his house until we were sure nobody was home and then slip the lock on the front door, see if we could find the camera or evidence of its purchase. I was considering this option as

I reached my car.

I was still doing online research on Cavendish when I got a call from Brad Munch, my computer guy. Munch had already received over a thousand replies to the "lost dog" items he'd placed on various web sites, while Snake and I had fielded a hundred-odd phone calls in response to our fliers and the newspaper article, so he was outpacing us by tenfold. He'd categorized the responses into seven groups: jokes, spam, sympathy messages, inquiries, possible sightings, probable sightings, and almost sure things.

"Funny thing is," Munch said, "you look at the time line for the probable and almost sure things and plot the coordinates of the sightings, and I'd say she's traveling."

"Around West Seattle?"

"Migrating clean out of the area. Started around five this morning."

"Where's she headed? Rat City?"

"Other direction."

"The other direction is the bay or downtown."

"Downtown."

After Brad took control of my computer remotely, he opened a map of Seattle on my screen and began populating the map with tiny figures I came to realize were dog silhouettes he had created for this purpose. It was the sort of attention to detail Munch brought to his work and which I appreciated.

The dog glyphs formed a trail that dribbled through West Seattle, down along Pigeon Hill through the Delridge corridor, and across the east Duwamish Waterway. Lord only knows which of the bridges she used—any of them could have been fatal for a dachshund. The sightings continued north along the waterfront, with several in downtown Seattle, each sighting represented by a doggie glyph on the map, military time alongside it. Together they presented a perfect trail leading north.

If these sightings were trustworthy, the dog had followed the waterfront, traveled through Myrtle Edwards Park, and followed a walking trail that extended farther north. From that trail, she must have crossed through the railroad yards toward Magnolia, an affluent residential area, part of which was situated on a tall bluff overlooking Puget Sound. So far, there had been a total of eight sightings of a loose dachshund in Magnolia, one by two kids who chased her for several blocks.

As determined as she was elusive, Pickles had traveled from West Seattle all the way to her old neighborhood, where Charlene McIntyre lived, all the while dodging traffic, bounty hunters, bigger dogs, and birds of prey.

"Where were the most recent sightings?" I asked.

"Right outside Discovery Park on Emerson Street. It doesn't make sense, Thomas. This is about as straight a line as she could take to West Emerson Street. Right through the heart of downtown. What do you think she's up to?"

"Pickles used to live in Magnolia. It's like the cat who gets taken two states away and six months later shows up at the old house."

"Wow."

"Yeah. Wow." I asked Munch to get the word out that Pickles had been spotted in Magnolia and might be near or in Discovery Park. There was no need to keep encouraging all the ten-year-olds prowling West Seattle in the heat if they had no real chance at the reward. With any luck, we'd have a fresh batch of hopefuls crosshatching Magnolia by morning.

I found Charlene McIntyre's home address on the net, two blocks from one of the Discovery Park entrances, on 39th West. As I recalled from visits in my youth, she lived in a brick rambler with a daylight basement consisting of a mother-in-law apartment. I'd been in the car with my father several times when he'd stopped at Charlene's that last summer before he vanished from our lives. The basement apartment was the same one Alex and Mick Kraft had formerly leased from Charlene.

I was headed downtown to drive Kathy home from work when I received a call from Anthony Throckmorton. "You got any more work for me?" he asked.

"I do, in fact. Tomorrow morning. Get as many of the guys from the other day as you can round up and meet us at nine in front of the Millionair Club. Can you do that?"

"Sure. How many guys total?"

"Eight."

"All day?"

"I'm not sure. We'll pay for half a day minimum."

"You got it, boss. We'll be there."

I drove home and pumped a hundred pounds of pressure into the tires on my Look bicycle, wondering all the while whether Herbert Cavendish might not be guilty of something worse than voyeurism. There was a standard progression in sex crimes, which often began with peeping, exposure, and maybe frotteurism and ended with rape, and in more extreme cases, kidnapping, or murder. Most rapists worked through the lower progression before they arrived at rape, though many whistled through the entire sequence as juveniles, which made collecting records from some of these individuals almost impossible, since the general rule in most states was to seal juvenile records. Not all voyeurs devolved into rapists, but most rapists had been or were currently voyeurs.

If Cavendish's crimes had morphed into something more heinous than peeping while he was residing in Washington State, he hadn't been arrested for any of it yet. On the other hand, there were plenty of people who got away with felonies, sometimes for years, sometimes forever. Maybe he'd perfected his technique so as not to get caught. Or maybe he'd been lucky.

After I suited up, I pedaled east from our house, then rode south carefully through Greek row, which was strewn with people tossing footballs and jaywalking. I made my way down a slight grade through the University of Washington campus, exiting the campus near Husky Stadium, then crossing the Montlake Bridge on the sidewalk, which trembled from heavy trucks drumming across the metal grating of the bridge. I then rode through the Arboretum and down the twisty roads to Lake Washington Boulevard.

It was a comparatively short ride, less than thirty miles round trip, and took me both coming and going past the marina where Snake was housesitting. I pedaled up into the neighborhoods above the lake on a residential route I'd been using all year, climbing the hills hard before dropping back down to Lakeside, encountering enough cyclists cruising in the August sunshine that I had friendly competition all along the route. I'd missed a few days of riding and, because of the layoff, felt rusty.

I spotted Snake through the window of a Starbucks coffee shop across the street from the marina. He appeared to be flirting with the same barista he'd been flirting with when I was with him there. Snake was much older than her, but oddly, she'd been interested in him from the beginning, interested perhaps in the same way people were interested in a chili pepper they'd been warned was too hot to eat.

Elmer had explained his battle strategy to me once, much of it based on a book he'd read outlining Don Juan's success with women. If you are observant, he said, it is far easier to make a conquest than people think. It is dependent on keen observation and forgoing a man's natural tendencies. The key is to approach only women who show an interest in you, and to forget about all the others, no matter how much you may be attracted to them. Be alert to an averted eye, a quickness of breath, a flushed face, whatever.

When done properly, the universe of rejections dwindles dramatically, while the success rate rises exponentially. It was the perfect technique for people interested in numbers and conquests, which was where Snake found himself despite his resolution to build a solid relationship with a woman.

His private life had been a shambles since the day I met him, something to do with the way he was raised: his twin brother stealing or trying to steal every woman he'd ever shown an interest in; and their mother, a woman— if Snake was to be believed— with two greedy babies and only one feeding port. The metaphor seemed to extend throughout their entire lives.

That same mother had been struck by an errant lightning bolt in the Sonoran desert when she was eighteen and had actually been dead for two minutes before being revived by a couple of movie extras working on a western being filmed nearby. It was hard to know which of the countless stories Snake told about his family were true and which were fabrications.

Kathy stayed up working long after I went to bed that evening, reviewing interview transcripts for a case she was hoping would never go to trial. I was hoping for some hanky-panky after she crawled under the covers, but I was already dead to the world by then and slept straight through until the alarm woke me.

That morning, the August skies over Washington State had dulled to a slate gray. Weather Underground predicted a chance of thundershowers, so I had Snake pick up the guys at the Millionair Club, while I shopped for eight disposable ponchos and four walkie-talkies. I figured we could split the men into teams. As I stared at the maps I'd already printed, I realized the project was next to hopeless. At over five hundred acres, Discovery Park was just too damn big.

I kept the receipt for the ponchos and walkie-talkies in the hope that we would find the dachshund sleeping on the doormat at Charlene McIntyre's house two blocks from the park, but when I arrived at Charlene's, long before Snake and the others, I saw no sign of the dog. I had never run into Charlene McIntyre when she didn't have her makeup on, and for just a few moments I thought I had the wrong house—or was looking at her mother.

"Charlene? Sorry to bother you so early in the morning, but Pickles is in the area. I was wondering if you'd seen her."

"How could she possibly be here?"

"One of those Darwinian miracles, I guess. Heading back to where she felt safe. Mind if I look around the yard?"

"I suppose this means I get the reward. Doda doesn't have to know."

"Let's see if she's here, first."

I didn't spot any traces of the dog in the shrubbery or the neighboring yards. Pickles was small enough to fit into the newspaper tube and could be hiding anywhere. I was thinking about renting or borrowing a thermal imager, something we could use to detect body heat from a critter as small as Pickles, when I got a brainstorm. Suddenly I knew how to find the dog, and it didn't involve men with maps or walkie-talkies, or legions of young boys and girls on bicycles.

I called Snake from the car. "Mobile Command to Scout One," I said.

"Thomas?"

"What's your ETA?"

"What the hell is Mobile Command?"

"Never mind that. What's your ETA?"

"A couple of these guys were starving, so I'm buying them breakfast here on Madison. Found an IHOP that's got a waitress with big cans. Why don't you join us for waffles? She's really quite exquisite."

"I don't think so."

"Your call, but you're making a mistake. I never been to Discovery Park. How big is it?"

"Get ready for some hiking. It's over five hundred acres. It's got bluffs, woods, paved roads, nearly twelve miles of trails, two miles of beach. It used to be Fort Lawton, a government Army base."

"She disappears in a park that big, we may never find her. How long do you think the old lady'll keep us on the payroll?"

"Call me when you're finished with breakfast."

"Will do, Tonto."

"Don't Tonto me. I'm not the sidekick. If anybody's the sidekick, it's you. Besides, we don't do sidekicks. But if we did, the sidekick would be you."

"Think about it. The Lone Ranger carries two guns. Tonto only gets one, and he has to wear it in front of his pecker. I've got four guns, and you don't even carry a cigarette lighter. You're definitely the sidekick."

"You keep this up, I'm going to start calling you Elmer like your mother did."

"You can call me Ke-mo-sah-bee. And my mother didn't call me Elmer very often. She preferred Knothead."

22

We are back to back, as first Snake tries to untangle the tape on my wrists and then I struggle to tear the tape on his. It's not easy, and after ten minutes we've made no progress. We are a couple of blind men playing Pick-Up Sticks. We keep working, hoping the rat's nest of tape can be unbound. My hands are tied so tightly the blood is pooling in them. I'm thinking there's a possibility of permanent nerve damage. But then, permanent is only until death, and my death is slated for sometime in the next hour.

The mobility in my hands is compromised to the point where, when it's my turn to pick at the tape on Snake's wrists, I'm having a hard time doing anything. I have a feeling he's in the same predicament but refuses to admit defeat, just as I do. I'm pretty sure we're both lying to each other. Then Snake lets loose another fart, and the air inside the enclosed space of the trunk heats up like a Saudi Arabian outhouse.

Being almost completely immobile is nearly intolerable, but complicit in my suffering is this stink which makes me want to scream. I want to yell through the back seat for them to stop the car, shoot us now, put me out of my misery. "Geez, Snake. Can you at least try to control the stench?"

"I don't appreciate that word."

"Control?"

"Stench."

"Well, I don't appreciate having my lungs scorched."

"Call it something else."

"I think you just burned out all my nose hair."

"Call it a gentleman's indiscretion. And I don't think they smell so bad."

"Are you kidding?"

"If only we could light a match. Blow the lid off the trunk and get out of here."

We laugh bitterly. I'm thinking this is really something, that we can laugh when we know we're about to be executed. Too bad nobody will ever see how cool we are.

The men in front are talking, at times chuckling, and seem as relaxed as we are tense.

Hell, they probably aren't even going to dig us separate graves. They'll pile our corpses on top of each other in a single pit . . . the final indignity, getting entombed in a grubby plot with Elmer Slezak. Despite everything, he's been a good friend and someone I have been able to put my trust in, even if to some he comes across as a trickster and a pathological liar. We've shared a brotherhood since the day we met.

I kick and try to stretch the tape around my ankles, but nothing budges, and then I get the glimmer of an idea. It's just the beginning of a plan and I'm not sure it will lead to anything, but I can't stop fantasizing about it.

As we struggle to untie each other, my ears pop. A few minutes later they pop again, and I realize the car is gaining altitude. We are headed into the mountains. We've driven too long and too far to be going through Snoqualmie Pass, which, at these speeds, would have been maybe forty-five or fifty minutes from our starting point. We may be heading up Stevens Pass, which is a longer jaunt and the next major pass over the Cascade Range to the north of Snoqualmie. Or we could be ascending the lower slopes of Mount Rainier, headed toward Paradise, aptly named for our present situation.

It would be a small consolation to this nature lover to spend eternity deep in the bowels of a national park.

23

It was just after nine-thirty when I pulled in front of Vereecken and Sons, now a branch of American Ingenuity, Inc.

Alex Kraft's former workplace was located on the west side of Queen Anne Hill at the southwest corner of a quiet intersection, alongside a cleaners and a pizza place that looked as if it might be going out of business. The morning was warming rapidly, but the heat didn't banish the rain clouds scudding in from the southwest.

According to my research, the architectural firm of Vereecken and Sons had once employed fifteen prize-winning architects, designing projects in the U.S., Canada, Mexico, Spain, England, Australia, and New Zealand. I'd found nothing online about cost-cutting measures, a take-over, or employees getting laid off.

Just as I reached Vereecken and Sons, Angela Celik returned my earlier call. I'd left a message and thought it a curious case of serendipity she would reach me just as I was about to visit her sister's former employer. "Angela. Thanks for calling back."

"Have you learned anything?" Her voice was impassioned, as if she wanted news but was afraid of the pain it might occasion.

"I wanted to ask if your sister complained about unwanted attentions from a neighbor."

Angela Celik sounded shocked. "No. I would remember something like that. I do know her boss at work made some kind of pass, but that's pretty standard, isn't it?"

"Her boss at Vereecken's or at McDonald's?"

"At Vereecken's. If somebody in the neighborhood was bothering her, she would have mentioned it."

"She mention any names of the people she was working with at McDonald's?"

"Just this one guy. I think his name was . . ."

"Huntzinger?"

"Yes. She was going to carpool with him. She was trying to cut costs."

"What can you tell me about him?"

"Nothing, really. All I know is McDonald's was a completely different atmosphere than what she was used to. She was all of a sudden working with high school dropouts and a couple of guys who'd done prison time and a woman from another state who was hiding from her abusive husband. Flipping two-dollar hamburger patties was quite a comedown from working on thirty-million-dollar projects, and Alex felt it. She told me she cried every day when she got home from work.

"To make matters worse, my sister had been a vegan since high school, and there she was cooking cow parts. I tried to give her as much encouragement as I could. I thought she should concentrate on getting back into her profession. She should have opened an office of her own, worked out of the house until she got established."

"What did she say to that?"

"Said they had too much debt. They'd already spent every cent of their savings trying to get out of the financial hole they were in. Then Mick took all their remaining money and lost it with that stupid investment. He even tried to talk John into investing with him. He was that certain it was going to make them rich. Thank God we didn't put any money into it. If all that wasn't bad enough, Alex still owed tens of thousands on school loans.

"You know John's theory, don't you? He thinks one of the bikers in the tavern spiked Mick's beer with PCP. I've read where PCP can make people do horrible things. It could have been the reason for the shooting. Maybe it was a prank or maybe he had an enemy who dropped it in his beer when he wasn't looking."

Years ago when I was in uniform, I came across a plasterer on PCP who cut off his ears with a broken mirror thinking they belonged on his dog, but Angela Celik didn't need to hear my war stories, particularly not that one. "As far as I know the medical examiner didn't find any drugs in his system. Is your husband there now?"

"He's at work, but I asked him about Mick's friends. He said Mick was only hanging out with that one guy, Manny. John doesn't know where to contact him. *Was* somebody bothering my sister? You think it might have been Manny?"

"I'm just trying to cover all the bases."

Angela gave me her husband's phone number at work, and after we hung up, I spoke to him briefly. He didn't know of any bothersome characters in Alex's West Seattle neighborhood, nor could he tell me much about The Dregs. He described Manny as an ordinary guy, Caucasian, not too tall, not too short. He didn't recall his eye color and said he almost always wore a watch cap. "Big guy? Small?" I prodded.

"Well, yeah. Kind of on the large side, but he was usually sitting at a table guzzling a soft drink when I saw him. He was a teetotaler."

* * *

Vereecken and Sons was housed in a single-story building constructed of painted concrete blocks, which I thought strange for an architectural firm. There was a small anteroom where a receptionist might while away the hours, but it was empty today and looked as if it had been empty for a while, probably a cost-cutting measure. I stopped in the main office area, where a young Asian woman nearby in her cubicle spotted me and stood up. "May I help you?"

"I'm looking into the background of one of your former co-workers."

"Alex?"

"Yes."

"Oh, God."

At the mention of Alex Kraft, a man walking across the large, open office space detoured from his original path and came at me like a torpedo. I was reminded of Angela Celik's allegation that somebody where she worked had been putting the moves on her sister. "Alex was so sweet," said the young woman, hurriedly. "And talented." She glanced at the approaching man and then in a whisper, added, "Alex should have been the last person we let go."

Just before the man intercepted us, the woman shut up, having rushed her last message, presumably so he wouldn't hear it.

"What's the problem?" the man asked.

"I'm a private investigator. I'm doing some background on Alex Kraft."

"Nobody in this company has anything to say about Kraft."

"Who am I speaking to?"

"Glen Masterton, vice president." He announced it in the same way he would have said, "Drop dead, buddy."

Intimidated by Masterton's bearing and loud voice, and possibly by his position in the company, the young woman sat down in front of her computer and pretended to work, though I could tell she remained intent on our conversation.

Masterton had the fleshy face of somebody who drank too much. He also had the kind of squinty eyes Kathy associated with a bully. He was thick-chested, his shirt sleeves rolled up on hirsute forearms as thick as Presto logs. He began crowding me in a pugnacious manner that made me want to crowd him back, but then, maybe that was the idea. I'd seen guys with years of martial arts training trying to intimidate people in the same way, itching to show off their skills. I wasn't sure that was his plan, but either way, I wasn't going to get what I wanted here.

"You're going to leave now," Masterton said. "We don't have anything to say to you."

"But she did work here?"

"Or I'll call the police."

"You can't confirm she worked here?"

"That's your last warning."

This level of vitriol over a former employee seemed unwarranted, but then, maybe the company was trying to disassociate from the whole Kraft storyline. It was the sort of course a public relations firm might advise a company to take, though probably not with this attitude.

Vereecken and Sons had a private parking lot separated from the customer lot in front, which they shared with the dry cleaners and the pizza place, and once I was outside I walked around the building until I saw a vanity plate on a lime-colored Volkswagen Beetle: "STFNSBG." Stephanie's bug. The nameplate on the desk of the woman I'd spoken to inside read, "Stephanie Chin."

It took five minutes on the Internet and some tricks Munch had taught me to find her home address. I would visit later.

A few minutes later I met Snake and the rest of the team in front of Charlene McIntyre's residence in Magnolia. There was no telling how Snake had managed to cram eight men into his truck, but he had. I recognized Anthony Throckmorton and several others, though there were new faces, too.

Throckmorton came bustling up to me. "Couldn't find all of the same guys, and you said you wanted eight, so I added two new swingin' dicks. I hope that's all right. I figured to take some initiative, you know?" He nodded at a pair of rough-looking customers who, upon first impression, resembled former boxers, both clad in gray raincoats that looked as if they'd just come off the rack at Walmart. These two certainly wouldn't have been my first choice, but I assured a nervous Anthony it was fine.

One of the new guys had well-kept shoes and a luxury wristwatch, or a copy of one, both anomalies with this group, but I wasn't in any position to pass judgment. These two resembled petty criminals more than they resembled transients. On the other hand, we were looking for a dog. It wasn't like they were going to pick our pockets.

After explaining our game plan, we split up and canvassed the neighborhood, blanketing phone poles with flyers and buttonholing anybody who would stop to listen. Having come up with what I felt was an alternate sure-fire plan to locate the dog without a search posse, I had pretty much lost interest in today's jaunt anyway.

Making almost no effort to be methodical about it, we divided up into three teams and went into the park, heading in three different directions. I deliberately split up the two new guys, keeping one with my group, sending the other with Snake's. Throckmorton captained the third crew.

The five-hundred-acre park consisted of twelve miles of walking trails running through thickly wooded areas, beachfront, sandy bluffs, and open meadows, so hiding places were abundant. I didn't see how we were going to have any success, but we made the effort because I'd already hired these guys and they needed the work and because sometimes you just get lucky.

We went in at the Forty-Third Avenue entrance. A hike around the forested circumference of the park could take well over an hour. I figured the dog would be worn out by the fifteen-mile odyssey from West Seattle. Like all dachshunds, Pickles had stubby legs, and the journey could not have been without stress, so I half expected to find her dozing near the park entrance. But we didn't.

After we completed our routes, I would pay these guys and we would return them to the Millionair Club. Then I would drive to West Seattle and find one of the dachshund's old blankets, which I would hand over to a friend who owned a tracking dog. I don't know why I hadn't thought of it sooner.

Just after noon, we used our walkie-talkies to confirm nobody had hit the jackpot, and we arranged to meet at the viewpoint above the bluffs overlooking the lighthouse. My group was the first to reach it. This was a logical central location where we could conduct a brief meeting, partake of a snack, and regroup. Besides that, the panoramic view over Puget Sound and west to the distant Olympic Mountain range, which stretched along the horizon, was just short of awesome.

Behind us was a huge, rolling field of wild grasses, maybe half a mile across. The hill at the far end of the meadow was dominated by a 75-foot tower with a huge geodesic dome balanced at the top. A relic of the Cold War, this radome was part of the 1950's Hercules air defense system and was currently used to track air traffic in Seattle.

Far below us, a gaggle of tugboats escorted a container ship south toward the Port of Seattle. They might have been ants carrying the carcass of a dead beetle.

It was mid-week, and the park was populated with joggers, dog-walkers, families, and small groups of tourists mostly speaking Eastern European languages. I heard a young boy asking his mother or nanny—I couldn't tell which—if the geodesic dome at the top of the hill, which he called "the big white golf ball" was part of a crashed space ship.

There were six of us gathered at the bluff when the rough-looking newcomer I'd had in my group, a man named Smith, appeared to take issue with Snake. The two of them were separated from the rest of us, standing not far from the rim of the cliff on the sandy soil overlooking Puget Sound. Snake had gone over to check out the view, and Smith, who'd followed him, was now pushing Snake angrily toward the cliff edge.

As I moved toward them, he began slapping Snake, first on one side of his face, then the other. My initial hunch that Smith had been a former boxer was reinforced by the way he landed the open-handed blows.

Snake was quick and alert and squirrely when somebody was after him, but he couldn't seem to evade these blows. It was frightening to witness, because if Snake couldn't get away from Smith, *I* wouldn't be able to sidestep him either.

Seemingly at will, Smith was nailing Elmer with his open palms, striking hard enough to knock most men off their feet. What Smith didn't know was that Snake had taken so much abuse in his rodeo days that something like this barely registered. When Snake had his appendix taken out, he told them he wouldn't need painkillers. It turned out he did, but the fact that he did surprised him. It surprised me, too.

If the boxer hadn't knocked him off his feet, he was at least keeping him from reaching for one of his weapons.

Two Miles of Darkness

Snake carried two large revolvers in holsters, one under each arm, along with a smaller semi-automatic somewhere on the backside of his belt or in a boot, just in case the magnum rounds didn't take down any charging elephants. He also had a fourth gun, a Derringer he was never without. Four pistols. It seemed nutty, but then, Snake *was* nutty. He was convinced the government had been listening in on his phone conversations since he was a child.

Snake was backing up quickly, trying to fend off the blows with his raised arms, coming perilously closer to the edge of the bluff. I'd been over there earlier to check out the view and knew the drop was sheer. If he got pushed another ten feet, it would likely be fatal.

Everybody else in the crew, aside from Anthony Throckmorton and the second new man, began heading out of the park at a ragged trot, avoiding trouble being second-nature to them.

We'd been told the second man's name was Ted Jones. Fred Smith and Ted Jones. Cute. These guys weren't homeless. They weren't Smith and Jones, either. And they weren't here to help us find a dog.

They'd arrived with an agenda. I didn't know what it was, but they had one.

I couldn't tell what they were arguing about, but the fight was decidedly one-sided. Considering the discrepancy in size and the probability that Smith was about to shove him to his death, few people would have condemned Snake for pulling out a pistol and firing it. But he couldn't reach his arsenal.

Throckmorton was an inch taller than me and outweighed me by fifty pounds. He looked like he'd taken a couple of solid whacks to the face in his time and might be able to handle himself, or at least absorb some punishment, so I was confident he could help me wrestle Smith to the ground.

Jones was another ex-boxer. I was sure of it, partly because he didn't appear surprised by the outbreak of violence and partly because he was moving toward me with two closed fists, looking as if he had some serious work to do.

I turned away from Jones and ran for the bluff, intending to separate Snake from his antagonist. For just a moment as I turned, I thought I glimpsed a calculation in Throckmorton's eyes that told me this had all been planned and that he was part of it. It was hard to be sure about such a minute inflection, but on the other hand, there it was.

Snake was almost to the edge of the sandy bluff now, getting his face slapped hard by a man who in all probability had been a professional boxer. They were three paces from a drop-off I calculated at almost two hundred feet, both men dancing along the rim of the bluff.

I'd only gone a couple of steps when Jones grasped the back of my shirt. It was enough to slow me but not enough to stop me. I could hear my shirt ripping. I pivoted while he held onto me and, without looking, ducked in time to feel his first blow whizzing across the top of my head. If I hadn't ducked blindly, he would have decked me and I'd have been out for the count. Ex pros didn't get clean hits on people like me without knocking them into next week. Hell, an old man once knocked me cold with an alarm clock, prompting Kathy to jokingly claim I had a weak brain.

As I ducked under his arm, I came up throwing a hard left jab at his windpipe. It wasn't the most accurate punch, nor the hardest I'd ever thrown, but it struck his throat solidly just under his chin and put him on his butt in the dirt, gasping for air. As I turned back to help Snake, Jones was gagging like a man who'd tried to swallow a wet dish cloth.

Throckmorton had been about to step forward when he saw me put Jones down. My success was due almost entirely to luck, but it probably hadn't looked that way from his angle. Throckmorton stopped moving and put his palms up in surrender mode, which was another indication that he'd been about to help Smith and Jones, not Black and Slezak.

By the time I got moving again, I was too late.

Snake was backed all the way to the cliff's edge, his head bobbing like a broken toy as Smith cuffed him.

Two Miles of Darkness

Hoping to distract Smith, I yelled. I had been planning to take out his legs, hit him hard from the side, maybe wrestle the bastard to the ground, with the hope that he wasn't as strong or as solid as he looked.

The two of them were teetering on the edge, well past the warning signs placed here after the last earthquake, during which a large section of the bluff had sloughed off.

As I sprinted toward them, Snake dropped onto his backside, moving quickly, as if he actually wanted to go over the bluff backwards. He fell and smacked the sand flat on his back, his hands gripping Smith's raincoat, pulling Smith with him in a Judo move I hadn't seen since college.

With Snake's help, Smith did a forward roll right over the edge of the bluff.

Snake had launched him head over heels.

I doubt Smith had been any more surprised in his life.

Moments later, we heard a whuffing sound partway down the cliff at the point where his body made first contact. There were more thuds, each growing more distant.

By the time I got to the edge and peered through the brush, the crumpled body had come to rest on a sandy knoll far down the cliff side, motionless limbs pretzeled into a shape that told me he was dead. Near as I could tell, he'd broken his neck, his back, both legs, and at least one arm.

"What happened?" I asked, as Snake dusted himself off and slowly climbed to his feet next to me.

"I don't know. He just started hollering and then hitting me."

"And then you killed him."

"I guess maybe I did."

24

As Snake peered over the edge, he said, "This is really going to mess up my day."

"It didn't do a whole lot for his."

"What happened with Throckmorton?" asked Snake, looking past my shoulder at Jones, who was still huddled on the ground nursing his throat. "He help you put that guy down?"

"We'll talk to Throckmorton in a minute. Right now, I'm more interested in what happened between you two."

"Maybe these new guys thought we were going to be divvying out the reward in cash. Maybe they thought we had five G's on us."

"Carrying that kind of cash would be stupid."

"Lot of people are stupid. Maybe they thought we were."

"He ask for the money?"

"No. He just started whaling on me. What happened over there with you? Why is Jones sitting on the ground like that? Looks like he swallowed an oyster without shelling it."

"I was coming over to help you. He tried to stop me." I didn't bother to tell Snake it had been a lucky punch. I never would, either. I might confess it to Kathy, but I wasn't going to admit anything like that to Snake. There were things you were better off keeping to yourself, and this was one of them. Besides, Snake didn't believe in luck. He would have tabbed the truth as both false modesty and ingenuous reverse braggadocio on my part.

"Throckmorton better have a pretty good fuckin' answer for why he brought these two assholes along."

I was keeping an eye on Snake, afraid he might be woozy from the pummeling, that he might faint and toddle over the edge. His face was red and his nose was bleeding, drips and drabs peppering his jacket. "I think that bastard was planning to push me off."

"I think so, too. But pushing you off wouldn't be part of the plan if he'd wanted to rob you."

"No, it wouldn't."

"By the way. That was a nice move, throwing him over your head like that."

"Judo I learned in the Marines."

"I didn't know you were a Marine."

"Dishonorable discharge. I had the hots for my commander's wife. She used to come into the office where I worked in the typing pool. It was a lot like the love story in *From Here to Eternity*. I'll tell you all about it some other time. You think he's dead?" Snake asked, knowing it had been a while since either of us had seen anybody deader. "Maybe we should throw him a rope."

"He moved like a prizefighter. So did his buddy over there."

Snake turned to me and said, "Hey, where are they going?"

Throckmorton and Jones were hightailing it out of the park, having gained a head start of almost two hundred yards. We broke into a run. As usual, Snake was bogged down with iron and spare bullets, so he dropped behind me right away. "What about the body?" he asked, hoping the run would be called off. "We going to call the police?"

"Not before we catch these two."

"What do you think is going on?" Snake shouted as we ran, swiping at his dribbling nosebleed with the back of one hand in a feeble attempt to keep it from ruining his shirt.

"Only one way to find out."

I quickly outpaced Snake and was soon gaining on the two men in front of us. I figured at some point they were going to split up and when that happened I would be forced to make a decision. Throckmorton was the one I wanted to talk to first, so he was the one I would follow. Besides, with all of his side-arms, Snake was a better match for the other guy.

We passed a smattering of tourists and a reedy, bearded man walking a dog; and then, just as I began closing in on my target, in one of those dreamlike coincidences that ironically convinces you you're awake and not dreaming, Pickles flew across the path in front of me, ears flying straight back, scurrying in a low scrunch as if she'd been flushed from her hideout—which she had been, for Jones had cut through the brush. She didn't appear wounded, but she did look more frightened than any animal deserved to be.

I was still thinking about the dog when a man I'd never seen before stepped around the bole of a large maple and pointed a pistol at me. From thirty yards away he fired one round, and then as I flopped onto my belly in the tall grass, I heard him fire another round over my head. I believed the second shot was directed toward Snake, who was a good ways behind by now.

Snake was an expert marksman and wasn't afraid to return fire, but I didn't want him shooting up the park. There were too many innocent people around, so I called out, "Elmer? Don't fire. You all right?"

"Don't call me Elmer."

"You okay?"

"So far."

"You see where that came from?"

"Man in the trees."

"Anybody there now?"

"I don't see anyone."

I took a chance and raised my head, saw the shooter running away from us. Throckmorton and Jones were already out of sight.

Snake walked to where I was sitting in the tall grass. "What's the matter? You all tuckered out?"

"No, it's just that I'm not getting into a gunfight in a city park with people everywhere."

"Especially since you're not carrying."

"That, too. Besides, you want to fight a war, you need a reason. At least, I do. I don't know what this is about. Do you?"

"No. But do you think Throckmorton's in on it?"

"Maybe."

"He sure can run."

"They all ran, but they couldn't have all been in on it. I think most of them were just scared. I will say this. For a minute back there, I thought Throckmorton was going to come at me."

"You shittin' me?"

"I think he changed his mind when he saw Jones go down."

"Yeah, you got Jones good. I would have put Smith down sooner, but I like to lull my enemies by letting them slap the shit out of me first."

"I noticed that. Good plan."

If things had gone differently, our lives might have ended a few minutes earlier. The thought was startling enough to give us both pause. When a woman with an Airedale on a leash came jogging past in revealingly skimpy shorts, Snake and I both stared at her a little too long. It was as if we'd both suddenly realized we were alive. "Thomas? You think I overreacted?"

"It was self defense. Pure and simple."

"I didn't realize we were so close to the edge."

"I think maybe you did."

"No, I actually didn't."

"Well, *he* did."

"That's right. He didn't have his back to the drop-off like me. He was getting set to push me off."

"Sure looked that way."

"This isn't about the dog, is it?"

"I don't see how it could be."

"People don't kill you over a dog."

"Some would kill you for a five-thousand dollar reward."

"When I picked them up this morning, Throckmorton vouched for those two. I didn't like the look of 'em, but he acted like they were long-lost brothers, so I let it pass."

"I used to like Throckmorton."

"So did I. You think this has something to do with the

Krafts?"

"I don't know. You got people after you, Snake? From something else?"

"Not that I know of. Usually when I have people after me, they're feds."

"The feds could have hired these guys."

"A couple of thugs off the street? You're beginning to sound almost as paranoid as me."

"I think they were planning to kill us—both of us."

"You think?"

"And I'm thinking Throckmorton was part of it."

"Yeah. Me, too."

"You know what else?"

"No, what?"

"I saw Pickles."

25

Claiming he didn't want the police to be uncomfortable should they find out he had them outgunned, Snake ditched his weapons in the trunk of my car, which was closer to the park entrance than his truck.

A few minutes later, we escorted the first uniformed officers through the park to the spot where Smith had gone off the bluff. The second group of officers cut the locks on the vehicular barriers and drove in, jouncing slowly across the meadow. Soon there were over a dozen vehicles parked at the site, the air filled with the odor of exhaust and the sounds of officers shouting orders.

Because the logistics of this particular death scene slowed the work to a crawl, we were still waiting for the body-recovery team to winch the corpse up from the base of the bluff three hours later. The fire department had lowered medics down to confirm the DOA and later cooperated with SPD in lowering crime-scene techs on ropes, hauling them back up after they'd taken their photos and used their swabs and so forth. In fact, there was a continual train of people going down and coming back up the ropes.

Smith's death had taken only a moment, but the intervening hours ballooned into a slow-motion circus with multiple fire and police units on standby, a medical examiner's wagon idling in the tall grass, reporters hustling about, and two news helicopters making large swooping arcs in the gray skies. The crime scene was going to make a great visual on the local news: the dead man, the bluffs, the lush park in the middle of the city, the blue-gray waters of Puget Sound, the mountains in the background, boat traffic below, all those winking blue and red lights, the feel of a massive and important undertaking in the air.

By luck of the draw, one of the investigators was Carole Cooper.

"Black?" she said. "What are you doing here?"

"We called it in."

"I heard it was a brawl. You the one who killed this guy?"

"It wasn't a brawl. And I was a witness." Before I could explain further, we were interrupted by one of the department suits, who called Cooper away for a confab. It was important for the top brass to think they were a pivotal force in any major ground operation. They could never stand out of the way and let the worker bees get the job done. I remembered that much from my time in harness, which seemed like a million years ago.

As Cooper walked away, she held up a stubby index finger to signify she would be back.

There was a time when I knew most of the upper echelon in the SPD, but I hadn't been a patrol officer in some years and a lot of the faces had been replaced. The uniformed officers who took our statements feigned disinterest in Elmer's entertaining demeanor. Then when they ran his name, it came up in a data base as a possible national security risk with an asterisk advising local law enforcement to hold him until contacted by the NSA.

Their attitude darkened after Snake was in cuffs and they were waiting for somebody from the National Security Agency to get back to them. News spread through the assemblage and acted as an additional draw for lookie-loos.

Snake mumbled, "National security has become another phrase for irrational panic attack."

"Keep calm," I replied. "And whatever you do, don't tell these people what you really think of the government."

"Me? I think the government's lovely."

Snake had long ago been placed on the national security risk list, a position from which there was apparently no escape. Five years ago he poked the wife of some guy in the State Department, who had heatedly vowed to get even. As was his lifelong habit, Snake favored high-risk behavior with high-risk women. It didn't help his standing with the SPD when they discovered Slezak subscribed to every conspiracy theory under the sun, from FDR conspiring to allow the attack on Pearl Harbor to Dick Cheney being in on 9/11.

Five minutes later, when Cooper found me sitting on the front fender of an assistant police chief's car, a steel button on the back of my pants scratching his paint, I gave her a thumb drive containing photos of the dead man and his friends. "Where'd you get these pictures?" Cooper asked.

When I told her about my custom of surreptitiously photographing everyone who passed through my investigations, she gave me a dubious look. "You took a picture of me, too?"

"Why would I have a picture of you?"

"Because you saw me at the Kraft house."

I pulled out my cellphone and scrolled through the "Pickles" album until I brought up a three-quarters profile of Cooper taken at the Krafts' front door.

"How did you get this?"

"It's a nice profile shot, don't you think? Want a copy?"

"Delete it." With her short, blunt-cut hair, fireplug figure, and eschewal of the cosmetic arts, Carole Cooper wasn't turning too many heads in Discovery Park. She seemed confident in her homeliness, a trait I admired in her. I gravitated toward people who were confident in who they were.

"By the way, thanks for showing me through their house."

"Still doubt it was a double murder-suicide?"

"Is that what I said?"

"You didn't look convinced."

"I'm thinking there's more to it."

"What else could there be?"

"I don't know yet."

"Don't tell me you think you were attacked today because you're snooping into the Kraft affair?"

"That's exactly what I think."

"What else are you two working on?"

"Just finding this dog."

"You didn't know the dead man before this morning?"

I shook my head. Thinking aloud, I said, "They might have been trying to frighten us. Screwed up and went too far."

"Frighten you to what end?"

"To get us away from the Kraft thing."

"No way. This is random. Your friend, Elmer, insulted the guy, called his wife or mother a whore—something like that. I wouldn't put it past him."

"Neither would I, but that's not what happened. There were two men. Both looked like professional boxers. The first guy picks a fight with Elmer, pushes him toward the edge. I come to his aid. His buddy follows and attacks me from behind. I'm guessing the other men we hired weren't part of it, but they weren't going to wait around to be witnesses, either. If two dead men were found at the bottom of this cliff and there were no witnesses, it would be easy to assume one lost his balance and the other went to help."

"How could they be sure the others would high-tail it?"

"Street people are easily intimidated. They knew that."

Cooper gave me a long look. "You haven't pissed off anybody in the past few weeks?"

"Just my wife, Kathy, but she doesn't have the money to hire killers."

Cooper stared at me.

"I'm kidding."

"With you, I can never be sure."

Cocooned in a yellow emergency services blanket and strapped firmly into a Stokes stretcher, Smith's body was eventually hoisted from the base of the cliff on a pulley system engineered by the fire department. While we watched, Cooper said, "You ever hear of a man named Eddie the Slugger?"

"Nope. Is that him?"

"Edward C. Turner. Eddie the Slugger. Ex-prizefighter. You were right on that count. He's a known thug who usually operates in the bay area. Four years ago he was implicated in the death of an ex-cop and private investigator in downtown Oakland. They couldn't pin anything on him, but he was definitely in the thick of it. He's known to work for a number of different law firms, mostly on the shady side."

"You got that awfully fast."

"He had a wallet on him. Plus, we took his prints first thing. He worked as a private investigator, but his license got yanked when he was convicted of manslaughter in a love triangle. Beat a guy to death. It's a long story. Served six years. We know he flew here two days ago, and we're still checking the flight records to see if he came up with a partner. Something else. Your buddy, Elmer? He's on high security watch list with TSA."

"I thought it was the NSA."

"Them, too."

"He's a crackpot, but you're wasting your time watching him."

"But he *is* a crackpot?"

"Let's just say he sounds nuttier than he really is."

Snake was across the way flirting with a female firefighter who looked as if she could play linebacker for the Seahawks. He'd been chatting with her for over an hour, playing up the fact that he was handcuffed and possibly dangerous. I knew how his brain worked. He would flirt with her, he might even get a date with her, pretending all the while he didn't give a hoot about our general situation or what had happened to us, pretending he wasn't even thinking about it, and then he would come over to me and explain what was going on in a way that I hadn't yet considered but which made perfect sense.

Snake was one of those players who loved giving the appearance of being the laziest guy on the field right before he hit the winning homer. I had to believe it had something to do with his long history as a bull rider, where his entire mystique was defined by the most dangerous eight seconds in sports.

"You have addresses for these guys who were helping out?" Cooper asked.

"Most of them don't have addresses. I have a cellphone number for Throckmorton. Anthony Throckmorton. At least, that's the name he gave us." I wrote down the number and she signaled a partner, a heavy-set male with a shaved head, who came over, took the scrap of paper, and told her he would check it out.

"They got one thing right," Cooper told me. "So far, we haven't been able to find any witnesses besides you and Mr. Slezak."

"He prefers to be called Snake."

"And I prefer to be called Your Royal Highness. Tell me about the shooter again."

I explained how we'd been chasing Throckmorton and Jones through the park when a man appeared out of nowhere and fired two rounds at us. I told her he was medium height, medium build, and Caucasian.

Cooper looked up at the sky, which was now a carpet of gunmetal gray. She had me lead her to the approximate spot where the shooter fired his pistol and then assigned two patrolmen to search the area for shell casings. On the walk back to the bluffs, she said, "Where did you find these homeless guys?"

"Millionair Club. Throckmorton found five of the guys we hired before, plus these two. He vouched for them. You can triangulate on his phone and pick him up, can't you?"

Cooper gave me a deadpan look. Law enforcement had been availing themselves of several new tools to track and apprehend suspects, and one of those tools they weren't too keen on broadcasting was their ability to triangulate on anybody carrying a cellphone. There seemed to be a group-think effort to keep that capability in their silent arsenal. Even though it was never spelled out, I'd seen write-ups in the paper about arrests in which it was glaringly obvious the police zeroed in on their subjects by tracking cellphones, a practice still fuzzy under Washington State law.

It was probably the same when fingerprint technology first came on the scene. Start bragging about your new crime-fighting tools, and suddenly all the burglars and murderers are wearing latex gloves. Or turning off their cells. Or using disposable phones.

Just before they released us, Cooper told me, "That

number you gave us for Throckmorton belongs to a Mrs. Edna Whitney. We called her on her land line to confirm it. She was under the impression her grandson, Jason Farnsworth, was using the phone."

"So Throckmorton's real name is Jason Farnsworth?"

"Farnsworth is eighteen and the drummer in a grunge band that plays all up and down the west coast. Right now they're in San Diego."

"Then the phone is stolen? Why wouldn't Farnsworth report it? Or has he?"

"We've yet to contact him."

Together we thought it over as Snake joined us, having been released from custody when the officer in charge of the scene received a call from national security officials back East. For ten minutes, we sat in the back of a squad car and wrote out our statements, then Cooper rejoined us. "These two guys you were fighting weren't homeless," she said. "Eddie the Slugger flew up here first class and was wearing a Gucci watch."

"And them was some handmade shoes," Snake mumbled.

As we walked through the park to where I'd parked the Ford, Cooper gave Snake a lingering look she probably thought nobody would notice. I couldn't tell whether she was trying to figure him out, or if she was thinking about him more in the way a woman thinks about a man she is interested in. I'd always assumed Cooper was gay, but I was no expert on such matters, and Snake had a certain scruffy charm that sometimes dazzled the most unlikely—to my mind—females.

26

Stephanie Chin lived with her parents just off Avondale Road in Redmond, on grassy acreage where rusted vintage tractors and hunks of decaying farm machinery were parked hither and yon. Alongside a two-story farmhouse stood a horse barn and smaller outbuildings, all picturesquely drenched in red paint with white trim. Two duns and a pinto grazed in a field behind the house. In another field, I spied barrels set up in a well-worn sawdust patch where someone practiced riding drills.

It was getting dark. I'd already gone back to The Dregs in West Seattle, but none of tonight's customers knew where I could find Manny or had any information on him.

Cooper had phoned with the information that Jason Farnsworth, whose cellphone Throckmorton was using, had been contacted and claimed he didn't know where his phone was. When asked what he was doing for a phone, he said he was using burners or borrowing from friends and band mates. Cooper thought there was something suspicious about this, and I didn't know what to make of the phone issue.

As I navigated down a long driveway shaded by elms and maples, toward the main house, I received a call on my phone from a number I didn't recognize, a 253 area code: South Puget Sound, possibly Tacoma, the city where I had been raised. "This is Black."

"Thomas Black?"

"That's right."

"Listen, ass hat, you don't be trying to tell people Mick didn't kill my sister or my mom. The last thing we need is somebody like you throwing your bullshit all over this. We're just now coming to terms with what happened, and

Two Miles of Darkness

I'm not going to let you put my father through hell one more time. I'm warning you."

I remembered a brother in the family and managed to recall the name. "Maksud?"

"That's right."

"Alex's brother?"

"We've got cousins, too. And they're just as pissed off as I am. You step away from this or you're going to be sorry."

Maksud Celik. "Maksud, where were you today at around noon?"

"I was at work in Olympia. Why? What the hell? Are you accusing me of something?"

"Where do you work?"

"You just stay away from my family. I hear anything about you poking your nose in our business, you'll be getting a visit of the kind I guarantee you won't appreciate. The police gave us the truth. Bugger off."

"Maksud?"

He'd severed the connection.

Just what I needed, angry relatives running interference in an investigation I should never have taken on in the first place. Here was somebody else who might possibly be linked to the two guys from California.

I kept thinking about the way Mick had lost the two jobs. Unless there are extenuating circumstances like a death in the family or a divorce, a person's performance at work usually slips gradually if at all, not suddenly and precipitously. Mick's problems had taken place in the space of a few short weeks: the complaints, the accidents, and then the failed drug test at his second job. I wondered if Mick hadn't received a head injury before it all happened.

While I was ruminating on this, Stephanie Chin drove onto the property in her Volkswagen bug and parked near the barn. It took half a minute to catch up with her.

"Ms. Chin?"

She didn't seem surprised to see me. "I was hoping to talk to you again. Can you help me with these?"

She was preparing to unload sacks of grain from the

trunk of her car. I hefted two of the bags while she struggled with one, and we carried them into the barn, where we deposited them in a crude wooden rack behind the door. I went back and got the last sack.

"I had a feeling you would be back," she said, slapping at the dust on the front of her workout tights, where powder from the grain had left a ghostly residue. She must have hit the gym on the way home from work, then the feed store. I dusted off my shirt and smelled the dry, gritty aroma of oats.

"This morning, I had the idea you wanted to tell me more about Alex Kraft," I said.

"I'm sorry about the way Glen treated you. At Vereecken and Sons, we've all been forbidden to talk to anybody about Alex or even concede she ever worked there. The new owners are scrupulous about enforcing all their little edicts, especially that one."

"Anything you tell me will be in confidence."

"Are you with their insurance company?"

"I'm looking into this for a friend of the family. By the way, who are the new owners of Vereecken and Sons?"

"It's a group called Guangzhou Central Brokers. A Chinese company, although we've never seen anyone from China. Listen, Alex's termination wasn't righteous. She didn't deserve it. Alex was the brightest rising star at Vereecken and Sons, and everybody knew it. She'd been there four years. It was crazy to fire her. When she left, it put a pall over the whole place. With her record of accomplishments and her work ethic, if they could fire her, they could fire any of us."

"What was their explanation?"

"There was no official explanation. When we pressed them, they said it was private. We all knew her husband lost his job, and we knew how much she needed to keep hers. It seemed so unfair."

She'd brought herself near tears thinking about her dead friend.

"She and Mick had been together since she was in college. They met in a co-ed softball league. She was dazzled by his athleticism. Funny how something like hitting a softball can cement a relationship. Later, he worked hard to put her through college. He joked about being a truck driver married to an architect. He said she designed the buildings and he delivered to the front steps. He had a great sense of humor. After Alex was let go, we formed a delegation and asked to bring her back, but Masterton wouldn't even hear us out."

"Who is Masterton exactly?"

"You met him. Glen. He's the flack for Guangzhou Central. Vereecken and Sons was founded back in the late forties and until recently was being run by the son of the youngest original partner, but he's in his late sixties now and wanted to retire, so when this offer came along from Guangzhou, he grabbed it. It turned him into a multi-millionaire but left the rest of us in the lurch. We're still waiting for more terminations, but so far Alex has been the only one."

"Alex knew they weren't terminating anybody else?"

"Mick was the one who got upset about it. Called the firm so many times Glen finally put a block on his number and told him if he showed up in person he'd call the cops."

"Guangzhou? What can you tell me about them?"

"We've researched the heck out of them and we can't find out who the new owners really are. As far as we can tell, it's some sort of shell company. Guangzhou seems to be a subsidiary of a subsidiary. Half the time, when we overhear him on the phone, Masterton is talking to people in England or Australia. Never China."

I made a mental note to get the phone records for Vereecken and Sons to see if Masterton had left any telltale tracks on the company line. "Is Vereecken and Sons being run any differently than before? Are they selling off pieces of it? Has anything at all changed except for Alex getting the ax?"

"Nothing else changed. Nothing."

"Maybe more cuts are coming?"

"Maybe, but it's been over five months and they seem to have lost interest in us. Masterton spends his day in his office practicing with his putter. It's like he's a babysitter."

"This morning when he heard me asking about Alex, he came at me like an off-course rocket booster."

"He's pretty touchy when her name comes up."

"So what's the real story?"

"They'll be furious if they find out I told."

"Nobody's going to hear it from me."

Stephanie Chin perched on a wooden fence just outside the barn's main door, as if she needed to be off her feet in order to dish out her tale. One of the horses in the pasture initiated a slow walk toward us. It would be a while before the horse arrived, lured by her, wary of me.

"One day, Alex was looking distraught. It was after this guy from corporate showed up. Geoff Hardy. He was Masterton's boss. Alex looked . . . well . . . as if she was in shock. I asked what was going on. She said Geoff Hardy told her he wanted to take her to the Virgin Islands."

"He was coming on to her?"

"Right. And she was worried."

"About her job, or about Hardy?"

"Both."

"Tell me about Geoff Hardy."

"Geoff Hardy was only there a couple of weeks. He would come in late, confer with Glen, then ask one or two of us into his office. We assumed he was going through the personnel files to see who could be let go."

"Anything ever happen between the two of them?"

"Of course not. Alex was all about family. I think Geoff pushed her out the door because she wouldn't play ball with him."

"He let her go personally?"

"Yes. I talked to her on the phone that same night, but she'd signed a confidentiality agreement and couldn't tell me anything. She did say she thought he got a kick out of firing her. I hate to think of something like that happening in our company. It makes me want to get out of there as fast as I can."

"What else can you tell me about Hardy?"

"We haven't seen him since Alex was let go. He was good looking. Drove a sports car all the men in the office envied. The worst part was Glen dissing her to prospective employers when they called asking for references. I never heard what he said, but it must have been bad, because she couldn't find another position to save her life."

As we stopped and considered the colloquialism she'd just used, the horse came up behind her and nudged her backside. No matter what else happened in her life, she would always have at least one friend.

27

A bus fire on the 520 bridge clogged the lanes and kept me from getting home until almost nine.

When I walked in the back door, I found Kathy relaxing with a book. She'd been working day and night on a case defending a woman who said she killed her abusive boyfriend in self-defense, a story disputed by the King County Prosecutor, who claimed she'd murdered him in cold blood. Kathy was also working on several cases of deceptive mortgage lending, trying to keep people from losing their houses.

"How was your day?" she asked. I hadn't given her any of the details over the phone, knowing it was better to deliver news of near-death monkeyshines face to face so I could leaven them with my dry wit, though I'd come to suspect recently that for most people the phrase "dry wit," particularly with regard to me, meant they didn't think it was funny. Kathy did. Or pretended to. Think it was funny. Think *I* was funny. Well . . . she laughed.

"I'm starved. Let me eat and I'll fill you in."

"Sure."

I lingered over my dinner, trying to think of some way to make the day's events sound more innocuous and less lethal than they actually were. I'd had an ex-prizefighter take a swing at me, had been shot at, and had watched Elmer narrowly avoid death by throwing a man two hundred feet off a cliff, a flight path he himself had avoided only by a whisker.

After I polished off my dinner, we sat in the living room listening to the occasional cars whistling along on 11th outside our windows, while I savored a giant chocolate chip cookie Kathy had brought me from the shop catty-corner from our office building on First Avenue. I tried to keep my story as simple as I could, but Kathy saw through my ploy and, staring at me with liquid violet-blue eyes, said, "These people must be old enemies of Elmer's."

"Somehow, I don't think so."

"What are you saying?"

"I think they have nothing at all to do with Snake's past or the dog, and everything to do with the three dead people in that house."

"Explain."

"There are lots of unconnected dots in the Kraft story. To begin with, the police didn't know there was a convicted voyeur named Herbert Cavendish living four doors down. They didn't know about the camera in the back yard, which is now missing, and which might be the tool of a convicted voyeur. Then there's the man named Manny, who dragged Mick Kraft into some intricate money-losing venture that, as far as I can tell, must have been the final blow to their financial stability. The police haven't located Manny, and I haven't been able to find him either. Word is, Manny loaned Mick the gun he used the day of the shooting. He helped trash Mick's life and then handed him the weapon he would use to end it. If, in fact, it *was* Mick who did the shooting."

"But the police are satisfied the Kraft killings were a double murder-suicide?"

"They're sticking to that."

"I'll tell you what you need," Kathy said. "You need a vacation. Put your mountain bike in the car and drive to Moab. You've been talking about that for years, but you've never gone."

"Nobody goes to Moab in August. Besides, my riding buddies come back from Moab covered in scabs from falling on those rock formations."

"Scabs are better than waking up in a box. Thomas, one of those men is still out there, and if you're not worried, I am."

"Somebody hired Eddie the Slugger and the other guy, and it probably wasn't our pervert down the street. I don't see Herbert Cavendish having the money or connections to fly leg-breakers up from California. One of them flew first class."

"Maybe he had miles or something."

"Maybe."

"Leg-breakers? Geez, I wish you wouldn't call them that."

"What if they're his friends? Or his cousins or something? If we had more operatives, we'd put a tail on Cavendish and see if he hooks up with the remaining prizefighter. Then again, I've been thinking maybe this business transaction where Mick lost everything was a drug deal. They were awful secretive about it. We have drug dealers involved, it might explain the muscle coming up from California."

"What I want to know, Thomas, is how somebody knew to put these two boxers in front of the Millionair Club. How did they know you were going to be there?"

"I'm glad you brought that up, because something's been bothering me all afternoon and you just articulated it. It's as if somebody was reading my mind, and the only person I know who can read my mind is you."

"Well, you're not hard to read. You're either hungry, horny, or bored."

"You make me sound like a goat."

"You are a little like a goat. But I'm so relieved you didn't get hurt today. At least you were able to drop the one who came at you."

"It was a lucky punch."

"You always claim it was a lucky punch, but you always seem to throw that lucky punch just in the nick of time."

"Except the time I got knocked cold by that alarm clock. If this fight had lasted three seconds longer, I might be dead."

"If that tidbit doesn't give me insomnia, nothing will."

"Sorry. I'm trying to give myself a pep talk in case I run into him again."

"A pep talk so you can punch him in the throat again?"

"So I can run for my life."

"I'm hoping the next time you see him it'll be in a line-up. Whoever sent those goons after you is going to think twice before sending them again. From their point of view, you and Snake must look pretty damn deadly. Think about it. They send a couple of prizefighters who've probably killed people before—one has for sure—chasing after what they believe are two hick private eyes who are out looking for a lost dog, and the two private eyes put one man down and throw the other off a cliff. Now the cops are looking for the guy who got away, and you two are unscathed. To quote one of our worst Presidents, they misunderestimated you."

"There's something else we need to think about."

"What's that?"

"They wanted what was supposed to have happened to us today to look like an accident. After today, anything they try won't look accidental."

"So you're saying they won't try again?"

"I'm saying they might as well come right out and shoot us on a street corner."

"Now I'm really not going to sleep. You need to go to Moab."

Moments later, Carole Cooper called on my cell. "We didn't finish our chat about the Krafts," she said. "Did you find anything else besides the camera mounting plate in the tree?"

"Just a convicted voyeur four doors down."

"Tell me about him." When I finished, she said, "My, my. You have been digging. I have to applaud you for that. I have something for you, too. I wouldn't normally be blabbing this all over town, especially with your pal on NSA's watch list, but in light of what almost happened to you two today, I think you need to know. We ran the rest of the names from the airline manifest on the flight Eddie Turner booked to fly up here. One of the other passengers had an extensive record. Burglary. Petty theft. Grand larceny. Assault. Kiting checks. Domestic violence. A lot of domestic violence. They weren't sitting together on the flight, but we're thinking he could be your missing guy.

"We matched their mug shots with the photos you gave us, and he fits the man you told us was calling himself Jones.

Real name is Frederick C. Lovell. Just as you thought, he's an ex-professional heavyweight. The two of them trained out of the same gym in Las Vegas. Lovell did time in Vacaville. Eddie was at Pelican Bay. We're looking for Lovell now."

"No progress on Throckmorton?"

"None."

"But you are looking for him?"

"We're looking for all of these people."

After Carole Cooper hung up, I called Snake. "You okay?"

"Why wouldn't I be?"

"Maybe because a guy twice your size spent part of the day bouncing your skull around like a powder puff."

"I've been thinking about the shooter in the park. My guess is he ran because he knew I carried enough heavy iron to outfit a Mexican drug cartel."

"Always a possibility."

"See? All them guns I tote around helped. I knew they would, eventually. Maybe now you'll give up your pacifistic ways."

"And our nuclear arsenal makes us all safer."

"Is that sarcasm?"

"Is the Pope Catholic? I'm not going to start carrying a gun." I explained about the angry phone call from Maksud Celik, then told him what I'd learned from Stephanie Chin and Carole Cooper, told him about Eddie the Slugger and Frederick C. Lovell.

"I think I need a woman," Snake said, more or less out of the blue. "After a near-death experience a man needs to spill some seed. It's a Neanderthal compulsion, probably the single greatest compulsion that's kept the species from going extinct."

"The Neanderthals *are* extinct."

"They are?"

"A long time ago."

"You know what I mean. You go jump Kathy. I'm going to call—"

"That barista from Starbucks?"

Two Miles of Darkness

"How'd you know about her?"

"I know all kinds of things. How did you make out with her last night?"

"We're going to sail to the South Seas together."

"On your friend's boat?"

"I'm pretty sure I can talk him into loaning it to me."

"He might put you in his will, too, and share his lottery winnings, but I doubt it. In the meantime, don't choke on your own backed-up seed."

"Anything happens, give me a call. That's her on the other line. Gotta go."

"Backed-up seed?" Kathy called out from across the room. "And how is Elmer?"

I tried to smile, but I think it was actually a smirk, then phoned one of my contacts at the phone company and asked for a triangulation on Anthony Throckmorton's phone, which could be done by tracing the cell registered to Edith Whitney. It was illegal, but I'd done it before and would probably do it again. The government did it every day. Hell, they'd probably come out with a free phone app for it within a month or two. I could only hope Throckmorton hadn't already ditched the cell, because if he was smart, that's what he would do.

My contact at the phone company would also run down the bills and numbers called from Vereecken and Sons. This was dependent on which carrier they were using and was going to cost an arm and a leg, but paying the freight was a hundred- four-year-old dowager who'd once dined with George Armstrong Custer's widow.

Earlier in the day, Snake had promised to contact some of his informants and ask if they had any information on Manny. Even though I thought Huntzinger was clear of involvement, he was going to track down and interview him, too. I knew if the murder-suicide had been staged, it was probably staged by somebody more knowledgeable about crime detection than a man training to be a manager at McDonald's. Also, as a general rule, a man didn't murder three people and then wait around to report it. Still, Huntzinger might well give us something Cooper and the newspapers hadn't. There were times when you got some little zinger from the man who discovered the bodies, and Snake and I were hoping for one here.

Without realizing it, my new working hypothesis was that we were dealing with a triple murder staged to look like a murder-suicide.

I called Anthony Throckmorton, but he didn't pick up, just like all the other times I'd called him that day.

28

At six the next morning, my cellphone woke me from a dream that was so racy I decided I could never tell Kathy about it. The caller was my phone company operative, Sheila, who was thoroughly corrupt and had a job which called for her to mostly sit and wait for problems in the system, which allowed her to read a romance novel a day.

Sheila rarely took on an assignment without waking me up with the results, which I had the feeling she believed infused an intimacy into our relationship that it did not, for even though she'd only met me face-to-face once and knew I was happily married, she invariably tried to inveigle me into a flirtation over the phone.

She told me she'd already e-mailed the phone records for Vereecken and Sons through an untraceable route Brad Munch had set up the previous year.

"We've triangulated your buddy. Near as I can tell, he's sleeping in the middle of the roadway next to the Pike Place Market."

"He's probably under an overpass, which would make it look as if he's in the middle of the roadway. How long can you watch him?"

"All day, if you like, but it's going to cost more to do this in the daytime. It's a lot riskier."

"I need you to stay on it until I catch up with him."

"Call back when you need an update on his coordinates. I'm sending a list of his calls, too. One month okay?"

"Three months would be better."

"I'll get those for you."

"Thanks, Sheila. Cash again?"

"You know I only take cash." She would receive the

money via courier when the case was finished, the same as she had in the past.

At eight, Snake met me at my house and I called Sheila for an updated location on Throckmorton, who was now up and about, roaming the Pike Place Market in downtown Seattle.

"I expected him to be in San Francisco by now," Snake commented.

"You think this is being run out of California?"

"That's where our prizefighter pals came from. My other contacts haven't reported back yet, but my brother's down there and he's going to give me a jingle if he digs up anything."

"You bring your electronics?"

Snake rattled a small plastic container with parts in it.

I'd done a cursory scan of Anthony Throckmorton's phone calls, and not surprisingly, they painted him as a frequenter of phone sex sites. One of the numbers turned out to be a woman in Ohio. Reading the texts, I could tell she was under the impression he was a CEO of a sportswear company who had just broken up with his wife, a wife Throckmorton claimed was a former Miss America. Throckmorton had been sending the woman twenty or thirty bucks at a pop, and in return she had been sending him semi-nude photographs that looked as if they'd been scanned from a magazine.

Sheila had e-mailed the photos to me under the heading "check me out, Daddy." Sheila knew that type of subject line would get a man in trouble should his wife happen to be privy to his e-mail, which only added to my sense that Sheila would be in high clover if she could stir up a fracas between Kathy and me.

Twenty-five minutes later, when Snake and I spotted him in the Starbucks at First and Pike, Snake roared, "Hey, Throckmorton!"

Throckmorton had been nonchalantly sitting at a table by himself reading a section of a latte-stained, three-day-old *Wall Street Journal* abandoned in the café, but when he saw us, he looked like a man who'd been hit a glancing blow by a speeding car. For a second, he looked as if he was going to bolt.

I'd left multiple messages on his cell since he ran from us in Discovery Park, and now the phone lay on the table next to a large blueberry muffin.

"Oh . . . Hey, guys! Thomas. I was about to call you back. The battery on this baby died and I just now got it working. I see you left some messages." He was using a nearby outlet to recharge his phone, but I knew he was lying about the battery being dead, because had it been dead, Sheila wouldn't have been able to trace him. It might have been low, but it wasn't dead. "Calling you was first on my list of things to do when I got this baby juiced up again." When neither of us spoke for a while, a thought occurred to him. "How'd you find me?"

"The questions," Snake said, pulling out a chair and spinning it around backwards so he could sit close to Throckmorton, "come from us, not from you. And the first question is, where did you find those jokers yesterday?"

"You said to get the same guys if I could."

"The new guys," I said. "You brought two new guys. Where'd you find them?"

"Hey, man. They said they needed work."

"And you need to stop lying," I said. "You told us you knew them."

"I never said I knew them."

"You vouched for them."

"I never did."

Snake slapped a palm down on the table so violently it sounded like a gunshot and made Throckmorton jump. Several customers turned our way. "Cut the crap and tell us what's going on. You ran from us. Why?"

" 'Cause I watched you throw a man off a cliff. I watched Thomas knock that other guy on his ass for no good reason. As far as I could tell, you two were going crazy. Hey, I gotta take this." Throckmorton's phone had begun humming.

Before he could reach it, Snake covered the phone with his hand. "I don't think so," Snake said.

"You guys. You guys . . . You don't think I was tied up with those two?"

"Actually," I said, taking the humming phone from Snake and looking at it, "that's exactly what we think." The call was from Cristiana in Ohio, one of the scam artists currently bilking him of pin money.

"Okay," he said. "Let me tell you what happened. And this is the truth. Yesterday morning I was standing on the street when they came over and threatened me. Said I was going to hook them up with you guys so they could help search for the dog."

"How did they even know about the dog—or us?"

"I guess people been talking about it on the street. That reward."

"How did they know we would be at the Millionair Club?"

"You called me."

"Not how did *you* know. How did *they* know?"

"I mighta mentioned it to a few people when I was recruiting. You told me to recruit."

"Tell us everything you know about them."

"They asked for work. I didn't see any reason to turn them down, and we were shy two bodies." While Snake and I waited, staring, silent, intimidating, he added, "Okay, they paid me."

"How much?"

"Two hundred."

"That was it?" Snake asked. "You gave us up for two bills?"

"It was two hundred each."

"Oh, well, I guess that makes it okay then!"

"No, no, no. It wasn't like that. First of all, they were scary. I was scared. And I tried to warn you. When we were in the park, I kept trying to get next to one of you so I could fill you in, but they were watching me. And you have to believe me when I say nobody ever said anything about throwing anybody off a cliff. I been a lot of things, but I never been no murderer. Honest. They said they just wanted to scare you."

"I thought you said they didn't tell you what they were going to do?" I said.

"Scare you. That's what they said."

"And that was all right with you?"

"Did you see them? There was nothin' I could do. They wanted to shit in my hat, I would have held it for them and then wiped their ass. Don't turn me in. I got a warrant out on me. My mom needs money. There's a jam I gotta help her out of before I go in. I'll go in, sure. I'll turn myself in. Right. I mean, I'm not trying to get out of anything. But first, I gotta help my mother out of this scrape."

"Give me your mother's number," I said, pulling out my phone. "I'll talk to her."

My offer rendered him speechless, which confirmed the mother gimmick was a ruse.

"You got a warrant out on you?" I asked. "Under what name?"

"Yeah, Throckmorton," Snake said. "What name are you using for your legal business?"

"Anthony Throckmorton."

"We checked. He don't exist."

"Okay. It's Brian Blair. The warrant is for Brian Blair. Hey, look. My blueberry bun is getting cold. And I gotta wash up before I eat. I'm a firm believer in hygiene." His chair made a shrill scraping noise on the floor. "I'll just be a minute," he said, gesturing toward the restroom in the rear of the establishment. He reached for his phone, which I'd placed in the center of the table. Snake snatched it up first.

"*We'll* just be a minute," I corrected.

The restroom was barely large enough for the two of us. Throckmorton expounded nonstop on the importance of cleanliness, especially for a "guy on the street," then launched into a story I could tell he was making up as he went along: about how bad off his mother was and how much she needed his help. It seemed she'd run up some gambling and medical debts where she lived in Aberdeen and had taken to shoplifting to pay her bills, got nabbed by a store detective, and was on the verge of doing time in the county lockup if he didn't get her a good lawyer. He promised to turn himself in to the police later if we let him go. I pretended to mull it over.

At one point, Throckmorton looked at me in the close confines of the restroom and for just a second I could tell he was thinking about rushing me—he was heavy enough that he could probably knock me into the wall with some force if he caught me by surprise—but then his look wilted and I knew he wasn't going to try anything. I kept him chatting until I figured Snake had completed his task.

I said, "So what do we call you?"

"Tony works. I'm going by Tony now."

"Okay, Tony. What happened to our buddy, Lovell?"

"Who?"

"The guy who called himself Jones. You scrammed out of the park with him."

"I told you I ran 'cause you chased me."

"Where did you and Lovell go?"

"He went one way and I went the other. I never saw him after that."

"And you didn't know the man taking potshots at us?"

"I heard some shots, but I thought that was you guys shooting at *us*. It made me want to get lickety-split outa there."

"What'd you use for transportation? It's a long walk from Magnolia to anywhere."

"Took a bus. Number twenty-four. I take the bus everywhere."

"Really?"

"Take my picture and show it to the bus drivers. They'll tell you."

"I may just do that."

"You'll see I'm telling the truth."

"I'll see what I'll see, but I doubt you're telling the truth." When we got back to the table, Snake was pawing through Tony's backpack, having already pulled out dirty socks, a package of raisins, and a couple of dog-eared, jerk-off magazines. Tony's face went red when he saw the magazines in the open on the table next to his blueberry muffin. It was funny how a guy could lie and conspire and maybe even try to kill you, all seemingly without an ounce of guilt, but bring out a magazine he'd been masturbating to and he acted guilty as hell.

Finding nothing of interest, Snake crammed the contents back into the rucksack and dropped it onto the floor.

We waited while Tony scarfed down his muffin, Snake and I letting the silence amplify the tension.

When Tony used the pad of his thumb to dab up the last of the crumbs, Snake leaned his elbows on the table so that his jacket fell open and both .44 Magnums revealed themselves. Tony stared at them while Snake gave him the same evil eye he'd used on animals and competitors back in his rodeo days.

"Now, Tony," Snake said. "You want us to break the law by not turning you in, we're going to have to get something for our trouble. You do realize Homicide is looking for you?"

"Homicide? I didn't kill nobody. Hell, I didn't do nothin'."

"You ran like you had fire ants in your britches. The SPD thinks that shows guilt. At the very least, you're a witness to an attempted murder and a death."

"Please, guys. My mother needs my help."

"Then I feel sorry for your mother," said Snake. "Now I suppose you're going to tell us she's a saint?"

"Saint? She ain't even no Sunday school teacher. She brought home men, lots of men, and some of them beat the living hell out of me. When she wasn't around, this one guy used to chase me bare-ass around the house with a hard-on. She ain't no saint."

"Then maybe you don't owe her so much. Maybe you should go to jail on that old warrant."

"No," he said, pretending to think it over dutifully. "I think I owe her."

"Tell us the truth," I said. "Who hired you to spy on us?" Throckmorton and I stared at each other for a minute.

"Ah, crap. I tell you, he'll kill me."

"Then I guess you're between a rock and a hard place,

aren't you, Tony?"

"You say he'll kill you?" Snake said. "Who is going to kill you?"

"I don't even know. He hires me to do jobs. A guy I bumped into in lockup hooked me up about two years ago."

"What kind of jobs?" Snake asked.

"On this one, he said I was to wait outside the Millionair Club and make sure you guys connected with me. That was it. I was to await further instructions."

Snake and I exchanged glances. "Wait a minute," I said. "You talking about one of the prizefighters from yesterday? Are they running you, or is it somebody else?"

"Like I said, I just met them two yesterday. This is somebody else."

"So you're talking about the first time we hired you?"

"Right. That first day."

"You were being paid by somebody who told you to stand in front of the Millionair Club and get hired by us."

"Yeah."

Snake and I looked at each other. "Just out of curiosity, how much did he pay you?" Snake asked.

"Three hundred bucks, but I don't have any left. I lost it at the casino."

"You check lost and found?" Snake asked.

Ignoring the bad joke, he said, "It was those one-armed bandits. I'm a sucker for those machines."

"Were any of the others on their payroll?" I asked.

"As far as I know, it was just me."

"You don't think those two new guys were on the payroll?"

"Maybe. I don't know. I'm not sure."

"So, who is this person who told you to stand out there and get hired by us?" Snake asked.

"I don't know. He calls me from time to time, and I end up doing jobs for him—or them. I don't really know if it's just one guy. I've never seen anyone, and the guy calls me never gives his name."

"How does he contact you?"

"By this phone here. He gave it to me."

"And how long have you had it?"

"Maybe a year. He had a guy on the street give it to me. He said it belonged to some kid who wasn't going to squawk. I never pay the bills or anything. He pays."

"Look," Snake said. "What did this guy do to you, Tony?"

"Nothing."

"He did something, or you wouldn't be this scared. Look at you. You're shaking."

"Okay. Yeah. Right. These two guys threw me in the trunk of a car, blindfolded. I never even saw them. Drove me two miles in the dark. I thought they were going to kill me."

"When was this?"

"Right before I was given the phone. They took me out in the woods somewhere. I don't know where. One of them dug a hole. They said they were going to put me in it. They were about done with it when the phone rang and somebody told them to call it off. They put me back in the trunk and drove me back to town. Those two miles riding in the trunk? I was never so terrified in my life. I could tell they were going to blow my head off. The crazy thing was, I never knew what I did wrong."

"And then you were hired again?"

"Told me to hold onto the phone and wait for instructions. Next time was the other day with you guys. The Millionair Club."

"You sleep on the streets?"

"Parks. I got places."

"I'm just wondering why this guy puts so much trust in you," I asked.

"I never failed him. Not once."

"He's so scary, why didn't you toss the phone and run?" Snake asked. "Should be pretty easy for someone like you to vanish."

"I got family. A son and my mom in the area. I can't just pick up and leave."

I said, "So he set you up with Lovell and Turner? Was this before we called for this second meeting, or after?"

"No. He never said nothin' about them. They just showed up and made me put them in the group."

"And the first time we worked with you? He called you and told you to be outside the Millionair Club?"

"Yes."

"You never saw this guy?"

"How many times do I have to tell you?"

"What about the guys who drove you into the woods?"

"They pulled a pillowcase over my head. It reeked of perfume. It musta belonged to some woman."

"What else have you been asked to do?"

"Weird stuff. Sometimes it's a burglary. He tells me to break in, trash the place. Even tells me when to do it. Once he sent me a key so I could break in. Had me take a guy's driver's license out of his wallet once while he was out jogging. Just the driver's license. One time they made me put a condom under this couple's bed and steal all the woman's jewelry. The condom had a spoonful of vanilla pudding in it. At least I think it was pudding. One time I had to bump into a lady was carrying all these groceries. Told me to knock her down. After I had her on the ground some dude came up and beat the crap out of me. I never found out if he was part of the act or not."

"You took a beating for this guy?"

"That warrant out on me? It's for breaking and entering. He told me to do it, and then he called the cops so I got caught inside the building. I know it was him called."

"But you still do what he tells you?"

"He pays good, and if you make him mad, you get a ride in the trunk of a car. Two miles of darkness. I don't see I have much choice. Besides, I get a free phone out of it. And I don't hear from him that often."

We continued to interrogate him, but his story about how he'd initially hooked up with us didn't vary much. I didn't think he was lying about that part of it. During the process, I excused myself to order a croissant, and while I was away from the table, I phoned Carole Cooper and told her we had Throckmorton. She said she was ten minutes away and would be there shortly. When I got back to the table, I quizzed him again on the identities of the men who put him in the trunk of a car. We were still grilling him when he asked to be excused to take a dump.

Snake and I looked at each other. "By rights it's my turn to go with him," Snake said. "But that restroom is awful small and things could get ugly."

"Could get downright gruesome."

In the end, holding onto his rucksack as insurance, we watched him from our table as he scurried to the restroom. We let him take his phone, thinking it might be interesting to see who he called once he was out of sight. Twelve minutes later, when Carole Cooper arrived with her partner, the restroom door was ajar and Tony Throckmorton, to our chagrin, was missing. He'd apparently squeezed through a tiny window above the sink, a feat akin to sucking a hard-boiled egg into a Coke bottle. When I poked my head out the window, I expected to see him in the alley with a broken neck, but he was gone.

Cooper wasn't any happier about being dragged from her office on a wild goose chase than we were about getting flimflammed by somebody we both considered our intellectual inferior. Before she went back to her car, we told Cooper everything we'd learned from Tony.

After she was gone, I looked at Snake. "You fix his phone?"

Snake opened his laptop computer and punched up a website, then typed in a password which brought up a map of Seattle showing a blinking X just outside the Pike Place Market and not far from our location. "That him?"

"Six hundred yards from where we're sitting. Traveling Northeast. Three miles per hour."

While I was monitoring Throckmorton in the restroom, Snake had programmed his smartphone with an app that allowed us to track the phone using the built-in GPS. From then on, we could trace his movements as well as every call he made or received in real time. It was a gizmo Snake had picked up at a trade show, part of the ocean of high-tech we were all floating in.

"What do you make of his story?" I asked.

"I don't know. There's something screwy about all this. How the hell did anyone know to tell Throckmorton to be there that first time?"

"Good question. I didn't talk to anyone."

"The only person I talked to was you."

"I think we might be in trouble."

"I'm thinking the same thing."

29

It was easy enough to trace Throckmorton's background on the Internet: under the name of Brian Blair, he had an accumulation of twenty-three drunk-and-disorderlies in Seattle, Tacoma, and Olympia, and had thrice been arrested for exposure while relieving himself in public. He had disturbing-the-peace arrests on his record as well. He'd never done any hard time that we could find, and his last day in jail was two years ago. Until then, he'd been on a first-name basis with jailors all over Western Washington.

"So, he did stop drinking," I said. "That's something."

"He set us up to get murdered," Snake said. "You gonna give him a merit badge for sobriety?"

"No, but we might nominate him for a stint at Ringling Brothers for the way he snaggled his big butt out that window."

We were hogging a Starbucks table other customers in the crowded store wanted, but we'd been slammed with a lot of information and we weren't leaving until we had time to mull it over.

"He's lying," Snake said. "Nobody took him for a ride. Nobody tried to kill him. And I don't think anybody but us ever hired him. He made up a story to throw us off the scent."

"I'm not so sure. He tells us he's on a retainer for somebody who tells him to break into houses and deposit used condoms under the bed? You think he could make up a story like that on the spot?"

"Throckmorton cobbled together that fairytale because he knows I'm partial to conspiracies."

"We know he was sleeping under a roadway last night, but the guy you threw off the bluff was wearing a Gucci watch. And at least one of them flew up first class. People who fly first class don't normally associate with people who sleep under elevated roadways. I think the guys from California were hired by the same person who was running Throckmorton. Throckmorton was the first tier and they were second. Remember the first time we saw him at the Millionair Club? He seemed to be looking for someone in particular."

"I thought he was just looking for work. That's what they do. They stand on the sidewalk and wait for somebody to come by and hire them."

"He was looking for us. Whoever's running Throckmorton knew we were going to be at the Millionair Club. How did he know we would be looking for workers, and how did he know we'd be there? We could have gone to Home Depot or any number of other places." It was the question Kathy had asked me, and I still hadn't come up with an answer. "I called you the night before and told you my plans. You were the only person I told. Did you mention it to anybody?"

"Not a soul."

"Not even the barista you're screwing?"

"All we talked about was her crazy ex-boyfriend."

"Then somebody was eavesdropping."

"How?"

"You tell me."

"Jesus H! This was a set-up from the beginning! I knew it."

I held up my cellphone and made a show of switching it off. Snake killed his, too, then leaned close and whispered. "They can track you on a smartphone if they have the resources and are willing to break the law. We're tracking Throckmorton right now. Why can't they be tracking us right now? Or listening in on our calls? The technology is out there. They can listen to you even when you're not on a call, Thomas. You think so, too, or we wouldn't have turned off our phones. Right now the feds are recording and encoding every phone conversation on the planet, storing it all on servers the size of the Pentagon in Utah. You say it on air, they've got it forever. This could be the feds."

"Why would one of the alphabet agencies have any interest in a missing dog or a husband/wife murder-suicide?"

"I don't know. Jesus. I just thought of something. I said things to Katrina over the phone I never meant for anybody else to hear. It was kinda sexy, but it was also kind of—"

"I don't want to know. But it is curious what a young woman her age sees in you."

"I make her laugh. I told her I was raised by wolves, can ride any bull in the world, and once caught a bullet in my teeth. She said if any part of it was true she would have dinner with me. 'Course at the time she assumed none of it was true."

"That's when you showed her your world championship belt buckle?"

"She looked me up on the Internet. She's a sweet little thing. Now she's got the idea into her head we're going to sail to the South Seas together. Claims she has a murderous ex boyfriend she needs to get away from. I'm going to be her sugar daddy."

"That's not even your boat."

"She doesn't know that."

"Okay, let's get back to Throckmorton. What he said about being a goombah for an unnamed individual or organization. They need something done, they hire someone like him over the phone using a prepaid cell on their end and a stolen phone on his. If he gets arrested, there are no links back to them because he really doesn't know who hired him. In addition, he's homeless, so the authorities aren't likely to believe him if he decides to rat them out."

Glancing at his laptop, Snake said, "He's already made two calls. Received one. He's walking south on Second Avenue."

"Let me see the phone numbers."

Comparing the earlier printouts Sheila had e-mailed me, it turned out Throckmorton's most recent calls were to the same number he'd dialed the day before within minutes of leaving Discovery Park. That number called him the night before we first met, and again the next morning just after we hired him outside the Millionair Club. It had to be the number of his alleged employer or at least an intermediary for his employer.

When we did a reverse directory search, the number tracked back to a company called The Auckland Group. "Never heard of it," said Snake.

"Like hell you've never heard of it."

"Who is it?"

"The people who were hunting Pickles before us."

"Oh, right. And how did Doda get hooked up with The Auckland Group?"

"We could call Charlene and ask, but we have to assume they'd be listening to our phones."

Snake pulled a hundred-dollar bill out of his billfold and offered it to a young man standing in the queue at the counter. "For five minutes with your Blackberry? Local call."

Using the borrowed cellphone, I called Charlene McIntyre. "Charlene? It's Thomas Black. A question came up. The people looking for Pickles before us? Who were they again?"

"Why, it was the Auckland people, but they weren't making any headway, which was why I convinced Doda to go with you." I was pretty sure she hadn't convinced Doda of anything, that my father had offered my services and Doda had jumped on the idea herself, but taking credit was something a good executive assistant did, and Charlene did it with relish.

"Where did you hear about them?"

"One of Binky's friends. Or maybe it was Binky himself. I don't remember."

When I punched in the number for The Auckland Group, I got a recording. All the message said was: "Leave your number; we'll get back to you." I left my own number, knowing I wasn't going to turn my phone on for a while.

"Damn," said Snake. "Maybe it's one of those ultra selective companies that cater to the super wealthy and do all their advertising by word of mouth."

Two Miles of Darkness

"Are there such things?"

"They're all over the place. My brother used to work for one. Guarded dot-com millionaires down in Silicon Valley. They carried automatic weapons in the trunk of their car."

During a more extensive examination of the last fifty numbers to and from Throckmorton's phone, we found calls from Charlene's cell and Doda's home phone. Several from J Compton.

I said, "If Charlene's in on this, I just gave away the farm by asking about Auckland."

"They're trying to kill us," Snake muttered, scanning the list of numbers and names. "J Compton?"

"My old friend, Binky. Joshua Compton."

"It's going to be interesting to hear what Binky says when you bring up The Auckland Group. I'd like to watch his face when you ask him why he's been chatting with Throckmorton a couple of times a week."

"Me, too."

30

 I phoned Charlene once more and asked if she knew where Binky was. She gave me his cell number, which I already had, along with an address for the house he was renovating in Des Moines, where she said he "camped out" last night.
 Camped out. Going without his heated, monogrammed Egyptian cotton towels was probably Binky's idea of roughing it. When I asked Charlene if she knew Tony Throckmorton or Brian Blair, she claimed she'd never heard of them, this despite the fact that her phone had been used to call Throckmorton several times over the past week. She also claimed it had been weeks since she'd been in touch with anybody from The Auckland Group.
 "Do you happen to have a contact address for them? Or a phone number?"
 She gave me a number, but it was the same one we'd found on Throckmorton's phone, the one that got us only a recording.
 Antsy over the course of our investigation and still shaky from the fracas in Discovery Park, Snake decided he wanted to run down some leads on his own: Huntzinger, the young man who discovered the bodies; Cavendish, the convicted voyeur who lived four houses away from the Kraft domicile; and Manny, who still hadn't popped up on anybody's radar.
 "We split up, we'll get this done faster," Snake said. "You talk to Binky. I'll run down these other guys."
 "I've already spoken to Cavendish."
 "Right. But I want to speak to him, too."
 "Knock yourself out."
 After stopping just north of the Market at Elliott Bay

Two Miles of Darkness

Bicycles to pick up a new chain for my bike, I drove south through downtown. On the way, I called a friend, a fire chief in a small town near the Cascade foothills. Mac Fontana owned a semi-retired police dog who'd been trained in Germany in a Schutzhund Club. As far as I could tell, Satan could track a thimble of distilled water across Lake Washington, which made me reasonably certain he could locate a dachshund in Discovery Park. Fontana was stuck all day conducting training fires at the state fire academy with his people, though he promised to get back to me when he was free.

On my way to Des Moines, I stopped at the Kraft house where I picked up a raggedy old blanket Pickles had slept on.

Charlie Hatcher came into the yard while I was there and said, "Hey, Mr. Black. The website you guys set up says she's in Magnolia."

"We spotted her inside the Forty-third Avenue entrance of Discovery Park on the south side."

"So you have her?"

"We only saw her. We were involved in something else at the time."

"Did she run when you saw her?"

"Oh, yeah."

"She would have come to me."

"That's probably true."

"Discovery Park? I don't even know where that is." Pickles had migrated out of his reach and was now on the other side of the city. I knew he'd been hoping for the reward money.

"Maybe you can get your mother to take you there on her day off. Or Mrs. Kennedy."

"My mother's not off until Sunday, and Mrs. Kennedy says her bunions hurt. Pickles is going to get picked up by somebody else for sure. This just sucks."

"I have to agree with you on that."

"The story of my life."

"You're twelve. Trust me. There's good luck and the other kind, but by the time you're my age, it all pretty much evens out."

"You think so? Really?"

"Absolutely." I was giving a pep talk I didn't really believe in to someone who would probably be handcuffed to the bottom rungs of the socio-economic ladder for the rest of his life, yet there was nothing else I dared to tell him. I wasn't the sort of miserable wretch who could pour dirt on the dreams of a youngster. My own position on the ladder wasn't much higher than where I figured he was going to end up, but I had the advantage of not giving a hoot. Even though there was a chance he would escape abject poverty after high school—if he even finished high school—history, common sense, and statistics told me it was only a slight chance. And now that the dog had migrated to Magnolia, Charlie was going to get skunked on the reward.

Pickles' migration across town was one of those miracle treks feature writers love to give ink to, the type of story apt to get picked up by the national media. I'd talked to Snake about it earlier, but he said he'd run out of chits with his feature-writer ex-girlfriend, probably because he came on to her over the phone the last time they spoke.

Charlie's relentless pursuit of the dog should have made the paper, too, or *Reader's Digest*, or *Christian Weekly*, but it wouldn't.

I was closing in on Binky's waterfront house south of Seattle in Des Moines when my phone chimed. I recognized Stephanie Chin's voice, or more accurately, her sobbing, because she didn't say anything at first. When she finally spoke, she said, "Mr. Black? I got laid off today. Glen gave me some song and dance about production and cutting costs, but then he let it slip he knew I'd been talking to somebody. I know it's why I got canned."

"How the devil did he find out we spoke?"

"That's what I can't figure out. I was wondering if you told somebody and it got back to Glen?"

"Stephanie, I only told two people: my wife and my business partner. Neither of them would have talked, and neither one knows Glen." Even as I disavowed my part in her sacking, I thought about the people who had been monitoring my phone calls and tracking my travels. Snake and I had gone over my car and his truck for GPS tracking devices and found nothing. It was likely they were using our phones, though Snake couldn't find any evidence of it on either phone.

The question now was, what was the connection between Vereecken and Sons, Glen Masterton, and the rest of this? Because it was all connected.

The thought that the people who tried to kill Snake might somehow be linked to Glen Masterton, or might have informed Masterton about my visit to Chin, came at me like an oil spill. Somebody was watching our every move and reacting with alarming speed: the missing camera plate in the tree, Throckmorton inserting himself into our search, the two prizefighters from California, and now Stephanie Chin getting the sack. I didn't for one minute think these people were trying to keep us from finding the dog. They wanted us away from the Kraft case.

It suddenly occurred to me what a bad idea it was for Snake and me to split up. "Mr. Black? Mr. Black?"

"I'm here."

"Glen knew we spoke. He alluded to it and then kind of turned the conversation around, as if he suddenly remembered he wasn't supposed to let me know he knew. I got laid off because I was talking to you. That is so illegal."

"All I can say is, I'm sorry."

"I still don't understand how he found out."

"Neither do I," I lied. I thought I did but couldn't prove anything. Also, if people were listening in on my phone calls that meant somebody was monitoring us right now. I couldn't let them know I was aware of it by telling Stephanie we were on a hot line.

"I'm going to get a lawyer and fight this," said Stephanie Chin. "They're talking about selling the company again. Why did they buy it if they were going to turn around and sell it?" For a few moments, her bawling got the better of her. When she finally got hold of herself, she said, "Now I know what Alex was going through. I feel like I've been thrown out of a plane without a chute. Oh, and there's something I probably should have told you last night."

"What is that?"

"It was back before Alex got laid off. I don't know why I didn't think to tell you before. It was Geoff Hardy from Guangzhou Central Brokers. He was only with us for about a week. I told you about him before. That he propositioned Alex. What I forgot was that he wanted to bet Alex a million dollars he could throw a crumpled Coke can into a waste basket from across the room. He told her she didn't have to risk any money, but if he missed she would get the million. If he made it, she would also get a million. But there was a caveat: If he made the basket, she would get a million dollars but she would have to sleep with him."

"What did she tell him?"

"She walked out of the room. She was never really sure if it was a joke or if he was on drugs or what. Doesn't that seem like a bizarre kind of proposal to you?"

It seemed like the kind of proposal Binky or Chad might make, but I kept that to myself. "When did she tell you this?"

"A few days before she was let go."

"So, her boss propositioned her, she turned him down, and a couple of days later he fired her?"

"That's the sequence."

"Why didn't she sue?"

"It was her word against his, and when she talked to an attorney, he said it was unlikely anybody was going to believe her story."

"She should have gone to another attorney."

"That's what I told her."

"You hear of any similar propositions from this Geoff Hardy to anyone else in the company?"

"No. But then after she was let go, Hardy wasn't around anymore."

"Thanks for passing this along. And I'm sorry about your job, Stephanie. If I'd known your job was on the line I would have thought twice before approaching you."

"I'm glad we spoke. I kept quiet all during the media buzz after the murders, and I still feel ashamed of myself for it. You want to know anything else, ask away. I've got nothing to lose now."

"Thanks, Stephanie. And good luck."

Joshua Compton's home was at the bottom of a long hill in a gated community, houses smack on the water, with magnificent views of Puget Sound and the Olympic Mountains to the west. For a few moments, I found myself blocked by the security gate, but then a woman drove through and punched in a code which I was able to glean through a pair of binoculars I keep in the glove box. Seven seven seven seven.

I punched in the code and waited for the gate to lift.

I could have phoned ahead, but surprise was a tool, and I needed to see the look on Joshua's face when I asked him why he was in contact with Throckmorton.

As a hired thug and spy, Throckmorton seemed an odd choice. For one thing, he really did appear to be homeless, which projected a certain air of helplessness one would hardly want in someone entrusted with all the secrets he'd been entrusted with. On the other hand, they probably thought of him as a stooge, a puppet to be manipulated. I guessed he'd been chosen more for his blind obedience and ability to be molded than for anything else, and we'd accepted him without question.

It was easy to identify Binky's house by the queue of construction trucks parked nearby and the multiple trails of mud from their tires in the narrow lane. As it turned out, Binky had bought the lot next door to his original house, had torn the place down, and was expanding his mansion in a manner that would give him a house running the length of two huge lots, all of it fronting Puget Sound. The sunsets would be glorious from here, I thought, with a touch of envy. I adored sunsets, but we couldn't see them from our little cracker-barrel house in the U District.

There was a buoy out in the still water, a small boat tied to it. I had the feeling the cabin cruiser docked at Doda's had been anchored here.

I parked the Ford up the street next to a neighbor's garage and walked back down the lane past both battered and immaculate pickup trucks driven into the enclave by framers and cement workers, and then past a couple of luxury vehicles, moving toward the sound of hammering and electric saws in the restless morning air. There were six or seven houses along the lane on the water side, the other side taken up by a nearly vertical, overgrown hill that served as a wall. This neighborhood wouldn't be accessible to casual burglars or door-to-door salesmen, or anybody else. You needed the code, a boat, or the ability to rappel to reach it, which made the eight houses about as private as any locality in the area could get.

When I found him, Binky was shouting at a man in white coveralls, belittling the workman in a way that astonished and saddened me and verified the cruelty in the story about Binky and the ducklings crossing the road. When he saw me, his eyes popped wide and his mouth erupted into his patented comic grin. The foreman had been weathering the tongue-lashing in a way that told me it wasn't the first time.

But now, with me, Binky was as charming as Santa Claus in front of a plate of cookies. "Thomas. Where did you come from?"

"Up the hill."

He laughed loudly. "Everybody comes from up the hill. What are you doing here?"

"Came to see my old buddy."

"Cool. Come on over to the compound. Let's get away from this mess." He turned back to the man he'd been cursing and spoke tersely, "Don't fuck up anything else."

31

The property sported five hundred feet of beachfront, which would soon be primed with gargantuan mounds of trucked-in sand, now waiting in front of the bulkhead just below the house. In the untouched part of the house, Joshua showed me artwork I could only marvel at. He spoke with affection about each painting and boasted of others in storage, told me he rotated the paintings because he didn't have enough walls to display them all at once. I hadn't expected art treasures, but then, Binky was full of surprises.

We found Chad Baumgarden in the kitchen making egg-salad sandwiches alongside a barefoot, bikini-clad woman I recognized from Doda's, her skin as smooth and liquid as café au lait. It was closing in on noon, but I could tell from their puffy faces these three hadn't been up long.

When we were alone on one of the decks looking out over Puget Sound, Binky said, "You find that mongrel yet?"

"I'm not here about the dog. Somebody tried to kill us yesterday." If he was part of the scheme, or if he even knew about it, he was good at concealing it. But Binky was a gambler, and part of being a gambler was the ability to put on a poker face when necessary. His face right now was as blank as a bucket of white paint. I was thinking about all the calls from his phone to Throckmorton's.

"Somebody tried to do what?"

"Kill us. They tried to kill us. My partner ended up throwing one of them off a cliff."

"Christ almighty. What happened to the guy he threw off? Is he all right?"

"He didn't make it."

"Jesus. You guys were on the news? That was the guy on the news? An exciting week. So I guess your partner's in the slammer?"

"It's been determined to be self-defense."

"That was lucky."

"It wasn't luck if it *was* self-defense."

"Christ, man. Why would somebody try to kill you?"

I gave him the least complicated and most remote possibility we'd so far come up with. "The reward money? The theory is they thought we had it on us."

"Hell, if they were going to kill you for that reward, they could just as easily kill me for my watch. It's worth a fuck of a lot more than that reward. What is it up to? Three hundred dollars?"

"Five grand."

"For that dog?"

"Doda wants her back."

"You weren't carrying the cash around in a paper sack, were you?" He chuckled grimly.

"You know a guy named Anthony Throckmorton?" I was throwing the questions at him out of order, the better to keep him unbalanced.

"No."

"How about Brian Blair?"

"No. Who are these guys?"

"They're the same con artist. Did you really run over those ducks?"

"Ducks? People can't stop talking about those ducks. Who told you? Giselle?"

"If you don't know Throckmorton, why do his phone records show multiple calls to and from your phone?"

"I tell you, I don't know the guy. Maybe one of the girls used my phone."

"What about The Auckland Group?" I asked.

"The what?"

"The people Doda had looking for Pickles before she hired me. What do you know about them?"

"I gave the name to Charlene. Somebody at the tennis club gave it to me. I don't remember who."

"You ever meet them?"

"I think they did all their business over the phone."

"So you don't know anything about them?"

"Not a thing."

"Word is, you and Chad had some sort of wager based on Alex and Mick Kraft."

"Pardon?"

"Is it true?"

"Hey, man. We make bets on everything. Sure, we put some money down on them. We met them at Doda's when they came over to adopt that stupid dog. Same day I won a thousand dollars betting Pickles could swim the length of the pool. Yeah. We saw them. Talked to them, too."

"What'd you do? Throw the dog in the pool?"

"Chad did. She started swimming the wrong way and we all placed bets. Chad thought she was going to drown."

"And if she had?"

"Then I guess I would have lost some money." Binky was so blithe about this second instance of animal cruelty he didn't even seem to realize what it was, or if he did, he didn't think there was anything wrong with it. None of this boded well for how he might treat people.

"You and who else were making bets?"

"Chad. Mark. Jason. The whole gang." I knew from chitchat I'd heard around the pool that he ran with a circle of trust-fund babies, young men who'd gone to prep school together, most of whom had graduated Harvard Business School in the same class. Only Binky and, by reports, Chad had gone out into the world to earn their way, each flamboyantly successful in his ventures, Chad as a hedge-fund manager, Joshua as the CEO of his father's oil company, a company he goosed into unheard of profits during the few short years he was at the helm.

"What kind of bets did you make involving the Krafts?"

"Just bets, man. It doesn't matter."

"Surely, you remember."

"I don't. And my name's not Shirley." He gave a weak laugh. His composure was beginning to crumble.

"Come on. Tell me about it."

"Oh, it was just that we saw them come and pick up the dog. We talked for a while. They seemed harmless enough.

Chad thought they seemed too happy together. He said it made him sick. That we should make some bets. I said he was a donkey dick."

"But you bet anyway?"

"Chad bet he could get them to a Mariners game and make her so mad she would go home alone."

"And did he do it?"

"We got them free tickets through an intermediary. Call it a good deed on our part. Chad arranged for this statuesque blonde to be seated next to them. Told her he'd give her a month's salary if she could break them up for the night. She had to be subtle but she had to be tempting."

"Was she?"

"She could have gotten a divinity student thrown out of seminary. Alex ended up taking the bus home alone."

"Why bet on people? Why not just go to the Casino?"

"People are more fun. Seeing what you can trick people into. It's a hoot. We've been doing it for years."

"So there were other bets involving the Krafts?"

"There may have been a couple."

"What did these other bets involve?"

"I don't recall."

"Why do I find that hard to believe?"

"We've got better things to do than to sit around reminiscing about all the money we've won or lost on the little people."

"The little people? Is this like dog racing to you? Get all the little peasants lined up and watch them race around a track?"

I could tell he wasn't sorry he'd used the phrase, and couldn't fathom why I'd focused on it. It was an idiom he probably used often and without thinking. *The little people.* I knew I was included in that category and he knew I knew it, and the startling part of it was he wasn't embarrassed at the hauteur. As far as he was concerned, he'd spoken a self-evident truth for which there was no rebuttal. I continued, "I'm investigating a murder-suicide that was preceded by a number of events that cannot be explained in any normal context. But right now I'm beginning to see my way toward an explanation for some of them."

"For instance?"

"Mick Kraft was a professional truck driver and had been for a number of years. Rarely had any kind of accident. Then one week vehicular accidents are raining down out of the sky. In fact, he had so many accidents he lost his job. Then lost a second job for the same reason."

"Maybe he needed glasses."

"Or maybe somebody was deliberately screwing with him because they made a bet." I was stabbing in the dark, but he'd handed me the road map and it was easy enough to follow the dots.

"Do I need my attorney?" Joshua Compton gave me a look that was half play and half tease.

"I'm just trying to understand."

"Hey, man," he said, glancing at his watch. "I'd like to talk some more, but I gotta run. Gotta get to the airport. Picking up a friend flying in from Bangkok. You're welcome to ride along if you want." He began walking briskly toward the cars out back, detouring through the kitchen to pick up his wallet and keys. I followed and was of half a mind to take up his offer and ride with him to Sea-Tac, but didn't. Before he walked out the main door of the house, he said, "Now that you mention it, I have been getting calls from people I don't know."

"What do they say?"

"Hell if I know. I never answer. Somebody's got the wrong number, that's all."

As I watched him climb into a Land Rover and race up the narrow drive toward the security gate, I thought about the calls between his phone and Throckmorton's. A few lasted only seconds; most went on for several minutes.

* * *

"You okay, man?" Chad Baumgarden asked. He was wearing a silk robe over swimming trunks. His lady friend was sunning herself on the deck outside the kitchen and wearing only the bottom half of her lime-green bikini, the top lying flat on the warm deck like a dropped blindfold. What a life. Sleep in. A little snack, and then right to the sunbathing. Laze around until you can think of a reason to do something useful, perhaps open a dividend check from the mail or wire some money to a friend in a foreign country. Baumgarden said, "Did I hear you say somebody tried to kill you?"

Though punctuated by the thumping of hammers and the occasional slam of a falling board next door, the August morning air was quite still, so it wasn't surprising he'd caught part of my conversation with Binky. "They tried to kill Snake yesterday."

"The spidery guy with the whiskers and the attitude?"
"Yeah. Snake."
"Jesus. By the way, I'm Chad. I think we met."
"Thomas. Thomas Black." I'd met him when we were both twelve, but I hardly expected him to remember. I'd also met him at Doda's within the past week. He may have been feigning social amnesia, something I'd noticed people of his ilk did to keep you in your place.

32

As we walked back through the house and out onto one of the decks where we would be alone, I gave him an edited version of what happened the previous day, running over everything in my mind as I spoke, trying in vain to knot it all up into a coherent theory. Tony Throckmorton. The ex-prizefighters from California. I didn't tell him about Stephanie Chin getting the axe twelve hours after speaking to me. How much of it was linked and what the crucial connecting factor was, I had no idea.

It was one thing to follow Snake and me and to attempt to injure us, but intimidating a person I considered a minor peripheral witness by taking her job after I spoke to her showed a more powerful net, a larger global intent, and a more malevolent presence than I thought possible. What magnitude of power were we talking about here?

Whoever was tracking me and listening to my phone calls may well have been doing the same to Alex and Mick Kraft. We knew somebody had gone to the trouble of installing a camera in their back yard.

I assumed Binky was lying when he denied knowledge of the phone calls, but I had no real reason for that assumption. On the other hand, I remembered one of the young women at Doda's borrowing his phone while we were poolside, grabbing it to call her sister, without fanfare or even asking permission.

"I heard Binky and you talking about The Auckland Group," Chad said.

I did my best not to let him see my renewed interest. Sometimes you could get a man's friends to rat him out without realizing what they were doing.

"Listen," said Chad. "I don't usually interfere in my

buddy's business, but when I hear people are getting assaulted the way you guys were . . . well, I don't like any kind of dissembling under normal conditions. Sure, we made a few bets, but we never did anything wrong. Not really."

"Maybe you can set the record straight then?"

"I don't think Binky was lying on purpose. Knowing Binky, I think he's just fucking with you, maybe setting you up to take your money on another wager. He spent eighteen million buying that house next door and all the property behind us here and then tore the place down without blinking, but lose two cents to you guys and he can't stop talking about how he's going to get even. Maybe that's what this is about. 'Cause he's really got nothing to hide."

"Charlene says he's a genius," I said, ingenuously.

"He tries to enjoy life, but it seems like he's pissed off a lot of the time. His father died at forty-five, and right now Binky's got the same high cholesterol and high blood pressure his pop died from."

"He looks in good health."

"And money's sure no problem. He lives to be a hundred like his auntie, he'll never be able to spend a fraction of what he's worth. He was born well-heeled, but if that wasn't enough, he has the Midas touch, just keeps making more and more."

"Midas gave up his gift."

"What?"

"Everything he touched turned to gold. He was in the process of starving to death."

"Oh, yeah, well . . ." Chad walked over to the deck railing, which was a good thirty feet above the sand-strewn beach, and he leaned against one of the Flamingo-pink rails. The house and decks had a Florida motif. "I won't say we didn't wager on the Krafts, because we did. After one of us lost, we'd go double or nothing on the next trick. We kept doing that until, frankly, the numbers got just a little outrageous."

"And Binky won the first bet at the ball game?"

"I won it. It was hilarious to watch Wendy work her

wiles."

"Wendy was . . . ?"

"The blonde I parked next to Mick Kraft. She kept rubbing her cannons against his arm and he kept sweating. Guys are such predictable idiots. We all are, aren't we?"

"I don't know about you, but I'm an idiot."

"Kraft was sweating before he even got out of the starting gate."

"And the Krafts went home separately?"

"Oh, yeah."

"What other bets did you make involving the Krafts?"

"I'm kind of ashamed to admit this . . . Binky bet twenty he could make Kraft lose his job inside of two weeks. The deal always was that we could mess with them in order to win, but nothing illegal."

"So Binky was responsible for Mick losing his job?"

"He lost it and Binky won the bet, so I'd have to say yes."

"I heard Kraft had a series of vehicular accidents," I said, feigning ignorance. "Wasn't he a delivery truck driver or something?"

"Drove for UPS. If I'd known he was a delivery truck driver, I never would have laid down the money. Forcing accidents is too easy. We hire stunt drivers."

"You bet twenty? Twenty what?"

"Thousand."

I whistled. "But causing an accident would be illegal, wouldn't it? Wouldn't that be against your own rules?"

Ignoring my question, Chad said, "Look, there are all kinds of ways to manipulate people for fun and profit. And it's hilarious to watch it play out. We've made a study of it."

"Is that how much you guys wager? Twenty grand?"

"We start small and work our way up."

"Up to what?"

"Whatever."

"Crazy."

"I'd rather bet with Binky than risk money in the futures market. Besides, it's a game. We'll see a couple, and one of us will bet we can break them up."

"And then you do it?"

"Most times."

"How do you manage that?"

"Usually starts with the guy. You get him into some sort of compromising position, film it secretly."

"And that's not illegal?"

"Is it? I don't think so. You get the video to the wife—put it on their computer or whatever. We got to the point where we could break up a marriage in less than a month. Sometimes less than a week. Our record is two days. It's crazy, man." He laughed boisterously, his mirth booming out over the water. A couple of gamboling kids and a limping grandma walked the tideline below us. Spurred by Chad's laughter and not realizing it was borne of cruelty, the grandmother looked up and waved to us. I gave her a small wave back.

"How many of those marriages did you put back together?"

Chad looked at me as if I wasn't making sense. "No, man. We lose a guy's job for him, we get that back. Or get him another job. But marriage? That's like putting a raw egg back together after you smash it. Can't be done. Besides, a guy would cheat with our hooker, he was going to cheat somewhere down the line anyway, and eventually the old ball and chain was going to catch him. We just shortcut the process. Hey, you can't cheat an honest man."

"You *can* cheat an honest man. Happens every day."

"Our people do their research."

"Who are Binky's people? The Auckland Group?"

"Who? No. He uses various agencies."

"You don't know which ones?"

"You think he's going to tell me?"

"Do you use The Auckland Group?"

"Me? I don't even know who they are."

"How do you pick your projects?"

"People we see. People we know. We got up to two big ones with the Krafts. We just kept betting."

"What's a big one?"

"A million."

Two Miles of Darkness

"You bet two million on the Krafts?"

"I still remember writing the check."

"How else did you manipulate the Krafts?"

He wasn't going to answer. That much was clear. He stared out at the water and then said, "You realize we could break up your marriage?"

Though not unexpected, the arrogance of it was astonishing. I'd stumbled upon a private game that had probably been going on for years. The sad thing was that, considering their bankroll, he was probably right—I had no doubt he and his friends could bring someone's life to a standstill. Given enough money, enough information, a ruthless operator could scam just about anybody out of anything, including a job, a bank account, their underwear. In some ways they were like boys frying ants on the sidewalk with a magnifying glass, the ants having absolutely no idea where the sudden heat was coming from—except in this case the ants were human beings.

I had to wonder if their actions hadn't driven Mick Kraft into a frenzy of anger, humiliation, and eventually suicide. If we could prove that was how it happened, the King County Prosecutor's office might be able to build a case against them. I wasn't sure what they could be charged with, but there had to be something. Then again, if these men got dragged into a court of law, their unlimited funds would make sure they were backed by the best legal defense team on the West Coast.

"It's not just marriages we mess with," Chad said, warming to the topic. "I took one of the best batting averages in the majors and ruined it. I screwed Binky bad with that one. Rodriguez was his hero."

"Alex Rodriguez? When he was with the Mariners?"

"Yep."

"You were responsible for the slump?"

"I won the bet, didn't I?"

"Seems like you guys would eventually get tired of this."

"What's to get tired of? It's like having your own reality show."

It was clear now why Mick and Alex Kraft's troubles

began the day they picked up Pickles.

"Listen, pal," Chad said. "I don't mean to make light of what happened to those people. Because we all felt bad about it. We still do."

"You trash somebody's life and they end up killing themselves? A normal person would feel a lot of remorse."

"Wait a minute. You're not trying to blame those deaths on us, are you?"

"I don't know anybody else who was messing with their lives."

"Oh, come on now. A guy shoots his wife and his mother-in-law, he's mentally ill. With or without us, it would have happened. Sooner or later."

"You don't really believe that?"

"Of course I do. It's just common sense."

"At the very least, you facilitated those deaths."

"We didn't facilitate shit. It was going to happen without us. Everything we ever made happen was going to happen anyway. People sink to their natural level. You don't know very much about people, do you?"

"The Krafts were going through the worst crisis of their lives, a situation you guys put them in. The next step was sleeping in their car. Were you responsible for her losing her job?"

"Hell, everybody's losing their jobs. It's part of the economy. Who's to say they wouldn't have been SOL without us? Besides, I kept telling Binky we needed to back off. The trouble with him is he makes everything so personal. He got all pissed when he lost that one bet."

"Which one?"

"That he could sleep with her."

"With Alex?"

"You ever see a picture of her?"

"How much did you wager?"

"I'm not going to tell you how much. But he was plenty pissed when I collected."

"It was well over a million. Had to be."

"How did you know?" I knew because Geoff Hardy at Vereecken and Sons had offered to give Alex a million dollars if she would sleep with him. He wasn't likely to make an offer like that if he didn't stand to win more on the wager. I was assuming Geoff Hardy was a pseudonym for Joshua Compton, my boyhood pal, Binky.

"Why are you telling me all this?" I asked.

"Because I was sitting over there listening to Binky lie and I couldn't stand it. He's not going to the airport to pick up a friend. He just didn't want to talk to you anymore. Besides, somebody looks into that murder-suicide long enough, they're bound to hear about our bets. I'm just glad it was you."

"Why is that?"

"Because you won't try to turn this into something it isn't."

"Just out of curiosity, what isn't it?"

"It isn't our fault."

"One more question. How did you find out they were dead?"

The question took him aback, and he pretended to try to remember. "Binky told me. I remember because we were down by the dock horsing around with the boat when he came and gave us the news."

"It wasn't entirely bad news either, was it? For one of you?"

"What are you saying?"

"I mean money changed hands over it, didn't it?"

"I'm afraid Binky cleaned me out on that one. Really cleaned me out."

"You know where we can find somebody from The Auckland Group?"

"You keep bringing that up. It might be something Binky set up when he was working with his father's oil company in South America. Don't quote me. Listen, I like Binky. He's my friend. He gets a little carried away, but he's got a good heart and he wouldn't do anything . . . really wrong."

"As opposed to driving somebody to suicide?"

"I told you we didn't cause that. The fact is Joshua's got a well-developed sense of justice."

"You guys are playing God."

"Is that what you're getting from this? If it is, I'm not telling it right."

I'd been around long enough not to cherish the conceit that if I had as much money as these guys I wouldn't eventually end up thinking and acting differently. Nobody knew what they were going to do until they were thrown into the cauldron, and by my reckoning nothing corrupted the soul faster or more thoroughly than too much cash. Anybody who thought otherwise hadn't lived long enough to be disappointed in themselves. Along with a lot of other things, including sex, I believed money actually altered brain chemistry, and the more of it the greater the alteration. I'd seen it happen too many times, but I'd never seen it happen like this.

"Hey. . . there is one other thing."

"What is it?"

"When we were kids? At Doda's ranch? We lied about you. It's embarrassing to bring it up now, but I've been thinking about it recently. I've felt bad about this for a long time."

Chad put his hand out to shake. He didn't remember my name, but somehow he remembered screwing me over when we were kids. He would destroy people's lives, rob them of their livelihood, and chortle about it, but now wanted to apologize for a boyhood slight. It was hard to believe he even remembered a malfeasance from twenty years ago. "There's no way to make it right," he said, "except to just come out and apologize. No hard feelings?"

I shook his hand. His confession and apparent remorse touched me more than it should have. I couldn't tell if it was because he'd uncovered an old wound, or if it was something else. Even though it happened ages ago, the sting was still there, and he'd offered the only balm I was going to get from anybody.

"Thanks," I said.

Funny how some of the stuff that happens to you when you're a kid gets hardwired into your brain. If the same insult had occurred when I was twenty, I might well have no

Two Miles of Darkness

memory of it by now, but because it happened when I was twelve it was right up there alongside "Rosebud."

33

Driving up the hill and away from the enclave of conspicuous wealth that had buried itself deep in the center of this middle-class area like a pearl inside an oyster, I phoned Snake, who answered, "Yup?"

"We have to meet."

"Where?"

We arranged to meet at Spud's on Alki, the same fish and chips place where I'd met Greg Rowsell. Snake said he needed lunch, and the beach was as good a place as any to talk. Without stating it aloud, we both knew better than to exchange any substantial information over the phone.

At Alki, we sat in Snake's truck, which he'd conveniently parked facing a quartet of lithe female volleyball players. Having already downed his meal in the manner of a python swallowing a goat, Snake watched the women slamming the volleyball around in the sand. They were tremendous athletes, and even a casual glance at their physical prowess told me an amateur cyclist like me wouldn't stand a chance against them.

Snake didn't say anything as I ate and watched two families with toddlers walking the shoreline in front of us in opposite directions. The sky had taken on a fuchsia hue, filtered by wisps of hazy smoke drifting over the Cascades from the increasingly common summertime lightning-strike forest fires in Eastern Washington. I could taste a faint tang of wood smoke in the back of my throat.

Snake said, "Whatcha got?"

"You first."

"Nothing on Manny. I went to the bar on California Avenue, same as you. I talked to this John Stacey character, the brother-in-law of Mick Kraft. He was home from work on a furlough day. I'm thinking of going back to The Dregs at night like you did and hanging out with Brunhilda. Somebody's gotta have a line on Manny."

"Brunhilda?"

"The barista. Real name is Katrina. She's been asking if she can do some detective work with me."

"You sure she's not part of the setup? That she's not working for them?"

"Damn! I wish you hadn't said that. And no, I'm not sure. Now that I think about it, she did take up with me on awful short notice."

"Plus, she's young and kind of cute, and you're neither of those things."

"Christ, Thomas. Now you got me doubting my own charms. You're worse than my mother. I hate it when that happens. By the way, I ran some computer searches on that man down the street from the Krafts. Cavendish?"

"I ran some, too. What'd you find?"

"Before he lived in California, he spent some time in Colorado. At the University of Colorado in Boulder, the cops caught him jacking off outside a sorority window. Same year they caught him making dirty phone calls to a housewife lived right down the block, telling her to take off her clothes and stand in the window, threatening to kill her cat with a pellet gun if she refused. But here's what's really interesting, the part that crosses the line."

"The rest of this doesn't cross the line?"

"Well, hell yeah. Sure. But check this out. The woman who's cat he was going to shoot? She later accused him of breaking into her house. They never proved it, but she was sure he burgled her place."

"So you're thinking Cavendish set up the camera in the back yard. Maybe even broke in to steal her underwear?"

"Whatever," Snake said, annoyed that I'd brought up one of his recent peccadillos, the underwear. "That's one theory, but we don't know for certain the Krafts were even on his radar."

"I'm going to get somebody to dig up all of his charge card records. That camera was his and had nothing to do with the murders."

"The fact is we haven't come up with a valid reason why it wasn't a murder-suicide. Just a lot of suspicions."

"Eddie the Slugger showing up isn't reason enough?"

"I'd feel better about it if we could prove what happened in Discovery Park was related to the Krafts."

"Eddie the Slugger didn't fly up here from California just to look for a lost dog. You know it had to be about the Krafts."

"We're not going to convince the cops to reopen the case without more evidence. You talk to Huntzinger?"

"Found him at his house in White Center, not two miles from the Kraft place. He didn't have anything to do with it."

"That your gut instinct, or what?"

"He's shook-up as a weasel in a dog kennel. Been having nightmares, seeing a counselor down at the free clinic. Barely functional."

"People get like that after they've murdered."

"No. For him, finding those bodies was like an acid trip that won't go away. He got there minutes after it happened. Blood wasn't even dry. He'd come any earlier, he would have ended up on the floor with a bullet in his head and he knows it. He can't stop thinking about it."

"Like I said, a guy might have that same reaction if he murdered three people."

"He might, but I don't think he did it."

"He see anything?"

"As far as I'm concerned, he's a dead end."

"What have you got?"

I explained about Chad Baumgarden and Joshua Compton wagering on their ability to tinker with the fates of strangers, the amount of money involved, and the length to which they'd gone in order to win. I explained the nature of their bets, at least the ones I knew about. It took a long time to lay out the details, probably because I was just coming to grips with the monolithic insanity of it. Chad was right when he said they were running their own reality show.

Snake told me he'd already spent some time looking up

background on Chad and Binky. He said Chad Baumgarden received a stipend from his family's estate worth just a little north of eight million a year. Despite my information that he once helmed a hedge fund, according to Snake, he'd never worked a day in his life.

Binky was ranked among the hundred wealthiest Americans and spent a decade heading a major oil firm the family had been associated with for over a hundred years.

"Of the two of them, I trust Chad more," I said. "Even though I don't know him well. He didn't have to tell me all that stuff. He won't admit it openly, but I have the feeling he's not taking his connection to those deaths well. I think underneath all the protesting he's feeling pretty lousy about it."

"Must be nice to be able to buy whatever you want," Snake said. "Including the total destruction of your enemies."

"How about the total destruction of somebody you barely even know, like Mick and Alex Kraft?"

"If this is what Chad will cop to, think about what he won't cop to."

"Like maybe murdering three people to win a very large bet."

"Unintentionally driving one of them to murder and suicide is bad enough."

"Sometimes I wonder at what I might do if I had all the money in the world. There was a scene in an old W.C. Fields movie called *If I had a Million*. Fields is given a million dollars. He hates road hogs, so he buys a bunch of brand new cars and has a line of chauffeurs follow him as he drives around town. Every time he sees a road hog, he plays bumper-car and totals the guy's vehicle at the expense of his own. Then he gets into the next new car in line and goes looking for another road hog. I've always admired that scene for its simplicity and emotional fulfillment."

Snake looked at me as if I'd lost my mind. "You serious?"

"Road hogs, tailgaters, people who can't be bothered to work their turn signals when they change lanes, people who stop in traffic circles for no reason, people at intersections who wave you on when it's their turn and then continue waving to you when you motion for them to take their rightful turn, people who can't pass a bicyclist riding on the dew line even though the lane is twelve feet wide? Are you kidding? If they let me, I could serve up some justice."

"Now I know you're joshing."

"Maybe. Just a little."

"There's no doubt we all have nut-ball projects we would like to get done if we had the money."

"There's nothing nut-ball about mine," I said, and we both laughed.

I told Snake about Stephanie Chin getting her pink slip, and together we speculated how her termination might be linked to our investigation. Before we got too deep into it, Snake fielded a call on his cell from one of his contacts in Colorado. He listened for a few moments, asked one or two questions, then closed the connection.

"More intel on Cavendish. He was wanted in Aurora, Colorado, for setting up a camera in a girl's high-school locker room, where he was working as a scab during a janitorial strike. He left the state when he found out he was going to be charged. How'd you like to be living four doors down from that dirtball?"

"How'd you like it if that dirtball was listening in to the call you just got?"

"Jesus, that's right."

My cellphone rang, not a number I recognized. "There he is now," I said, and we both chuckled. "Yeah?"

"Mr. Black?"

It was an adolescent's voice. "Speaking."

"Mr. Black? This is Charlie Hatcher. I'm kind of in a jam. I'm using a borrowed phone, and I was wondering if you could help me out."

It wouldn't have been trouble for most of us, but when you're twelve years old and you get a flat tire on your bicycle on Alaskan Way and you're six miles from home and don't have a cellphone or a nickel in your pocket, or a spare tire, you might call it a jam.

Two Miles of Darkness

At the Seattle waterfront, I spotted him on the broad sidewalk next to the ferry terminal at Colman Dock. He was nearly invisible among hundreds of tourists and probably could have stood there for a very long time before anybody noticed. Double-parking, I jumped out and threw the bike into the trunk and then drove Charlie two blocks away to a half-empty lot, where we had some space.

Snake showed up in time to kibitz. "Let him walk," Snake said, winking at Charlie. "He got himself down here. It'll do him good. It's only six miles. Let him figure out how to get out of this."

"He did figure out how to get out of it."

"By calling you?"

"That's right."

"You said I could call you if I needed help," Charlie said.

"And you can," I said. "You did the right thing. But what are you doing down here, Charlie?" I asked the boy.

"I was on my way up to Magnolia to look for Pickles."

"That's a pretty long bike ride through some heavy traffic for somebody your age." He opened his knapsack and showed me two sandwiches he'd slapped together, white bread and peanut butter, along with a bruised apple. He had water in an old plastic cranberry-juice bottle.

"I already fixed one flat," Charlie said. "I didn't have any more patches and didn't know what else to do."

"When you fixed the first one, did you check the inside of the tire for nails or a piece of wire?" I asked, removing his rear wheel. "You get two flats in a row on the same tire, there's usually something in the tread poking through."

"I didn't know that."

I pried the tire off, letting Charlie assist, and ran my fingers along the inside, where I detected a minute piece of wire lodged in such a manner that it would prick a third tube if left in place. I inspected the patch he'd already put on—it was a worn and much-used tube—for integrity, then slapped on another patch from a kit in my car and waited for the glue to dry. While I was doing this, Charlie borrowed my phone so he could call his mother at work to tell her he was all right; he'd called earlier from a pay phone when he was still trying to figure out how to get home and promised to call back so she wouldn't worry.

"Why didn't you call Mrs. Kennedy?" I asked. When he didn't reply, I said, "She doesn't know you're here, does she?"

"You're not going to tell, are you?"

"Not if your mother doesn't."

"Mom's trying to move us out, but she can't find anybody who'll take four kids. And she doesn't want to split us up."

He was still holding my phone as I pumped up the tire, put the wheel back on, and adjusted the brakes. He said, "Hey. You got a bunch of pictures on your phone."

I peered over his shoulder. He was looking at the Pickles file.

"Go ahead and look through them if you want." I hadn't taken a picture of the corpse yesterday, so it was all G-rated.

After a bit, he said, "Hey, there's Mrs. Kennedy. There's me. And Mrs. Boulanger from next door."

"Everyone I've spoken to."

"You even have Manny."

"What?"

"There's a picture of Manny here."

34

When I looked at the photo, I felt like a butterfly had parked on my nose, that I didn't dare move, that this new piece of information, arriving so gently and unexpectedly, would flitter away if I even breathed.

"This is Manny?"

"Yes, sir."

"Are you sure?"

"He was friends with Mick."

"Did you happen to see him on the day of the shooting?"

"No."

"And you haven't seen him since?"

"Just with you guys when you had all those men putting up fliers and looking for Pickles."

"Snake," I said. "Come here. Can you track Throckmorton?"

"Why?"

"Charlie knows him as Manny."

"Anthony Throckmorton. Brian Blair. Now he's Manny? You shittin' me?"

"Tell him we're not shitting him," I said to Charlie.

"We're not shitting you," Charlie said, a half smile playing on his lips.

Snake opened his computer and, after a moment, exclaimed, "Son of a bitch."

"What is it?"

He turned the laptop toward me. "Check out where the blinking X is."

"Lakeside Avenue?"

"The bastard's on my boat."

Even though his stay on the boat was short term, Snake

had built the same sort of camera set-up at the marina that I had at my home. His paranoia meter dialed to high alert at all times, Snake could not pitch a tent or throw a blanket down for a picnic without setting up a security perimeter that would do justice to a harem master.

He said, "I don't see anything right now. He must still be on board. I got no cameras on board."

"You sure?"

"Well, there is one in the bedroom, but I usually don't turn it on unless my partner gives the okay. Come on, Thomas," Snake said, slamming his truck door and firing up the engine. "If he's in the marina, he's gotta be on my boat. Goddamn Throckmorton. We should have been tracking him every second."

I'd been planning to drive Charlie to Discovery Park to show him where I'd spotted Pickles, and then to make sure he got home okay, but now I had to settle for sending him back home on his own, which made me feel a little like a nervous hen, seeing as how he seemed perfectly competent at navigating the streets on his bike. Still, he was awfully young. With some trepidation, I sent Charlie away and climbed into Snake's truck. "What do you mean you 'usually' don't turn it on unless your partner gives the okay?" But he didn't answer me.

Seattle was sandwiched between two great bodies of water, Puget Sound on one side and twenty-mile-long Lake Washington on the other; saltwater to the west, fresh water to the east. As far as I knew, only one street linked both bodies of water and that was Madison, but we weren't near Madison. Yesler did almost the same thing and we were only a few blocks away, so Snake detoured to Yesler and raced up the hill and out of downtown.

He blew through two stale yellow lights, and then negotiated the steep gyrations of Lake Dell Avenue, threading his way down the hill to Lake Washington.

At the marina, he double-parked and sprinted along the dock. I wasn't far behind.

When we got there, the sailboat was free of intruders, though we could see where somebody had been pawing through his possessions.

"He's gone," Snake said. "He musta got tipped off."

"You think?"

"Look. You can tell. He wasn't finished. I wonder who tipped him off?"

"We did."

"What do you mean?"

"We know somebody's tracking us by our cellphones. They saw where we were headed and warned him."

"I guess we should have turned off our phones. I was too jacked up to think of it."

"Me, too."

We went back outside and stood at the open door of Snake's truck. Snake logged onto the site we were using to track Throckmorton and quickly found the blinking X. Throckmorton was fleeing north on Lake Washington Boulevard, only a mile or so down the road. His last two incoming calls had come from the same number we'd earlier traced to The Auckland Group. No help there, since they refused to answer our calls and we didn't know where to find them.

The question now was whether or not The Auckland Group had figured out we had a tracking device on Throckmorton. It was one thing for them to warn him; it was another to realize how we'd known where to find him, because once they realized his phone was rigged they would tell him to dump it and we wouldn't be able to track him.

After we turned off our cellphones, Snake backtracked through the security photos on his laptop and found a picture of three men exiting the sailboat in a hurry. According to the time-stamp on the photo, we'd missed them by less than four minutes. As expected, one of the three men turned out to be Throckmorton, aka Manny. He was the only figure I could positively identify and had the terrified look of a man fleeing a burning theater.

A second man was heavy and wore a white Denver Broncos baseball-type cap, the bill pulled down low and effectively screening out his identity. He was probably more muscle for hire, and I was pretty sure he hadn't been part of our dog posse. The earlier photos of the men entering the marina showed all three only from the rear.

I was pretty sure the third man was Frederick C. Lovell, the ex-prizefighter, the man I'd throat-punched yesterday, which meant Throckmorton lied to us about knowing him. But then, what hadn't Throckmorton lied to us about? The third man's face was a little blurry, but I had faith that a lab technician could clean it up enough to make him recognizable.

Following the tracker in Throckmorton's phone, we tailed him and his pals across north Seattle, first to the Northgate Mall parking lot, where they dallied for only a few minutes, then through Wedgewood, a pleasant residential neighborhood in the north part of the city. Whether or not Throckmorton was still with his friends, we had no way of knowing. They may have gone to the mall parking lot to switch vehicles. Or he might have gotten onto a bus there. We were dealing with a lag time between the GPS on the computer and Throckmorton's actual position, so we weren't going to get real close until he remained in place.

For three hours, we followed Throckmorton's cellphone through city streets in the August heat. By the time rush hour began to congeal and harden the arteries of the city, his blinking X had perched on a single spot. "Where is that?" Snake asked. "He's stopped, but where is it?"

"It's the rose garden at the entrance to the Woodland Park Zoo."

"Which entrance? There's a lot of entrances."

"South entrance, just off Fiftieth. Haven't you ever been to the rose garden?"

"Why the hell would I go there?"

Laboriously working our way through the afternoon traffic, we arrived twenty minutes later. When we pulled into the parking lot, I expected the blinking X to have changed positions, but it hadn't moved. I could only speculate on Throckmorton's purpose for coming here, but I knew it would be easy to meet up with somebody while pretending to browse the hybrids, mingling with zoo visitors and amateur gardeners. The rose garden was where I first encountered Whiskey Mac and Voodoo, along with a dozen other rose varieties I now grew in my yard.

We parked near the entrance.

I had a sick feeling this was going to be trouble, but neither of us made any noise about backing off. As far as we knew, there were three thugs in front of us, at least one of them an ex-pro boxer. Snake was armed, but they probably were also. We were doing one of those things two guys did together without either of them, as a point of pride, mentioning how nervous it made him.

As we walked through the parking lot to the rose garden, we spaced ourselves twenty feet apart. The garden was crowded, a blur of nearly motionless adults and running kids. Farther inside, near the gazebo, a group of elderly Japanese visitors stood in sun hats discussing the roses. The sweltering heat had stirred up the fragrance from dozens of rose varieties and mixed it with the exotic tang of wild animal dung from the adjoining zoo.

As always, I was unarmed and Snake was not, though nowhere in the rose garden was there a backdrop that would allow him to shoot a weapon safely; there were simply too many people within range of a bullet. I said as much to Snake, who replied, "I know about backdrops. I ain't stupid. It just angers me that I carry all this iron and never get to heat it up."

"Maybe you should work in the desert. More open spaces."

"Artillery impresses the women, though, don't it?"

"Only the women who are already bat-shit crazy."

"My favorite kind."

There were so many people, we were having a difficult time locating our quarry in the two-acre garden.

I had just about given up on the idea of finding them when my gaze was drawn to a group of six or eight teens surrounding the butt end of the reflecting pool. I signaled Snake and we headed toward the teens, all of whom were staring at the wet concrete rim of the pool. As we drew close, the teens parted.

The center attraction was a man who'd fallen into the water, most of his skull still submerged. His eyes were open underwater and staring at the lily pads. Koi were nibbling lazily at his face. One of the kids said, "Is he holding his breath?"

I knelt and, using both hands, gently pulled his face from the water. He was extremely heavy, and I could feel the intimacy of our touch, his unshaven face rough against my palms. His frozen look was one of surprise, the same dumb, open-mouthed grimace he'd given us that morning when we ambushed him at the Public Market, except now he was dead. Throckmorton. The elusive Manny.

A middle-aged woman burst into our group, sized up what she thought was going on, and spoke to me harshly, "You should be ashamed of yourself. Keep your drunken friends out of our zoo."

"Mom," said her daughter. "He's not drunk. He croaked."

"That's even worse," she said.

While I was getting chewed out, Snake leaped up onto the rim of the pool and used the slight raise in altitude to scout the surrounding gardens for Throckmorton's killers. We both knew it had taken more than one man to hold his head underwater long enough to drown him, though it was just possible he'd had a heart attack and fallen in.

Easing Throckmorton onto the lawn on his side, I hopped up beside Snake and together we scanned the crowds for almost a minute. "Must have made their getaway about the time we arrived," Snake said.

"That'd be my guess."

The remaining teens—one had been dragged off by her mother—weren't going to disperse anytime soon. They'd run across a dead man, and such events did not present themselves with regularity in this town. Their parents or grandparents had dragged them to the rose garden in an attempt to entice them with botany, but instead of cataloguing roses or gently chasing koi in the pond with sticks like the younger children, they'd discovered a corpse amid all the quiet splendor, and the story of a corpse was

Two Miles of Darkness

something they would invoke to astonish their friends.
"Any of you kids see what happened?" I asked.

35

Carole Cooper arrived not long after the first patrol car, Elmer escorting her in from the parking lot while I remained with the body and told the first uniforms his name and his aliases. Snake hadn't been able to get away from the corpse fast enough. He once told me that while lost in the desert, in order to survive he'd eaten the raw innards of a coyote that had been knocked into the afterlife by an eighteen-wheeler, yet he couldn't bear to spend a few seconds around a perfectly intact corpse that a group of giggling teenage girls had no trouble ogling.

The first uniform blocked the entrance to the garden and began collecting names and addresses of possible witnesses, while another policeman cordoned off the death site.

After she'd examined Throckmorton's body and the surrounding area, Carole Cooper came over to where I was standing beside a Dancing Flame. "The vic is Brian Blair?" Cooper asked.

"Also known as Anthony Throckmorton," I said.

"Why don't you start from the beginning. You first, Thomas. You can wait over there, Mr. Slezak." Separating suspects and witnesses was always a good idea, but Snake gave Cooper a snarl as he walked away. Sometimes Slezak thought he'd been brought into this world solely to irritate the authorities.

I gave her the whole story, including the part about turning off our cellphones to keep from being tracked.

"So you were shadowing the deceased?"

"After we saw them breaking into the marina where Snake is housesitting."

"You have any photos for me? You always have

photos."

Besides the surveillance pictures from the marina, I'd snapped random photos of tourists in the rose garden, the corpse, and the group of kids, all of which would eventually go into my collection for the case.

"Explain again how you were following the deceased," Cooper said.

"We inserted a tracker in his phone."

"Which allowed you to . . ."

"Track him. At a distance."

"And when did you insert this tracker?"

"This morning."

"At the Market?"

"Right."

"So when I showed up and you said he'd sneaked out, you actually knew where he was?"

"No, but we could have found him."

"God! You guys!"

I pretended to examine the Dancing Flame. I'd had one in my garden until last year, when it succumbed to an unidentified blight. I was thinking I should replant.

"Why didn't you tell me you were tracking him this morning when we were all looking for him?"

"Must have slipped my mind. Sometimes I get overwhelmed in all the excitement."

"You thought he would lead you to the higher-ups, didn't you?"

"I don't know what we were thinking."

"No?"

"You're not trying to blame this on us, are you?"

"Black, you do realize this is the second day in a row where you called in a murder? I'm just wondering how the rest of the week is going to lay out."

When I didn't say anything, she continued, "Maybe next time you'll let us handle it. Murder is no game for amateurs."

"Wow. 'Murder is no game for amateurs.' I like that. Isn't that a line from a Pink Panther movie?"

"Yesterday your partner threw a man off a cliff. Today

you come up with another body, and on top of everything else, you insult me."

"You're the one who called me an amateur."

We glared at each other for a few moments. Maybe the heat was getting to her. Or maybe it was getting to me. "Point taken. But you are an amateur." Less than a year ago I'd reversed her verdict on a murder she had written off as a suicide, and although she'd been semi-gracious and businesslike about it at the time, it must have embarrassed the hell out of her, as had my remark about the Pink Panther. I was putting myself on the wrong side of my favorite conduit into the SPD and should have kept my mouth shut, should have apologized profusely, yet I did neither. She was right. Solving murders was *her* job.

On the other hand, we were uncovering fresh links in the Kraft case she should have known about.

Cooper gave me a dour look. She said, "I don't see his phone."

I hadn't searched the body, but if whoever killed him had taken his phone with them, we couldn't have traced him to the rose garden in the first place, so it had to be nearby. I wondered if he hadn't dropped it into the shrubbery or in the koi pool while struggling with his attackers. In fact, I wondered how much of a struggle it could have been, since there didn't seem to be any witnesses.

I got out my own cell and punched in Throckmorton's number.

Moments later, we heard it ringing in the vicinity of a group of teenagers. He was about fourteen, with a smear of a mustache on his upper lip and a sneer that hadn't left his face since we arrived, as if to prove to himself and the nearby girls that corpses were no big deal to him.

When I grabbed his arm, he pulled away roughly and started running, Tony Throckmorton's phone still chiming in his pocket. I gave chase, but before we went too far, his pants— which he wore gangsta-style with the waistband low around his skinny ass— dropped to his ankles, taking him down like bolas. I could hear Snake laughing behind us. The phone lay in the grass next to the boy's outstretched hand.

Two Miles of Darkness

When Cooper picked it up by the edges, I said, "It's the one Throckmorton was carrying this morning. You check recent calls, you'll see where I called it just now."

"How'd you get this?" Cooper turned to the kid, who had a crooked grin on his face as he corralled his pants. He got up and tried to step back, but a patrolman grabbed him. "I think we're going to get you for tampering with a crime scene," said Cooper. "And theft. How much time do you want to serve? Three years sound about right?"

"Three years? I don't want to go to jail."

"Then answer up, smart ass," said Cooper.

"I found it over there next to the body. I was only gonna call my cousin in St. Louis. I was gonna put it back."

"It was evidence in a murder investigation, you dumb cluck," said Snake. A moment later, Cooper followed me while one of the uniforms cuffed the boy, who was still doing his best to look nonchalant, though anybody could see he was on the verge of tears.

Cooper stepped close and turned to me. "Two days. Two bodies. It's getting so I'm afraid to take a vacation day."

"At least you don't have to climb down a cliff to reach this one. Maybe we'll deliver the next one to your office."

"That would be nice."

"We'll do our best."

"I want you to tell me everything you know about this."

She let me explain our tale one more time, how Edward C. Turner, the dead man and ex-prizefighter from yesterday, had been brought into our search crew by Throckmorton, aka Brian Blair. I told her about The Auckland Group and gave her their phone number. I mentioned Throckmorton's confession that morning, how he claimed to have been performing illegal acts for some time under the direction of unknown parties.

I didn't tell her about the calls on Throckmorton's phone to Charlene and Binky. She had the phone. She could figure it out herself. I would have told her more, but she kept looking at me as if I were lying and she was going to catch me at it, and the attitude was beginning to piss me off.

Friends in the department had warned me that she pissed off people, sometimes for no reason. An acerbic personality, they called it.

When I finished, she said, "What were you planning to do when you caught up with them?"

"We were playing that part by ear."

"And the other two guys? Where'd they go?"

"We're not even sure they were here. He might have come alone. Nobody we talked to saw a fight."

"But you think his partners killed him? In front of all these people?"

"I don't know."

"How does any of this connect to that dog you're hunting?"

"I wish I knew."

"He told you he was breaking into homes?" Cooper asked.

"Under the direction of the party who gave him the phone."

"You believed him?"

"I had no reason not to."

"Who do you think he was working for?"

"Your guess is as good as mine."

"Anything else you want to get off your chest?"

"Remember the man who loaned the gun to Mick Kraft? Manny? We found a wit today who claims Throckmorton is Manny. *Was* Manny."

"Hell, he was Brian Blair, too. So our victim was hanging out with Mick Kraft?"

"Kraft lost a lot of money in a financial scheme cooked up by Manny. My guess is that the whole thing was a scam to take Kraft's money and masterminded by Throckmorton's controllers. I'm going to show a photo of Throckmorton around the tavern where they used to spend time together to confirm Throckmorton was Manny, but I'm reasonably sure he was."

"Why do you think he was killed?" she asked.

"I haven't had time to think about it."

"You think it was because maybe he knew something

and people were afraid he would talk?"

"Maybe."

"Why not just kill you?"

"They tried that yesterday."

"Why not try again?" She said it as if it wasn't a bad idea.

"Maybe we're next."

An hour later in the heat of the afternoon, Cooper cut us loose.

We climbed into his truck in the parking lot, where Snake switched on the engine and the air conditioning. "So what do you think happened to Throckmorton?" Snake asked.

"If this was a pre-planned decision to get rid of him, they wouldn't have done it with a million wits."

"Except there are no wits."

"Somebody'll step forward."

"One would hope so. But they definitely did not come here expecting to drown him. Nobody plans to drown a man in a rose garden. And I don't expect they were here to look at the roses. Nobody cares about roses."

"I do."

"My guess is they were here for a meeting, and while they were here, he said something he shouldn't have."

"Take a look at the surveillance photos from the marina. Throckmorton looks spooked."

"Their handlers must have phoned and told them we were on our way. That was our bad."

"I'm guessing he was spooked and threatened to walk out on them. He probably thought with all these people around, they wouldn't do anything."

"But they did."

"Maybe they put him in a choke hold and pushed him into the pool after he was unconscious. You can put a guy out with a choke hold in less than ten seconds. Years ago, they routinely used the choke hold in the King County Jail. Killed several people by accident before it was banned."

"The way we boogied on over to the marina, maybe they thought he was the one warned us. They didn't know about the tracker in his phone, so it would be natural to suspect somebody tipped us off. I think you should arm yourself, Thomas. At least until we get this settled."

I had some serious baggage when it came to firearms. I continued to maintain a concealed-carry permit for the few times I hired out as a bodyguard, but I didn't like the weight of a sidearm and didn't want one now.

36

Snake and I didn't know where to turn next. I had a feeling Binky had already coughed up all the answers he was willing to cough up. I needed some sort of leverage before approaching him again. Chad had given me part of the picture, but I needed more. I was pretty sure if I put any more pressure on Binky and his pals, they would clam up and sic their lawyers on us; Binky had enough money to keep us tied up in court for the rest of our lives, notwithstanding the fact that I was married to an attorney.

A year's simple interest on Binky's pile was more than I could spend in my lifetime. When we were kids together, I'd yearned for a cabin cruiser and an island and my own jet and all that preposterous and pathetic pie-in-the-sky stuff young boys dream about when they get old enough to realize what's even remotely possible. In my case the accent was on "remotely." Now, twenty years later, Binky could buy and probably had bought everything we'd ever talked about. He also found a hobby we'd never dreamed of: making high-stake wagers on his ability to ruin the lives of strangers.

As an adult, I found myself more worshipful of the Native American school of thought, in which Indians gained stature in the eyes of the community by giving away wealth. In early American Indian communities, anybody who hoarded goods was considered mentally ill. This made a lot of sense in a society where you picked up everything you owned every few months and carried it on your back or on a travois. Even though I hadn't moved in years and didn't really have much to give away, it made sense to me, too. Or maybe it made sense only because I didn't have a whole lot to begin with.

That evening after I was finished updating Kathy on the

day's events, we began washing dishes, working quietly together for a few minutes. Finally, she said, "I suppose if I asked you to quit this thing, you would say no."

"You suppose right."

"Why?"

"Because there's a little dog out there crying for a home."

"You know what I'm talking about. And it's not that dog."

"Somebody sicced two prizefighters on us, and it makes me furious. I'm going to find out who."

"You can't go around doing things because you're furious."

"Sure I can."

"If you had any sense, you would be scared out of your pants right now."

"You want me to take off my pants?"

"Maybe later. You think your friend, Binky, is tied up in all this?"

"The phone calls to and from his phone certainly point to him. That and the fact that he lied to me about several things."

"Couldn't it have been somebody else making those calls? Weren't some of them from Doda's phone and Charlene's?"

"True. I checked with each of them earlier today, and neither knows anything about those calls. Wherever he goes, Binky tends to be the ringleader. By the way, maybe you should stay at your sister's until things get sorted out."

"You mean until you're either dead or you're not?"

"I didn't say that."

"I'm not going anywhere, mister. You stay, I stay."

"Okay, but I have to warn you. At some point my pants might come off."

"Looking forward to it, buster. Looking forward to it."

After we finished cleaning up the kitchen, I went to the gun safe and removed a Glock 9 millimeter. Kathy wasn't going to carry it, but she knew how to fire it, and I could tell she felt a vague sense of relief seeing it armed and ready outside the safe.

I left the gun on the table, kissed Kathy goodbye, and drove through the sparse evening traffic to West Seattle and up Fauntleroy to where it bisected California Avenue.

When I arrived at The Dregs, the front doors were open and letting in heat off the sidewalk. As usual, a row of Harleys was parked in front. I went inside, found the man I'd spoken to the other day and showed him the photo of Throckmorton, aka Brian Blair. "You recognize this guy?"

"He's been in. Sure."

"Recently?"

"Nope."

"Know his name?"

"Sure. That's Manny. The guy everybody's been looking for."

"Anybody in here tonight who might know him?"

He gestured with his chin to a table near the dart board, where four massive bikers were slugging down beers in front of a ball game on the huge television screen. As I walked across the neon-lit room, it occurred to me that The Dregs might be at the center of this, that Throckmorton and the others might have been recruited from this miasma of bikers, ex-cons, derelicts, and wannabes; that I might actually be showing Throckmorton's picture to some of the people who had been working with him, or maybe even the people who drowned him in that koi pool. Although I had yet to recognize any faces in the tavern, it was possible I had stepped into the viper's nest.

Two of the bikers who said they knew Manny turned out to be corporate attorneys. "Sure. He used to come in all the time. Used to hang out with that bastard who murdered his wife."

"Mick Kraft?"

"That's the one."

"Did you know either of them?"

"Nope. I just saw them in here occasionally."

Before I left West Seattle, I called the house next door to the Kraft place. "Mrs. Kennedy? This is Thomas Black, the private investigator."

"I know who you are. Am I getting my reward money? Have you found that mutt?"

"Not yet. I was wondering if I could speak to Charlie."

A moment later Charlie came on, sounding sleepy and worn out. He'd ridden his shabby bike quite a few miles that day, probably enough to earn a merit badge of some sort. "Hello?"

"This is Thomas. I just wanted to make sure you got home okay."

"Yeah. I did."

"Your guardian still doesn't know you went anywhere, does she?"

"No, sir."

"Did you go straight home like I told you?"

"No, sir."

"You went to the park?"

"Yes, sir."

"You see the dog?"

"Didn't see the dog. I saw the park."

"The bike holding up?"

"Yes, sir. When I find Pickles, can I call you? Because I don't think I can carry her on my bike."

"By all means. And thanks for telling me about Manny."

"You guys sure took off."

"Yes. I guess we did."

He racked the phone unsuccessfully so that the line didn't close; I could hear Mrs. Kennedy screaming at him. "Hang up the receiver! Hang up the gol-durned receiver! I'm expecting Martha to call any minute. Can't I have a sister? No wonder nobody ever calls this poor old lady! Hang up that durn phone!" Eventually the phone line went dead.

I turned off my phone and drove across the I-90 floating bridge to Stephanie Chin's place. I half expected her to be out with friends, commiserating over her job loss, but she answered the door before I knocked, having heard my car tires making popcorn noises on the gravel driveway. She told me her parents were out of town and invited me into the kitchen, where she had been in the process of feeding three small dogs, all of whom sniffed, pawed, and licked me. I liked dogs—a lot—but I mostly liked my own dog.

"I want to show you some pictures," I said, opening my laptop on her kitchen table.

She examined each of the photos as if trying to identify a Presidential assassin. After a few moments, she said, "Oh, my God. How did you get a picture of him?"

"You know this man?"

"That's Geoff Hardy. The guy from corporate. The guy who propositioned Alex and then fired her. I haven't seen him in weeks, but that's him."

"You're sure this is the man who wanted to bet Alex Kraft a million dollars he could sleep with her?"

"Except he wasn't wearing a swim suit when I saw him, and he had a mustache and glasses."

I'd shown her the photos of everyone involved in the case, including Charlie Hatcher, the manager of The Dregs, the bikers and lawyers in the tavern, the homeless job seekers who helped search for Pickles, even the police detectives, but she recognized only one face: Binky's.

Joshua Compton had gone to an enormous amount of trouble to make life miserable for Alex Kraft, including, I suspected, buying her company for what he would probably consider chump change and then handing her a pink slip when he couldn't coerce her into bed with him. The wagers were definitely getting out of hand.

Even though I had been expecting this to tie itself into a loop that made some sort of sense, it made me sick to my stomach to learn that Binky had played the part of Geoff Hardy, inserting himself into Alex Kraft's workday world solely to seduce her, and squandering a small fortune to dismantle her life. I wasn't sure how much those two had been betting, Chad and Binky, but it must have been a lot. I wondered how much they would be willing to spend to get me out of their lives on a permanent basis.

On the drive back into Seattle, I phoned Chad Baumgarden. "Chad, old boy."

"Thomas?"

"I'm just wondering about the nature of that last bet

you guys placed on the Krafts?"

"I'm not sure I should talk about this anymore. When Binky came back, he kinda went off his nut. He's pretty mad at me right now."

"Your last bet. What could it hurt? He's already angry."

"Hell. Everybody around here knew what it was. He bet they both wouldn't be in the house by the end of the week."

"He bet they wouldn't be living together in that house by the end of what week?"

"The week they died."

It took a moment for the implications to sink in.

"Black? Still there?"

"He bet they wouldn't be living together in their house? What does that mean, exactly?"

"I was on the other side of it. I knew the bank couldn't take a house that quickly. I mean, they were foreclosing, but it takes time. As it happened, it was the week Mick Kraft went mental and shot everyone. Who could have guessed he was mentally ill? If I'd known he wasn't playing with a full deck, I don't know . . ."

"So Binky won that last wager?"

"On a technicality."

"They were no longer living in the house together because they were no longer alive."

"Right. I had been thinking more along the lines of Alex moving out, or kicking Mick out. Or Mick setting fire to their house for the insurance. Or Binky buying the mortgage paper and moving on it in a matter of hours. I never expected them to end up dead. It was a shock."

"Was it a shock to Binky?"

"What are you getting at?"

"How much money did you have to pay out when you lost the wager?"

"I'm not sure I should tell you."

"You just keep telling the truth and you'll be fine. I'm going to find out, anyway."

"A little over ten million."

"You bet ten million dollars the Krafts would not be living together in a week?"

Two Miles of Darkness

"I bet they *would* be living together. At the time, it seemed like a sure thing. Besides. Binky would win one bet and then I'd win the next. We were basically just exchanging the same money back and forth."

"Until that bet?"

His voice dropped. "Right. That was the last in a series of bets on them."

"After they died, you paid him ten million?"

"That was the agreement. We don't welsh."

"Were you guys using an investigator to keep track of what the Krafts were up to?"

"Binky must have had somebody. He always seemed to be one step ahead of me."

"Just out of curiosity, you wouldn't happen to know about a camera hidden in their back yard, would you?"

"What? No."

Oddly enough, I believed him.

Elmer called me on Kathy's phone just after eleven. "Got a call from my brother," Snake said. "He was checking out Lovell and Turner. He found a bunch of stuff which I'll go into tomorrow, but get this: they belonged to a gun club down there, the San Leandro Rifle and Pistol Range Club."

"A lot of people belong to gun clubs."

"Guess who was also a member."

"Why don't you tell me?"

"Herbert Cavendish."

"You're kidding."

"The pervert down the street from the Krafts. Makes you stop and wonder, don't it? Guess what else? I got hold of some of his credit card statements. Three months ago Cavendish bought something from a spy shop over the Internet. I called them, but they won't tell me what it was without a court order."

"That camera set-up?"

"I can't tell from the credit card statement, but the price is about right."

"Think they knew each other? Cavendish and Lovell and Turner?"

"I think they were all buddies and have been for a long

time."

"Or maybe belonging to the same gun club is just one of those coincidences that seem to crop up in every investigation. There's always some neighbor of the dead guy who went to school with the head of the CIA or something in that vein." The line went quiet. "What are you thinking?"

"I'm thinking I should have told you this in person."

"You're not on a safe phone?"

"I borrowed Katrina's."

"And you called Kathy's. We should be all right. We'll talk in the morning."

"In the morning."

37

It was almost 2 a.m. when Snake called me, urgency pulling at his nasal, somewhat atonal, nighttime voice. It wasn't unusual for him to be awake at that hour, since he existed on four or five hours sleep a night, squandering the nighttime hours when normal people were recuperating from their workday in the search for new watering holes and new friends he would forget by morning, or cleaning his guns, writing letters to lost relatives, doing on-line ancestry searches— having gone all the way back to Charlemagne, or whatever. Logging onto dating websites in search of married women.

He had never actually run off with another man's wife, yet he fantasized about it until it had become an obsession, perhaps because his first two wives had been stolen by his brother, or because his distant father had been a womanizer of mythic proportions.

"You need to get over here right now," he said, gruffly. "I found something you'll want to see."

"Just e-mail it to me, pal," I said, but he'd already signed off, and when I called back he didn't pick up.

"Where are you going?" Kathy asked, reaching out for me as I cleared the bed. I dressed, sans socks, which I would later regret.

"The marina. Elmer thinks he's discovered perpetual motion or the fountain of youth or something. Fifteen minutes down. Fifteen back. Ten to tell Snake he's a genius. Be back in forty minutes, give or take. The gun's on the night table on my side of the bed."

"Don't you want it?"

"I'm not going to need it. Just don't shoot me when I come back."

"When *should* I shoot you?"
"Any time I ask my father to come live with us."
"That's a given."
"But not tonight."
"When you come home, how will I know it's you?"
"Your heart will flutter when I get close."
"If it doesn't, I'll shoot."
"Use your own best judgment."
"Don't worry. When you're around, my heart's like a metal detector over a city water main. Just come back in one piece. You realize there are people wanting to do you harm."
"I'll lock up on the way out. Love you."
"I love you, too. And I'm going to try really hard not to shoot you when you come back."
"Good, because that's my primary goal in life right now. To not get shot."
"Glad to hear it, bub."

I laughed, perhaps a little too enthusiastically.

Because it was late and it was a week night, the streets were more or less empty and the lights were off in all the houses I passed. I called Snake twice, but each call went to voicemail. It was one thing to come up with a brainstorm in the middle of the night, quite another to force your partner into driving all the way to Lake Washington just so you could tell him about it. On the other hand, we both knew anything important could no longer be relayed over the phone, and at this time of night, he was probably too drunk to drive. It was ironic that he would summon me, because just before I'd fallen asleep I figured out who killed the Krafts. In fact, I figured out the whole puzzle.

I drove the winding road through the Arboretum and dropped down to Lake Washington Boulevard on the same route I used on my bike.

Beyond the gated marina entrance were several docks, boats gunwale to gunwale like hogs in a cattle car. Only a few of the boats had full-time squatters like Snake, so there weren't going to be a lot of people around. Far across the glassy black water of Lake Washington, I could see the lights of downtown Bellevue. It was always interesting to be up at this hour. I'd had third watch most of the time when I was with the SPD and still associated the wee hours with adventure. And danger.

Snake was housesitting a thirty-six foot sailboat named Princess Diana, a boat he said slept one captain and six female sailors, his description tailored to a lifelong fantasy of traveling to the South Seas with an all-female crew. He made daily attempts at recruitment for this fantastical voyage, even though he didn't own the boat, couldn't navigate or sail, and the owners wouldn't trust him to push a cork across a duck pond, much less sail to Tahiti.

As I walked along the floating docks, the only person I saw was an old man in a big hat, making his way in a stooped, heavy-gaited slouch, a pail in one hand, a pipe wrench in the other. Emergency plumbing duties in the middle of the night? I nodded at him, but he didn't look up.

It was always a bad sign when a man refused to make eye contact, especially in such a lonely sector of the city and at this time of night. It was also strange that anybody in this tight little boating community would be so uncommunicative. We were probably the only two people within a half mile who were still moving about.

I prided myself on my situational awareness, a trait that had kept me safe and informed many times in the past, and as I squeezed past him on the narrow wooden walkway, I couldn't help feeling a little superior when I decided to turn around so I could see what he was up to. I had the vague feeling he wasn't an old man at all, but was feigning decrepitude, acting a part. Maybe he was breaking into boats.

My backward glance wasn't quick enough.

The pipe wrench came at me like a meteor shooting out of the sky, struck me across the skull and knocked me cattywampus.

I hit the wooden deck like an errant kite in a crosswind, zigzagging crossways, landing on my knees, then my hips, ribs, and face, slamming hard into the planks. My cheeks were numb, my brain spinning with images of brightly colored lightning, oblongs, trapezoids, gigantic insects. I knew I could take this guy in any kind of a fair fight. I would simply get back up and duke it out with him.

But I was groggy and too momentarily stunned from the blow to get up. I reached for his leg.

New plan. I would wrestle him to the ground, get him in a stranglehold, make him cry uncle. Before I could implement it, I slid a hundred miles into the ether. I didn't realize it then, but he'd thumped me again, the second blow not as hard as the first. Later, when I couldn't recall anything else, I remembered hearing the pipe wrench connect with my skull. It sounded like a short buzz on a waterlogged doorbell.

38

Because my movement interfered with his and his with mine, we alternated trying to untangle each other's bonds. First, Snake would fiddle with the tape binding my hands, then I would jigger the tape on his, neither of us seeming to forge much progress. With our hands taped behind our backs and our legs bound, the contortions required for even the most remedial movements chafed my wrists and jarred my nervous system. I was quickly growing to hate the men who'd done this to us. My bare ankles were already raw from the tape. It didn't help that being stuffed into the trunk of a moving car was making me carsick. The last thing I wanted right now was to vomit all over myself, and I was pretty sure Snake didn't want that either, but I sensed it coming on.

On top of everything else, my headache was pounding away like a Laguna surf in January.

I was pretty sure of two things: The first was that the old man with the pipe wrench wasn't actually an old man and was probably sitting in the front of the car now. And secondly, he'd fractured my skull, which meant I needed to get to a hospital as quickly as possible. Along with the massive headache, I could already feel a steady and gradually escalating pressure inside my skull. If I didn't get some medical attention soon, I was going to die. But then, that was the whole point.

As we worked, I managed to separate my ankles, but not before they were bloody and raw. Any slight air movement on them made them sting. Getting out of any of it seemed like a minor miracle. Now, instead of being hog-tied the way Snake still was, my legs were free. Once the trunk of the car opened, I would be able to stand under my own power, maybe kick one of our captors in the knees.

On the other hand—feet loose, hands free, it didn't matter which—once the trunk yawned open, we would be facing at least three men with guns. Even without our hands taped behind our backs, three men with guns could easily control us.

I found myself smothered in a feeling of dread. It was impossible to express just how much I resented the nonchalance of the men in the front of the car, men who continued to natter and guffaw as if on their way to a ball game, while Snake and I suffered in the cramped, fart-filled trunk. As the minutes passed and as I continued to contemplate our impending fate, I grew more furious, more full of hatred.

My ears popped for the second time, which told me we were at altitude and proceeding higher. Judging by the speed of the vehicle and the sound of the tires, we were on a relatively smooth highway, though an empty one, for I did not hear other vehicles traveling in either direction. It was the middle of the night. Presumably most highways were largely empty.

The taillights brightened the inside of the trunk enough so we could see each other, Snake and I struggling in a neon nimbus of rage, confusion, and uncertainty. The tangerine-colored lights, which in another circumstance could have been downright cheery, seeded a deep melancholy in my gut.

"My feet are loose," I said.

"That ain't going to help nothin'."

"Sure it will. You distract them. While that's going on, I'll run."

"And leave me?"

"No. I'll carry you on my back."

"Go ahead. Run. They're gonna love a moving target. Turn this into a game for them instead of work. They're hauling us out into the dingles so they can bury us. It's going to be pitch black out there. Where you going to run?"

"Hell, I don't know. We need some sort of plan."

"I got a plan. Had one all along."

"Thanks for sharing it."

Two Miles of Darkness

"Let's get this goddamned tape off first."

"Tell me what your plan is."

"We need to get the tape off first."

He didn't have a plan any more than he had a ham radio in his pocket. He was bluffing for my sake and for his own. Even though I knew it was a bluff, I felt better hearing him lie about it. Funny, the little lies we cling to when we're in extremis.

There were three men in the front of the car, talking and laughing and listening to Emmylou Harris, the stereo system cranked so loud Snake and I had a hard time hearing each other. There were ironies to this that I couldn't get out of my head. In my last conversation with Kathy I said I wouldn't get shot, and now I was pretty sure I was going to break that promise. Also, as I had fallen asleep that night, long before Snake called, I had an epiphany concerning what happened to the Krafts. The police had it down as two murders and a suicide, but it was three murders. I knew who killed them all, and it wasn't Mick Kraft.

As I worked out the scheme, it surprised me a little bit. I knew who was behind the prizefighters attacking us and I knew who ordered Throckmorton's death. The entire fandango had been staring me in the face.

"You recognize any of those boys when they took you?" I asked Snake.

"They hit me too damn fast. I was expecting Katrina. I just stepped out of the shower and was in my jammies and boots. I like to keep my boots on when I'm making love. Better traction. Plus, I got ugly feet. I felt somebody moving around on the boat and thought it was her. I told her to come down the hatch. My back was turned. I had my shirt off. I was going to accidentally let her see my scars. Gets the women hot. Did you know she's got song lyrics tattooed all over her ass, takes up almost one whole cheek?"

"I saw some lyrics on her shoulder. I didn't get a look at her ass."

"You should see it."

"I don't anticipate that happening."

"Hell, she'll show her ass to anyone. And there's

245

nothing wrong with a married man doing a little window shopping. I told her if she gained some weight, she could put more songs back there."

"When did you realize it wasn't Katrina?"

"Two guys jumped me like linebackers. Tased me a couple of times and threw a sack over my head. Before I knew it, I was all taped up like a birthday present in an insane asylum. Then they told me they had Katrina up on deck and they were going to gut her like a mackerel if I didn't do exactly as ordered. Turned out they didn't have her, but I didn't know that."

"They made you call me?"

"I'm sorry, Thomas. I thought her life was in danger. If it had been just me, I would have told them to go fuck themselves. I tried to make it sound like there was something wrong at my end, but I didn't do a very good job."

"It didn't make a whole lot of sense that you would tell me to come over and then hang up. I should have guessed something was wrong."

"Right. And now here we are, reliving Throckmorton's worst nightmare. Two miles of darkness. Except this ride is more like forty miles of neon. He told us it was dark in here, which now makes me think he was making the whole thing up. It's not dark."

"Maybe they didn't take him at night."

"What difference would that make?"

"No lights."

"He lied about a lot of things, and I think this was one of them."

The car slowed momentarily, then the driver gassed it and we took off again. He did that two more times, as if searching for a turnoff.

"They're looking for something," I said.

"We need to get our hands free. And we can't let them know. The only thing we got on our side is surprise."

"We don't get our hands loose, we're not even going to have that."

"Even if we get untied, it's still three against two."

Two Miles of Darkness

"And we're not armed."
"Except we are."
"We're armed.?
"I got my Derringer."
"Are you kidding me? I'd kiss you if you had a gun."
"Pucker up, stranger."
"You said you just got out of the shower when they jumped you, and you're in your jammies. You're not even wearing a shirt. Where's the gun?"
"My left boot."
"You keep a gun in your boot when you're at home?"
"Bet you're glad I do, eh?"
"Can you get to it?"
"I think so. But here's the bad news."
"It's not loaded?"
"The bad news is there's three of them and I only got two bullets."
"Wait till they're lined up. You can shoot two at once."
"Funny."
"I'm trying."
"And here's another problem. Unless we can get my hands free, I'm going to have to fire behind my back. I'll need you to direct my fire."
"Even if we execute this perfectly, there's going to be one man left standing."
"We'll face that when we get to it."
The car slowed, slowed some more, and turned left onto a bumpy road.
"We're going to face it a lot sooner than we want."
"Jesus," said Snake. "I haven't even brushed my teeth."
We spent the next few minutes bouncing along an unpaved road which climbed steeply in a manner that threw Snake against me heavily, winding along one tortuous incline after another. I figured we were on some ancient logging road or maybe a forest service road.

When they turned off the music in front, Snake and I stopped talking. Without the noise, they would hear our conversation through the thin material of the back seat. Despite our half-formed plans and the bluster we were

247

displaying, we both knew they were going to kill us, and we knew something far worse—they were going to get away with it. Eventually, Snake's brother would show up and poke around, and he might even find somebody upon whom he could wreak revenge. He would never get the whole truth, because the whole truth was too complicated and our bodies would be too far in the hills to be dug up and exhumed.

"Better get out that artillery piece now," I whispered.

I could feel him behind me trying to dig the gun out of his boot. I vowed silently that if we somehow came out of this unscathed, I would never again poke fun at Elmer's paranoia-driven inventory of weapons.

The road, which had been climbing steeply, finally became more or less level. Then we stopped, and three doors opened and slammed shut, though the engine continued to idle.

"You got everything ready?" one of them said.

"It's all ready."

"I'm going to do this myself, right?"

"We said you could."

"But I am going to do it?"

"We said."

"I don't want any misunderstandings."

"No misunderstandings, pal. They're all yours."

"Good."

I recognized the voice, just as I knew I would. He'd already arranged one attempt on our lives, and now he was going to kill us personally, was as jittery and high with the prospect of cold-blooded murder as a brainless, sugar-addled kid was high on the prospect of another candy bar.

"Listen, I've gotta take a shit," he said. "You two stand guard at the car."

"What are we guarding?"

"Just guard."

"There's nobody here but us. We could have executed them right in the middle of the highway back there and nobody would have seen."

"Just stand guard. These two are slippery."

Two Miles of Darkness

"Sure. We can do that."

Soon the conversation was reduced to two voices, neither of which I recognized. The mastermind was off taking a nervous shit, having gotten the jitters at the happy prospect of murdering two human beings.

"You ready?" Snake whispered.

"As ready as I'll ever be."

"They ever going to open this trunk?"

We waited a few more seconds. "Maybe not," I said.

"I wish I knew who they were," Snake said.

"I know one of them."

"You do?"

I kicked the inside of the trunk lid, hollered and kicked some more.

Snake snarled like some sort of wounded animal and thunked at the inside of the trunk lid with his skull. I didn't generally get nervous before physical confrontations—I'd been in more than a few of them and found I was generally too stupid, or too busy calculating the odds, or perhaps my brain just didn't register anxiety—but I was twitchy now and found myself shaking like a wet dog, my torso perspiring heavily, trousers damp against my legs.

Unless an asteroid streaked out of the sky and killed our captors, chances were about a thousand to one Snake and I would be dead within minutes. We had some cheesy ideas about outwitting them and a half-baked plan, but as far as I was concerned, the most we could do, if we got really lucky, was to wound one of them. Still, that was better than going quietly into the cold dark earth.

Our deaths weren't going to be pretty or noble or even clean. Nobody was going to attend our funerals or ballyhoo our passing with oratory or floral arrangements. When we were listed at all, we would be listed as missing. The only possibility of anybody finding out what happened to us hinged on one of our killers spilling his guts, and I didn't see much chance of that. To begin with, I firmly believed only one of our killers was going to go home from this. Throckmorton's fate was a hint these other two should have heeded.

The sketchy story of our disappearance would be trotted out and rehashed every ten years or so, maybe in a back-page newspaper article—no leads, no clues, no witnesses. No bones.

Like imbeciles locked in a closet, we continued kicking and hollering, as if it was going to get us somewhere.

Then the car shifted incrementally as somebody sat in the front seat and released the trunk lid. I looked up through the chink in the partially opened trunk but could see nothing at first; then as my eyes adjusted, I recognized fir trees and a smattering of stars, the stars burning in thicker as my eyes became accustomed to the night sky.

Both men had mag lights. One said, "He probably doesn't want us to pull them out until he gets back."

"Fuck that shit. I been up two nights in a row trying to put an end to this. The sooner we get this done, the sooner we get home. Dumb fuck's out there dropping a deuce, and I got a six-pack waiting at the motel."

"He's going to be pissed."

"We ain't gonna shoot 'em. He'll shoot 'em. We're just saving time. Besides, what's he going to do about it?"

The trunk lid yawned open to its highest point. One man leaned inside and jerked Snake out, throwing him to the ground, where he landed like a sack of dry cement. He hit so hard I was afraid he might have dropped the Derringer, if he even had it.

The man closest to him waved his hand in front of his face like a fan and said, "Jesus, you stink. What ya been eating?"

"I eat bullets and I shit fire," said Elmer, game right up to his last breath.

When they pulled me out of the car, I remained on my feet leaning against the fender, keeping my legs together as if they were still securely taped. There was no point in giving away the fact that I had mobility. One of these men I recognized in the murk from the headlights and the glow of the trunk lights as the prizefighter I'd throat-punched two days before. It was easy enough to see he was happy to be completing the job he failed in Discovery Park. He glowered

Two Miles of Darkness

at me in a manner that told me he had no intention of fulfilling his promise to let the other man, the man who was off in the brush emptying his bowels, kill me. He was going to finish me himself. And he was going to relish it.

The second man I didn't recognize, but he didn't have the features of a former fighter.

On the ground, hands taped behind his back, Snake rolled over until his forehead and knees were all that was touching the loam, until he formed a trestle, angling around in a crab-walking motion while pointing his skinny buttocks at the starry sky.

In the darkness I could see the Derringer in his fist, but only because I was looking for it. I was hoping the others wouldn't notice until it was too late. "Now?" Snake asked.

The stubby little Derringer with its .38 Special cartridges was pointed at my belly. The man with the knife was moving toward me. "Your left," I said. Snake swiveled left. "One more click."

Even if they'd been looking, I'm not sure they would have seen it in the dim starlight. And they certainly didn't seem to understand what Snake and I were talking about. They had flashlights, but they weren't focused on us. Instead, they were scanning the woods. "Now!" I said.

Funny how even when you're expecting it you can be startled by the pop and flash of a gunshot. The Derringer was dead on. The man standing next to me let out a gasp and doubled over, sagging to his knees. I wasn't sure how badly he'd been hit, so I kicked him in the head. It flopped him over backwards, but other than that it didn't produce much of a reaction.

Now, we only had Frederick C. Lovell, the ex-prizefighter, to deal with. He had brought out a knife, was clenching it in one hand after the gunshot, one of those three-inch blades, serrated on one side, wickedly sharp on the other. He hadn't quite digested what was happening, and I knew I needed to take advantage of the split second of surprise Snake and I were enjoying. It was a small doorway, but it was mine. During that fateful second when he was too surprised to move, I braced myself against the car and kicked him hard in the side of the knee, cartilage crackling as he spewed out a string of profanity and dropped to the ground, grasping his leg with both hands.

I'd assumed he'd brought the knife to cut our throats with, or to cut the duct tape, since tape could preserve fingerprints and these guys were thorough enough they wouldn't want to take a chance of leaving prints in the grave with us. But now, for just a moment, he lay curled in a fetal position, stunned by the pain.

Before I could do anything else, Snake rolled over twice and pressed the little gun up against Lovell's spine.

I heard another pop, this one muffled somewhat by the victim's shirt, for the barrel of the gun was jammed firmly into his back. Two shots. Two hits. Two men down.

We'd used up the element of surprise, but our hands were still taped behind our backs, and worst of all, we had no idea where the third man was. Still, for the time being, we were two points ahead in a three-point game.

39

The first of our captors wasn't moving, probably because the bullet had center-punched him somewhere near his solar plexus. The man whose knee I destroyed was still moaning, even though Snake had pumped a round into his back close to his spine.

Moving like a half-dead traveler in the desert, the second man began crawling away from us. My guess was he was trying to achieve some distance from the tangle of bodies and from me before he pulled his gun and killed us both.

I walked over and booted him in the ribs, then kicked him a second time so hard the force of it knocked me off balance and to the ground.

Hands still bound behind my back, I pressed my forehead against cold fir needles, struggled to my knees, and picked myself up. The man had stopped crawling but was now reaching inside his coat for a weapon. After I kicked him in the head twice, he went as limp as a dishrag.

I searched the dark ground for the knife he'd dropped somewhere along the way.

Not far from one of the fallen mag lights, I spotted his open knife amid a thick carpet of conifer needles. I sat heavily on one hip, grasped the handle of the knife, and began sawing at the duct tape balled up around Snake's wrists, hoping I didn't slice his hand in the process. It was dark and our hands were behind us, so we were both working blind.

There was one man left. He could be on us at any moment, so speed was of the essence. As I worked, I looked around but didn't see anything but shadows and the vague silhouettes of trees. The gunshots from the short-barreled

Derringer had been incredibly loud in the quiet mountain air. As we worked with the knife, we both listened for footsteps in the darkness.

Hands free, Snake took the blade from me and slashed at the tape binding his boots together, then quickly sawed through the duct tape wadded around my wrists.

When I brought my arms around in front of me, trying to work some life into the muscles, I found my shoulders stiff and sore, my hands moving in odd arcs as if they belonged to someone else. I would have lost an arm-wrestling contest against a Girl Scout.

Snake had a gun in his fist, having pulled it from the belt of the first man he'd shot. It turned out to be his very own Smith and Wesson with a seven and a half-inch barrel and enough juice to take down a grizzly, one of the twin .44 Magnums he carried everywhere he went. He verified the cylinder load, then clicked the cylinder back into the frame and moved from the rear of the car toward the bole of a large tree, where he crouched, quickly making himself close to invisible in the shadows.

"Arm yourself, Thomas," he whispered. "It ain't over."

I picked up the mag light, turned it off, and found a gun on the other man, a Glock .40 caliber. As far as I could tell, both men were still breathing, though neither had put up a fight or even stirred while we relieved them of their weapons.

After inspecting the load in the semi-automatic, I crept around the car and shut off the lights, turned off the motor, and stuffed the keys into the pocket of my jeans. Without the headlights illuminating the trees in front of us, the area was darker than I thought possible. In less than two minutes, we'd gone from battered prey to shrewd hunters.

My clothes were wet from perspiration, and my shirt was sticky on the back of my neck from what I later learned was a trickle of blood, where I'd been clubbed with the pipe wrench.

The back of my head felt as if a horse had kicked me, and the night air was icy on my wet clothes. All in all, it was an uncomfortable feeling, though probably not as uncomfortable as getting rolled into a grave with a bullet in my gut.

The choreography of our violence had worked out far better than we had any right to expect, and later we would both mull over our luck at length, because that's what it had mostly been—luck. Overly confident in their superiority over two beaten and hog-tied prisoners, our guards had been taken unawares.

Still, one heavily armed man would be returning for us, and we had no idea from which point or points of the compass he would be coming. We were both stiff and awkward and shaky from having been trussed up so long, and as far as I was concerned, the odds were still in his favor.

Shoulders aching, head throbbing, I wasn't quite settled behind a thick tree trunk when he appeared over a small rise, closer to Elmer than me, his silhouette bracketed in the dimness by starlight, a small, dark object in his right hand. He stopped and crouched amid a stand of trees thirty yards from the car, realized the car lights had been doused, the motor silenced, and grew still.

"Larry?" said the newcomer. "What's going on? Freddie? You there?"

I didn't move. Neither did Elmer. The man on the hillside came down the slope toward us, moving slowly, stepping off a narrow trail he'd used earlier, closing in on us until I could hear his hollow-sounding footfalls on the thick forest loam. He was trying to be sneaky, but he was walking right into us. He'd heard two staggered gunshots, and now, instead of coming back to friends and headlights and a convenient little execution scene, he was greeted by silence, darkness, and some dissonant moaning. He had to know something was seriously wrong, but he wouldn't know precisely what. The last thing he would guess was that the prisoners in the trunk were aiming weapons at him.

More likely he would be thinking his two friends had disobeyed orders and disposed of us.

"Freddie?"

Snake fired a round from his .44 Magnum. I was not

certain whether he was trying to hit our man or merely trying to scare him. The noise of the gunshot reverberated in the quiet mountain air, a fearsome sound compared to the earlier sharp-sounding pops from the Derringer, the gunshot accompanied by a flash that split the darkness and seemed eight feet long, bright and angry looking. For just a split second the flash lit up the trees, the car, and the two men on the ground. Behind the fir tree, it lit up Snake's crouching form, in pajama bottoms, cowboy boots, and nothing else.

The man in the trees fired three rounds, one of which thwacked the sheet metal on the car, which wasn't close to either of our positions. It told me he was shooting blind. Snake fired again.

Aiming as carefully as I could in the darkness, I cranked off two rounds from my position and then quickly got back behind the tree. One of the bullets in the return fire spit up some dirt ten feet from me.

Snake fired again, the boom reverberating in the mountains, the flash lighting up all the space around him. To our opponent, it must have looked as if his friends had turned on him.

It was six minutes before we heard or saw him again. It was hard to tell whether he was circling back on us or fleeing through the woods, and for a long time I didn't know which. Then I glimpsed his silhouette, closer than ever. He'd been slowly and carefully closing in on us. He thought we were his people, thought he knew his enemy, thought he could outmaneuver us.

As he drew closer, Snake hollered, "Drop the gun, fucker."

"Who is that? Larry?"

"Who do you think?"

"What happened? Larry? Freddie? Talk to me."

I was glad Snake and I were spaced apart. It was good to have at least two angles of fire. It was good also to keep our location and disposition undisclosed for as long as possible.

After a long silence, I yelled, "Why don't you come on in?"

Two Miles of Darkness

"Black? Is that you?"

"Come on in and take this damn tape off me." I was free, but I didn't need him to know it.

"Larry? Freddie? What's going on?"

"They're not going to answer," Snake yelled. "They're taking a little siesta."

I knew our man had probably taken pistol training courses from experts, had belonged to a popular gun club in California, loved to shoot. If he should happen to outgun the two of us and leave our bodies here in the mountain dirt, he would probably get away with it. Nobody else was on his trail. In fact, at some point he might even pursue Kathy, particularly if he thought she was privy to my investigation.

I tried to reason through the setup from his point of view. As he was hunkered over a log in the cool darkness of the mountain air, he'd heard a couple of staggered pops in the distance, at which point he had to assume the execution had taken place without him, that the hogtied men in the trunk of the car had been assassinated. That he had been excluded from the festivities. "Throw your gun out, and we won't kill you," Snake yelled.

"Who is that?"

"The name is Elmer, but you can call me 'sir.'"

"Bullshit. Turn the car lights back on, Freddie."

Just as he spoke, one of the wounded men behind the car made a loud barking noise as he coughed up something, probably blood. It was clear he was in agony, and what was more, there was no mistaking his gruff, idiosyncratic voice. It was Larry.

"Throw down your weapon," Snake said. "This is the only chance you're going to get."

The gunman answered by sending six bullets down the hill in the general direction of Snake's position, firing in two-shot bursts the way he'd been trained by his instructors. The treetops above him lit up with each shot as if they had a strobe light on them.

My guess was he had at least sixteen rounds in his magazine and was probably carrying a spare mag, perhaps two spares. That was a lot of firepower, and somewhere in all of the exploding gunpowder he might just get lucky and connect with one of us.

Snake returned fire, one shot, which meant he had two left in his Smith and Wesson Model 629. The man on the hill sent two more rounds down the hillside. It was obvious he was planning to fight it out toe to toe, that he believed he was going to outgun us. Just to show him it wasn't going to be easy, I fired two rounds in his direction, carefully aiming just behind the point where I'd seen the last burst from his gun.

I either hit him or came too close for comfort, because without turning his light on, he dashed up the dark hillside, crashing through underbrush, tearing at brambles, forging up the hill through the fir trees, trampling everything in his way like a bull elk in rut.

Snake and I followed, jumping from tree to tree, keeping under cover. We moved in concert, each covering the other. We didn't use lights, just guesswork and the dim blanket of starlight shining down through the treetops. Even so, it was hard to make out what we were seeing, both of us still blinded by the flash from our pistols. The moon, which had been visible when we were in Seattle, had either already set in the mountains or was hidden behind a nearby peak.

I could hear our man a good distance away now, maybe a hundred yards, continuing to run from us at a rapid pace.

I followed at a careful trot until I reached the top of a small hillock. I couldn't see him, but I could hear him scrambling down the other side of the slope, making his way through the forest. After some minutes had gone by and he was well out of pistol range, he turned his light on and we could see it flickering through the woods far down the backside of the mountain. I assumed he was on a service road or an old logging road, because he was moving in a straight line away from us, his light flashing in the treetops from time to time.

Snake eventually appeared alongside me and, seeing the tiny, bobbing light in the distance, said, "That him?"

"Yep."

"He's moving pretty good."

Two Miles of Darkness

"I'd say if one of us hit him, it wasn't a good hit."

"Wonder who he is. You said you knew."

"Cavendish."

"The creepy neighbor?"

"That's right."

"You sure?"

"I figured it out last night. I was going to tell you this morning."

"How'd you figure it was him? I thought it was going to be one of the rich kids. Or that phantom investigating agency."

"Those pictures your security cam took at the marina. One of the men was identifiable as Throckmorton. Another may have been the second prizefighter."

"And the third one had a hat covering his face."

"It was a Denver Broncos cap."

"So?"

"The day I interviewed Cavendish, he was wearing a Denver Broncos hat. It was a different color, but it was a Broncos cap. He'd lived in Colorado. He was still a Broncos fan."

"There are a hell of a lot of Broncos fans in the Seattle area."

"I know it's not proof, but I had Brad Munch figure out the statistical probability Cavendish would be a Bronco fan and another guy breaking into your boat would also, coincidentally, be a Broncos fan."

"What were Munch's odds?"

"About eight thousand to one we'd have two different, unrelated prime suspects wearing a Broncos cap."

Snake looked off into the darkness and the slopes where Cavendish had vanished. "We going to chase him? He's way the hell down there. I can't even see his light."

"I can't chase anybody in my condition. My head is killing me. I can feel my heartbeat in my skull."

"So we're going to leave him for the police?"

"Or maybe the bears'll get him."

"That would be poetic justice. Guy was going to blow our heads off one minute, and the next he's running like a little girl."

"Bullies are like that."

"I wouldn't have expected him to shoot it out."

"I think he was going to shoot them from behind, Lovell and the other goon they brought along. I believe he was planning to kill them both. Leave four bodies up here. Nobody left to rat him out. When he found out it was us and realized we were fighting back, he panicked."

"I guess we've got a rep."

"Maybe that was it. Or maybe one of us wounded him."

"Hell, yes we do. We've got a rep."

We were back at the car now, walking as we talked. Neither of the men we'd left on the ground had moved, one because he was dead, the other because he needed medical attention even more than I did.

40

We figured the first man Snake shot had bled out while we were exchanging gunfire with his compadre, a theory borne out by the crusted pool of blood-soaked dirt under the body.

The second man, the one I'd stomped, Lovell, was barely conscious and breathing raggedly. In addition to my beating, he'd taken a bullet from Snake's Derringer at point-blank range. He either couldn't or wouldn't answer any of our questions, so we carefully maneuvered him into the back seat of the car. Snake proposed putting him in the trunk, but I vetoed that. Our plan was to get help to him as quickly as possible.

"We're alive," Snake said, as he slid into the driver's seat.

"That we are."

"Can you believe it?"

"Just barely."

We were stumbling around in that haze of disbelief and raw ache that often follows a near-death experience, our brains filled with gruesome mental pictures of how it could have gone wrong. By rights we should be dead.

Carefully avoiding the body we'd left on the ground, I guided Snake as he turned the car around, and then we slowly traversed down the steep, bumpy road back to the highway.

"Crazy, huh?" I said.

"I can't hardly believe it myself."

"You think there might be another reality where we're actually dead, but we got mentally stopped in this parallel universe where we both think we're still alive?"

"Funny you should say that. It feels that way to me. As

if maybe we really are dead but we just haven't realized it."

"We were damned lucky," I said.

"Don't fool yourself, Thomas. Luck had nothing to do with it. I been practicing with a shooter behind my back for ages. It's a well-honed skill."

"Was it skill that the first two disobeyed orders when they were supposed to leave us in the trunk?"

"Well . . ."

"Did skill cause Cavendish to go off and take a shit so he wouldn't be around to gun us down while we were fighting the others?"

"Well . . ."

"There's no doubt your shot rivaled any Wild West Show gunslinger's, but most of it was bald-faced luck."

"You might be right, but it ain't over. We still got Cavendish running around out there in the dark. He gets away, how are we going to convince the cops it was him? Neither one of us got a good look at him. Maybe this guy here'll talk."

"I recognized Cavendish's voice," I said.

"You think that's going to hold up in court?"

"Probably not."

Somewhere out there, as he wandered the mountainous terrain, Cavendish would be trying to work this out in his head just as we were; he would be trying to figure out what he was going to say when the authorities found him, where he would go if they didn't. He might even concoct a believable tale to account for his presence here, turn it all around a hundred eighty degrees and convince the cops we were the bad guys and he was the victim.

I was relatively certain our side of the story would hold up under scrutiny and his would not, but you never could tell. I knew one thing: The authorities weren't going to be happy finding a gunshot victim in the back seat and a dead man up in the hills.

Sprawled across the bench seat behind us, Lovell had wet his trousers. That alone told me he was hurt badly. I tried to make him as comfortable as I could, but every furrow and loose rock we drove over brought him visible pain.

Once we arrived at the highway, we located our cellphones in the car, along with our wallets and keys, found a map, a couple of jackets which we donned against the crisp mountain air, an empty Krispy Kreme box, and some secretly-taken street-scene photos of Elmer and me, which Cavendish had apparently used to show the third man what we looked like. As far as I could tell, they'd been taken two days ago. I found a rolled-up blanket and wrapped it around Lovell, who murmured, "Thanks."

The car stank of sweat, stale coffee, body odor, and cigars. None of the phones were operational. We were obviously out of range of any cell tower.

I soon recognized the roadway in front of us as a stretch of Highway 410, which ran south out of Enumclaw toward Mount Rainier. We were on the lower slopes of the mountain. I had earlier guessed as much from the terrain and cold air. Our bike club pedaled this highway at least once a year, sometimes twice, and I'd been on those rides and knew the roadway well enough.

"What makes you think this is Four-ten?" Snake asked.

"Because that's the back side of Mount Rainier right over there."

Snake ducked his head under the visor and squinted up at a section of the majestic, starlit mountain, a halo of altostratus clouds sitting atop it like a slipshod tiara. "Son of a bitch. I coulda sworn we were in Eastern Washington."

"Well, we're not."

Before we proceeded up the highway, we marked the service road entrance by stacking some dead branches. I was sure our kidnappers had also marked the site, but I couldn't identify their marker, so perhaps they'd removed it on the way in. I said, "Keep driving. I'll tell you when we get cell coverage."

As soon as my phone had a signal, I called 911 and told the dispatcher we had a GSW with us and needed a medic unit and the police, that there was a dead man in the woods, as well as an armed fugitive who'd already fired on us. The dispatcher asked us to wait where we were with the patient till aid crews arrived to assist the injured man. We were to signal with our headlights when we saw the emergency vehicles.

I called Kathy, who was still awake and worried sick. "Where are you? I've been scared half to death. You said you would only be a few minutes."

"We're somewhere in Yakima County."

"Where?"

"Near Mount Rainier. We'll be talking to the police, probably for a few hours."

"What happened?"

I told her briefly, leaving out the worst parts, but it was hard to tell the story without revealing how close we'd come to getting executed.

"Somebody slugged you?"

"Don't worry. It was only a pipe wrench. And they didn't hit me anyplace important."

"In the head?"

"I love you, but that just might be the concussion talking." I did, too. I loved her more than ever, which I didn't think was possible. I had a feeling it had something to do with chemicals released into my bloodstream when I thought I was going to die. Or maybe it was on account of the blow to my brainstem and the headache that was growing more and more appalling by the minute.

When Snake dialed Katrina, she was wide awake, loud rock music and a male voice in the background, a voice she claimed belonged to her brother. Snake said, "Hey, baby. This is the snakester. I ran into some trouble. I wanted to make sure you were safe."

Katrina was furious at having been stood up. She didn't believe a word Snake told her about our kidnapping or about having to wait for the police. She said when she arrived at the marina he was gone and his boat looked as if a couple of rabid dogs had been fighting on board. Even from the passenger seat, I could hear her screaming into the phone. After a few minutes of listening to her verbal abuse, Snake rolled his eyes and hung up without signing off. There were times when he was as goofy as a peach-orchard boar and he proved it then by saying, "I was thinking about marrying that gal. No matter now. My brother would have cuckolded me. She was more his type."

"I'm thinking maybe *her* brother would have cuckolded you. Or he already has."

"Yeah. Right. That guy in the background wasn't her brother. I suppose she's too much like a graveyard to make a good wife."

"Like a graveyard?"

"Takes on all comers."

"That's kind of how you are, too, isn't it?"

Ignoring my quip, he continued, "At least we're alive. You got women yelling at you, you know you're alive. Tell you the truth, Thomas, me boy, I never thought I would see another sunrise."

"I didn't either."

A few moments later, I turned around and realized our passenger in the back seat was dead. I checked his carotid pulse, but it was gone and he'd stopped breathing. Short of finding a non-existent emergency room around the corner, there wasn't much we could have done for him. The drive to Enumclaw from here, the first place that might have a suitable hospital, was probably a half hour away, perhaps further. The emergency vehicles we'd summoned would reach us long before we could have found a hospital.

We'd done all we could for Lovell. There was almost no external bleeding, so there had been nothing to staunch, no wound to patch. We'd placed him in the shock position, feet higher than his head, and made him as comfortable as we could, but too much time had elapsed.

For reasons difficult to understand and embarrassing to admit, his death seemed to relieve the almost palpable tension in the air. Odd how having a corpse in the back seat could relax you, but there it was. I was almost asleep when Snake said, "Can't you put him out in the dirt? It's creepy having a dead man in the car."

"I'm not putting him out in the dirt."

"Okay, then. Explain this. I'm still trying to figure this all out. Explain to me what you think happened to the Kraft family? Are you saying Cavendish did them?"

Without opening my eyes, I said, "He did. He put up the camera which we thought Chad or Binky was responsible for. He was spying on them—or more accurately, her. He's a voyeur. Don't forget in California he actually broke into a woman's home. He was escalating the degree of his crimes. I think he went into the Krafts' home to assault Alex. He may have seen the gun Mick borrowed from Manny through his camera. Knew where they kept it. He broke in, went for the gun, and thought he could control Alex with it. Or maybe Alex grabbed it to defend herself and he took it away from her. Then Mick showed up. Now he has two people under the gun, but he doesn't know how to extricate himself without going to jail. Maybe he shot Mick in the chair and when he did that Alex ran, so he shot her, too."

"And the mother-in-law?"

"The mother-in-law showed up unexpectedly while he was trying to stage it as a murder-suicide."

"But how did he get the gunpowder residue onto Mick's hands? They said he had residue on his hands."

"To get a positive on the paraffin test all Cavendish would have had to do was wrap Mick's hand around the handle of the weapon."

"Who would know that besides an ex-cop like you?"

"It's online. It's probably been on a million TV shows by now. Cavendish tried to make it look like a murder-suicide, and it worked. He probably took his camera down from the tree in a hurry once the police were gone. He left the plate thinking nobody would look up there. But then he saw me in the tree and took the plate down, too."

"Yeah, you said you saw him watching you with binoculars. I just figured him for the self-appointed block-watch nut at the time."

"When we showed up canvassing the neighborhood with all those guys from the Millionair Club, he must have got our story from them. We got him worried enough to call in help— Lovell and Turner, who he knew when they were all members of the same gun club in California. He knew enough from talking to one of our guys that first day to send his men to the Millionair Club and to have them hook up with Throckmorton. Throckmorton was telling the truth when he said they strong-armed him into hiring them to work for us. I think they were still strong-arming him yesterday when they broke into your place at the marina."

"And then they killed him. So who was Throckmorton working for?"

"Throckmorton was working for the people Chad or Binky hired to manipulate the Krafts—The Auckland Group—although, like Throckmorton told us, he didn't know who he was working for. They only contacted him on that stolen phone they couriered to him."

"So he'd been doing Chad and Binky's dirty work before and after the deaths, manipulating the lives of unsuspecting victims just so one or the other of them could win the stupid bets they were making."

"And then we got hired to look for the dog, and Chad and Binky were afraid we'd uncover their manipulation of the Krafts, which was what they thought drove Mick Kraft over the edge to murder and suicide. In spite of their disavowal of any responsibility in causing the deaths, they knew they would be blamed if the whole scenario came to light—or maybe they just didn't want the media to connect their names to something like that. So they spied on us, learned of our plans, sicced Throckmorton on us, traced us through our phones. They believed the suicide story and thought they were indirectly responsible for the three deaths. They didn't know any more about Cavendish than anyone else did and were just trying to cover their asses. Or at least one of them was—the winner of the bet would be my guess."

Snake thought things over for a while, then said, "Who won this last bet between Binky and Chad? The phone calls on Throckmorton's phone were tied to Binky and Charlene and the old lady."

"If Binky was running the surveillance on us, he wouldn't have been leaving traces back to his own phone or to Doda's. He's too smart for that."

"You think it was Chad?"

"Chad told me Binky won that last ugly bet, but Chad's been trying to play me since the first day we saw him at Doda's, and he's been all too eager to place blame on Binky. I don't trust anything he says. I'm guessing it was Chad who got paid off when those people died, not Binky. I think he was the one who was betting on the Krafts not lasting in their house together, and he already had The Auckland Group working toward that purpose. Then we came along, and he had them listen in on our phone conversations, so he knew we were getting closer to knowing all about the way he and Binky had both been messing with the Krafts. Chad didn't want us showing up at his doorstep with the police."

"I'm sure he didn't."

"When I talked to Binky and Chad, I kept looking for discrepancies in their stories. I suspected one or both was lying to me, but wasn't sure which. Then I remembered when we took on the case, Charlene told us Chad was the one who told her about the murders. She said he told her he heard it on the radio in his car. She said she told Binky and he was genuinely surprised. Later, Chad swore Binky and the others told him about the murders, implying that Binky knew first, that Chad was last to get word. Charlene had no reason to lie about it. But Chad did. He didn't want to look like he was knowledgeable or gloating, wanted to look as if it was a surprise. It was a little lie and he didn't have to tell it, but he used it to distance himself from the murders and from the Krafts."

I tilted my seat back further. Snake tilted his forward, putting as much distance between him and the dead man in back as possible. He said, "I can't believe how tired I am."

After some time had passed and we were both almost asleep, a cellphone rang. We weren't sure which of our former captors the phone belonged to, but the incoming call had a 415 area code, which I recognized as San Francisco. Snake answered it, but the caller quickly realized the voice wasn't the expected one and hung up. Snake turned to me. "It's disconcerting getting phone calls for a dead guy."

"Yeah."

Two Miles of Darkness

"Sure you don't want to put him outside?"

"We're going to leave him right where he is."

"You're right. He's too heavy. Remember what a bitch it was getting him in here?"

We were quiet for a while longer, waiting for sirens and flashing lights to race up the highway, presumably from Enumclaw, the closest town of any appreciable size.

My headrest was now butting up against the corpse in the back. I hoped it didn't leave an imprint on the torso that we were going to have to explain to the medical examiner, but I didn't hope it hard enough to tilt the seat back up. I said, "At one point, Binky bought Vereecken and Sons and passed himself off as an executive so he could put the moves on Alex—all to win another bet with Chad. When she didn't cooperate, he fired her."

"Buying the company probably cost more than he would have won."

"It was never about the money."

"You know what, Thomas? I think influencing people's lives must get intoxicating."

"How could it not?"

We sat back and waited. After a while, I rolled my window down to let in some fresh air. Snake muttered, "That one wasn't me."

"Maybe it was the guy in the back."

Snake made a sound that was almost a chuckle. "I guess if I kept a dead guy in the back seat all the time, I could blame him for a lot of things."

"Great conversation starter, too," I said. We laughed at the absurdity of it. At least I was laughing at the absurdity. I noticed we were both laughing a little too hard. I'm not sure Snake wasn't trying to figure out how he might make himself more comfortable around the dead so he could actually make it work for him on a regular basis.

41

  The first State Patrol unit whizzed past us and then skidded seventy feet until his tires were blowing white smoke from the wheel wells. After he reversed, blowing more white smoke, he got out and marched over to our vehicle, his sidearm pointed at my face. For a moment or two, I was afraid I'd survived six kinds of hell only to be gunned down by a trigger-happy state patrolman who looked like he was about seventeen years old. Still, it was hard to blame him. We'd reported involvement in multiple shootings, admitted we were armed, and now we had a stiff in the back seat.
  And the trooper was alone.
  The trooper woke Snake by tapping on the driver's side window with the barrel of his pistol. I had long since placed both hands on the dash, where he could see them. In the end, he had us step out of the car and put our hands on the roof. We were still in that pose when the next official vehicles careened around the curve.
  The rest of the night and early morning fitted itself together like a kaleidoscopic nightmare with a dozen missing pieces. It was easy to see nobody was really believing our wild tale, including the State Patrol investigators, who seemed to get more annoyed each time one of our allegations was borne out by fact.
  Probably because of my head injury, my memory of the particulars continued to be hazy. After we directed them to the turnoff where we were to have been slaughtered by Cavendish and company, the State Patrol and county deputies placed us in separate patrol cruisers so we couldn't coordinate our stories any more than we already had.
  Wearing a jagged crown of blood from my head wound,

Two Miles of Darkness

I caught a few glimpses of myself in the reflections in car windows. I looked like a ghoul. Snake looked more like a clown in pajama bottoms and cowboy boots, his lean torso a display board for all sorts of scars and tattoos, including the one that said: *In Case of emergency, do not resusitake.* I guess neither of us looked particularly reputable.

They removed Lovell's body from the back seat and placed him in the rear of an ambulance, where he was pronounced dead. Within fifteen minutes, they found the second corpse up the hill, where we'd left him on the ground. They initiated a systematic search of the woods but failed to find a trace of the third man, Herbert Cavendish.

None of the officials wanted to believe we'd been kidnapped, hogtied, and driven into the hills by three men and then had managed to kill two of them in self defense. The story was simply too strange, and Snake's ragged look and the way he mouthed off irritably when they asked their questions, along with my growing confusion, which must have looked like dissembling, reinforced their doubts.

They barraged us with questions designed to expose lies, changing the tone and coloring of their inquiries without any apparent rhythm, rephrasing their requests, badgering us, all in an effort to trip us up, and then conversed among themselves at a distance, continuing to shoot jaundiced looks our way. They didn't want to believe any part of our story, including Snake's claim that he kept a loaded Derringer in his boot "because that's how I roll."

Piece by piece, the evidence bore out our story and wore down their reluctance to accept it. They would find additional film of our kidnapping from the surveillance cameras Snake had set up at the marina where he was housesitting, making this the second time in a week Elmer's paranoia paid a dividend.

They collected strands of duct tape from our limbs and clothing. They photographed my injuries and the patches of dried blood streaking my skull.

I'd had a ferocious headache since waking up in the trunk, but after the police arrived it began to really blossom. I had to assume adrenaline had been keeping the worst at bay until then. At first I fended off medical help, but by the time the sun came up, I was riding in the back of a Medic unit and on my way to Harborview Hospital in Seattle, where I was to undergo a brain scan and minor surgery. Kathy camped out in a low chair next to my bed for the duration, while she monitored my well-being and worked on her upcoming court case. It wasn't the first time she'd nursed me through a hospital stay and, as it had in the past, it made me feel like a child. I told her to go home and get some rest, but she refused. Even though I assured her there was little danger now, she kept the loaded Glock in her purse under the chair. She'd had a carry permit for over a year now, though this was the first time I could remember her making use of it.

"We don't know where Cavendish is or what he's planning," she said. "And here you lie, helpless. We don't know how many confederates he's still got out there."

"You going to shoot them when they show up?"

"I'll shoot Mother Teresa if she comes in here and looks at you crossways."

"I feel all warm and fuzzy when you talk like this. You should carry a gun every day. You love something more when you're forced to defend it with a gun."

"You're drugged, and you're talking nonsense."

"Drugged out of my gourd, but I love you soooo much."

"I know you do."

When Cavendish was not located in the first twenty-four hours, the State Patrol put out official warnings and expanded the search grid. Everyone in the state was on the lookout for him. It was hard to see how he would remain free for long. But he did.

Somewhere toward the end of that first day, a string of thunderstorms blew through the region and drenched the Cascades with a couple inches of summer rain. Miles from the site of our prospective grave in the hills, hard men with dogs picked up Cavendish's muddy trail for a time, or thought they did, then lost it when additional showers swept through the area and sluiced the mountain paths.

Two Miles of Darkness

The police tried to home in on Cavendish's cellphone, but didn't get any pings. The cell company told them he was either out of reach of their towers or his phone was switched off. There was some speculation his battery may have shorted out in the heavy rains.

We all knew that in court my voice identification of Cavendish could be put into question by any good defense attorney. Without fingerprint evidence, his attorneys would be able to make a good case that he hadn't been there at all, that my ID was faulty.

To my relief, Cavendish's fingerprints were found in the car that had taken us into the mountains. They found other items corroborating our story, bullet holes in the sheet metal, blood splotches from my busted head in the trunk, along with pieces of duct tape we'd cut off our wrists and ankles.

Carole Cooper interviewed me several times while I was in the hospital. I had the feeling she was hoping my head injury and the drugs in my bloodstream would produce an alternative psychotropic storyline, one that made more sense than the one Snake and I were spinning.

What Cooper had on her plate now was a dead man in Discovery Park who may or may not be involved in three deaths she'd already cleared as a murder-suicide, another dead man at the Woodland Park rose garden with a similar but stronger involvement to the Kraft case, and now this wild tale about us being hogtied and driven to the mountains where we "allegedly" blasted our way to freedom against almost impossible odds, in yet another park, Mount Rainier National Park. She had no idea what to make of our claims against Cavendish and had even less inclination to believe two local millionaires were toying with people's lives in order to play out their own mind games.

Our contrary theory on what happened to the Krafts must have galled Cooper, too, because it was just outrageous enough to have the ring of truth—or the sting of truth— and because it was a hundred eighty degrees from her theory.

When she attempted to interview Binky and friends

about the wagers, the whole community closed up like a clam and she found herself stonewalled by unanswered phone calls, maids who said the principals weren't in, staggered and delayed appointments with high-priced attorneys, and superfluous legal motions.

The general recalcitrance to talk and all the lawyering up excited her suspicions, but was not enough to get her to buy fully into our story. Carole Cooper grew a little prickly around me. It didn't help that Kathy twice turned her away from my hospital room when she felt I was too doped on painkillers to be responsible for my statements. Apparently, the more I told Kathy I loved her the more she thought I was under the influence, which, when you think about it, was a sad state of affairs. I vowed to tell her more often after I got out of the hospital.

When my father showed up, Kathy barred the entrance to my room, said it was doctor's orders. Kathy had always viewed my father as a freeloader and charlatan, but more than that, she feared his visit would annoy me at a time when my defenses were non-existent. She knew I was peeved that he'd spent the last twenty years believing, or pretending to believe his only son was a weenie wagger, and she didn't want him reminding me of it at a time when I was apt to respond, because of all the dope in my system, by telling him how much I loved him.

Before she shooed him away, I heard him in the hallway trying to get Kathy to invest in a guano mine in Bolivia. "Guano's like gold," he said. "Those bats might as well be pooping bolivianos." Later, a nurse he'd cornered in the hallway told me at length what a wonderful father I had. He must have given her his standard spiel about how his children didn't appreciate him, because she really pressed the point. Taking his victories where he could find them, it was typical that he could schmooze the socks off the support cast while the main actors shunned him.

The doctors ended up drilling a hole in my skull to alleviate the pressure of an internal bleed that started when I got slammed in the head with a pipe wrench. The doctors scolded me for not coming in right away. I didn't bother to explain that I'd been hogtied in the trunk of a car.

When Binky showed up at my hospital room, accompanied by a small entourage, none of whom said a word, Kathy woke me. I hadn't expected a visit from Joshua Compton, but I wasn't going to turn him away, either. If he was refusing to talk to the cops, maybe he would talk to me. He was more tan and fit-looking than ever, while my head was swaddled in bandages and my skin pale and sickly. I was half sitting up in bed, feeling greasy and bloated with hospital pudding and ice water, groggier than a dying dog.

Whatever Binky claimed about their shenanigans, he was never going to be entirely guiltless. Not in my mind. Not in the mind of anybody who heard my story—provided they believed it.

After we exhausted the small talk, he said, "Wow. I can't believe everything that happened."

"Why not?"

"I knew Chad was cheating on our bets, but I never figured . . ."

"What do you mean cheating? You both used operatives to ruin people's lives. You told me about the Mariners game yourself."

"We used operatives. Sure. That's not cheating. That was the whole point. We fixed it so something changed in a person's life without that person realizing we changed it. But there were rules, man. Nothing illegal."

"At least not too illegal."

"Yeah. Right. That's what I said."

"But you could crash vehicles into a man's work truck until he lost his job?"

He gave me a look that told me he was wondering how much more I knew. "Kraft was going to get a better job in the end."

"After you had him living in his car for a few months?"

"I don't think you understand what we were doing."

"No, I don't think I do."

"I guess some mistakes were made."

"They didn't happen by themselves; *you* made mistakes. And what's this I hear about you not talking to the police?"

"My attorneys told us to keep mum. We'll get it straightened out. I just came here to see what's going on. Find out how you're doing."

"You sure you didn't come here to find out how much I know?"

Binky gave a weak smile and glanced around at his companions and at Kathy, who'd put ear buds in and was moving her head to some music only she could hear, pretending to be oblivious to us, though I knew she had the gun handy and the music low.

He gave Kathy a long look. I shuddered to think what sort of wagers he would have made with regard to us if Chad were here to goad him. I said, "Tell me something, Joshua. Which one of you stood to benefit when the Krafts died?"

He thought about it for a few seconds, his tan set off by a white designer T-shirt and the ubiquitous magenta neon sunglasses perched atop his head. "I'll admit Chad won a lot of money on that. I thought he would cancel the bet after we found out what happened, but he insisted, so I paid him. I felt sick about what happened to them. I still do. I was even thinking for a little while that we might have helped cause it."

"You think?" I said, sarcastically.

"Hey, I thought it over—I even talked to some of my people—and we didn't. We didn't do anything. A guy wants to commit suicide and take his wife with him, you can't stop something like that. Nobody could possibly blame us."

"If you really thought you were blameless, why go to extremes to cover up your involvement? And I almost hate to tell you this, but it wasn't suicide. A neighbor named Cavendish killed them. The police are going to prove it." We'd already heard from one of my sources inside the SPD that they'd found a print inside the Kraft house they were matching to Cavendish. "If it *had* been a suicide and two murders, you would have been responsible. You can't systematically destroy people's lives."

"You're saying one of their neighbors killed them? So we really *didn't* have anything to do with that shit. I'm sorry

Two Miles of Darkness

all this happened. I guess we were so busy trying to win our bets, we never thought about what we were doing. But I swear we were going to make it right. We always make things right when we're finished."

"You were at Vereecken and Sons for a couple of weeks, weren't you?"

Our conversation had been one small shock after another, but this was the biggest shock I'd given him so far. He was startled that I knew he'd been at Vereecken and Sons but tried to hide it by pretending it was common knowledge, that it had never been a secret. "I lost that bet. And then we found out she was stealing from the company. That was why I was forced to can her."

"Who told you she was stealing?"

"Chad."

"You took his word for it?"

"Chad wouldn't lie. He'd do anything to win a bet, but he wouldn't lie, not to me."

"How about Stephanie Chin? Why was she fired?"

"I don't know anything about that."

"You want to do something honest, give her job back."

As he was exiting the room, Binky turned back and said, "Chad told me he apologized. For that summer we sent you away? He said he told you it was my idea."

I said nothing.

"I don't suppose it would do any good to tell you it was his idea."

"I thought you just said he wouldn't lie."

"I shouldn't have gone along with it, but he was the one who cooked it up. He was the one who wanted to get Doda to send you away. Every time I rode Thunderbolt that summer I thought about how we screwed you over. Thunderbolt was your horse. I wanted to call and ask you to come back, but Doda said I had to live with what I'd done."

"Blackballing a twelve-year-old is one thing, Joshua. But this other? You two should be in prison."

After he left the room, Kathy removed the ear buds and said, "I thought you said he was funny."

"He was once."

42

The day I got out of the hospital I got a call from Mac Fontana, whom I'd contacted earlier. Fontana was a fire chief in a small town east of Seattle and had a police dog, Satan, who'd received his training in a Schutzen club in Germany. Satan took a whiff of Pickles' blanket and then, in a workmanlike manner, zigzagged and backtracked the paths in Discovery Park until he pinpointed Pickles' lair, taking less than an hour to do a job we'd been working on for the better part of a week. It was hard to know why I hadn't thought of it earlier.

When we found her, the dachshund was tired, hungry, and nervous, but we netted her and she quickly calmed when she saw the other dog. We had her examined and treated by a veterinarian, and then we placed her in our fenced backyard with our own dog, LC, who was glad of a new friend, his tail wagging furiously. Though wary at first, after a day with LC, Pickles relaxed amidst the companionship of another canine and the security of a fenced yard.

When I phoned Charlie at Mrs. Kennedy's house and told him the dachshund had been retrieved, the disappointment in his voice was palpable. He'd been making daily pilgrimages to Discovery Park on his bicycle.

Using volunteer search teams, two spotter planes, and men with tracking dogs, the authorities launched a monumental manhunt for Herbert Cavendish, combing the mountainous terrain surrounding Mount Rainier each day until the light gave way to darkness. When a search helicopter scoured the area, they found a small plane that had been missing for eighteen years, three moldy skeletons still strapped inside, but still no Herbert Cavendish.

The surveillance tapes from the marina showed me getting cold-cocked with a pipe wrench and then, a few moments later, Snake, bound hand and foot, a sack over his head, being carried out to the car by three burly men who punched him in the face when he offered resistance.

Carole Cooper and her team were unable to find any traces of an organization called The Auckland Group, and Charlene could only give a vague description of the person she'd been in contact with. Chad, under advice from his attorneys, refused to talk at all and took an extended vacation to the Cayman Islands.

Fingerprint experts put names to the two dead men in the hills. Just as we thought, the man who'd died in the back seat of the car was the second boxer from California, Frederick C. Lovell.

The other dead man was a former federal law officer, an ex FBI agent who'd been drummed out of the service for drug use and sexual misadventures with a witness in the Justice Department's protection program. His name was McIntosh, and he was found to have had a connection with Turner and Lovell in the past.

Searches of Lovell's, Turner's, and McIntosh's living quarters in the San Francisco Bay area revealed evidence related to other crimes which were now being investigated by California authorities and the FBI.

Two years earlier, all three men from California had been implicated in a massive fraud in Denver, where hundreds of investors in a new professional sports franchise were scammed out of tens of millions of dollars. The three men had apparently played a part as hired muscle by intimidating regulators who were on to the fraud, although after a series of strung-out trials, all three men were freed without convictions.

Among other bits in a growing mountain of evidence against Cavendish was the mounting plate and Tecktrixonic Remote camera we'd known all along had been in the Kraft's apple tree. The camera showed up during a warrant search of Cavendish's storage locker in the Interbay area in Seattle, complete with footage taken through the Krafts' bedroom window.

On Friday of the next week, I drove Snake and Pickles to Doda's. On our way, we stopped in West Seattle to pick up Charlie Hatcher, who wore a clean, button-down shirt and freshly laundered jeans for the occasion. In the car he renewed his acquaintance with Pickles while he chattered about the most recent library books he'd been reading. He was researching the Old West at the moment, possibly because earlier in the week I'd told him Doda was a hundred and four and had known several celebrities in her time, including Wyatt Earp. More than ever, he reminded me of me at that age, for I'd haunted the local public library, too, still did.

Mac Fontana, the owner of the German Shepherd who'd tracked the dachshund in Discovery Park, had generously gifted the reward money to Charlie after I told him about the boy. When Doda found this out, she applauded Fontana's generosity and asked if she could present the check in person.

The mansion was quiet, no Maseratis in the drive, no pool parties, no uniformed maids scrubbing the floor, and nobody at the bottom of the pool holding his breath. It was more like a mausoleum than a frat house, and because the stillness was so pervasive and overwhelming, I could almost see why Doda might welcome the raucous diversion her nephew and his friends provided.

We were greeted at the front door by Charlene, who seemed older and more enfeebled than she had just the previous week, but then, so did I. I'd just come out of the hospital. Upstairs in her office, Doda once again presided behind her grand antique desk as if she were royalty, smiling when Snake and I entered the room with Charlie Hatcher. As was the case with a lot of the elderly, she appreciated youth in a way many of us did not. "I understand you're the young man responsible for recovering Pickles," she said, without taking her eyes off him.

"No, ma'am. I can't take credit for that. Somebody else found her. I guess you could say I was in second place. The silver medal."

"That's no matter. From what I've been told, you did

an admirable job."

"Thank you."

"With that in mind, I'd like to present you with this bankbook. We've set up an account for you where your Mrs. Kennedy can't lay her hands on it."

"You know Mrs. Kennedy?"

"No, but Thomas filled me in on your situation. When we're finished here, he'll take you to the bank for signatures. I trust you'll be responsible with your money."

"I'm going to save it for my education."

Doda nodded, surveying him steadily with her rheumy blue eyes, then turned to me.

"While you're here, Thomas, tell me about Binky. How was he related to all this trouble you've managed to uncover while you were looking for Pickles?"

"SPD has reopened their investigation of the Kraft killing. Mick Kraft did not kill his wife or his mother-in-law. He didn't commit suicide, either. A neighbor murdered all three of them during a presumed attempted sexual assault on Alex, whom he'd been stalking. And as a result of those murders, Binky paid out ten million dollars in a wager with his pal, Chad."

Charlie hadn't heard any of this yet, was staring at me in wonder.

"But why?" Doda asked.

I explained Binky and Chad's game of wagering on their ability to manipulate the lives of ordinary people, turning them into puppets, and then detailed their escalating wagers with regard to the Kraft family.

Doda was incredulous—as was everyone who'd heard the tale—over the thought of people trifling with lives of others for the perverse fun of it.

To have had all this going on under her own roof—for Binky had been living with her for most of the past year—was particularly disturbing to Doda. It was equally disturbing to me to realize how little it would ultimately cost Binky and Chad.

"Just tell me something, Thomas. And I need to know this from your heart. Was Binky involved in the killing? Tell me the truth."

"The neighbor, Cavendish, killed the Krafts and her mother, then he sent for his thug friends from San Francisco on the pretext of collecting the reward for the dog, which he told them was fifty thousand, not five. They were trying to eliminate Snake and me as competition for the reward money, but Cavendish's true motivation for getting them involved was to get rid of us before we could expose him as a murderer."

"Thomas. Send me a bill for all this. I want to pay for your medical expenses and your lost work time, too. And young man?" She turned to Charlie. "Do you have any questions?"

"I do, ma'am. Just one."

"And what is that?"

"Did you really know Wyatt Earp?"

A hundred years of wisdom and kindness radiating from her eyes, Doda smiled at Charlie. When she asked Snake and me to leave them alone, the two of us went downstairs and stared at the historical photographs on the walls. It was close to an hour before Charlie joined us. I was hoping Doda had seen in Charlie what I'd seen, for she had it within her power to change his life with a casual wave of her hand. Funding an education account for him would mean next to nothing to her financially and pretty much everything to him, but then I remembered reusing paper napkins at the ranch in Wyoming, getting socks for my birthday, and re-gifted religious books for Christmas. Like a lot of the wealthy, she'd always been tight with a penny.

"Well?" I said, when Charlie rejoined us, his face beaming.

"She said Wyatt Earp was an old man when she knew him. She said he was a pimp. And not everything he was cracked up to be in the newspapers. She said he smelled bad. She knew General Custer's wife in New York. Custer once shot his own horse in the head by accident. She said that was all she ever needed to know about him. How could you shoot your own horse by accident?"

"He probably had his finger on the trigger of his gun while he was riding," said Snake. "Horse hits a bump. Bang.

First lesson of guns. Keep your finger off the trigger until you're going to shoot."

"What else?" I asked.

"She gave me these." He fanned out a handful of recent issues of the *Christian Science Sentinel*. It was unlikely Doda would bypass a potential recruit without burying him in religious pamphlets. She'd done the same to me when I was a kid. She felt she had the truth and didn't want us to miss out on it.

Two weeks later a pair of hunters scouting an area just northeast of Mount Rainier prior to hunting season came across the bloated and decomposing body of Herbert Cavendish. The location was more than nineteen miles from where he'd taken us to be killed and buried. Beside the body lay a cellphone with a dead battery. The corpse wore a pistol in an expensive hand-made holster and was missing one shoe. Authorities matched the gun to a bullet pulled from one of the trees near our shootout, which gave them the last piece of evidence to confirm Cavendish had been shooting at us and that our story held water.

He'd wandered the mountains for over a week before succumbing to exposure and bad mushrooms the Medical examiner guessed he must have eaten out of desperation. It turned out a bullet, probably the last one I fired, had taken a chunk out of one of his ears, sawed it half off, so that it was dangling off the side of his face while he wandered the hills, lost and disoriented, hiding from the search parties he should have been hailing, feverish from the infected ear and dehydrated from lack of potable water.

It was a lousy way for anybody to die, but then, the manner he'd intended for us wasn't all that rosy.

Once again Snake and I were questioned by Carole Cooper, who appeared to be looking for something to pin on us. It was hard for her to believe all those people were dead and Elmer and I weren't, that they were all guilty and we were blameless, or at least blameless enough not to get charged with anything. I found it hard to believe myself. I liked to think that in the end good always won out, but I had to admit it didn't always happen that way, not that either Elmer or I was particularly good.

"Gonna take more than three hardened killers and thirty feet of duct tape to get rid of me," Snake told Carole Cooper.

Pondering our narrow escape, I was not nearly as sanguine as Snake, though I suspected Snake's boasting was mostly hot air, a pose he'd taken on so his brain didn't have to accept how close the two of us had come to disappearing without a trace. It bothered me. It became something I thought about late at night when I should have been asleep.

We'd escaped and ultimately triumphed through a combination of factors which probably would never repeat themselves, not if we replayed that night a hundred times. I'd had other close calls in my life, but I'd been able to shake them off. I wasn't so lucky with this one. There were times over the course of the next year where I had the feeling Snake and I had entered an alternate universe, a universe wherein we were allowed to keep on living, while our former selves got dispatched and buried in the first universe. It was a strange feeling, but I couldn't shake it.

It took several weeks, but Stephanie Chin found another job at a larger company. The people at Vereecken and Sons offered to hire her back, but she refused, saying she could no longer tolerate the place.

The extent to which Chad and Binky had been manipulating people and destroying lives bothered me as much as the predatory neighbor who'd been spying on Alex Kraft and who eventually broke or conned his way into her house with plans to assault her, murdering the whole family in the end.

I was also aware that if the deaths had actually played out in the manner posited by the police and media, Chad and Binky would have been morally responsible, though it was doubtful either would subscribe to that view. I wondered if either of them felt any guilt over their actions.

Kathy's love-hate relationship with Elmer revealed itself late one evening when she asked me whether Snake still made a practice of sleeping with married women, usually those with drinking or drug problems. I told her his girlfriends were typically running away from something, either a husband or an addiction, or in some cases, both. "It's a question of like searching out like."

She let out a grunt of disapproval and said, "But he did save your life."

"Absolutely."

"And he helped you save my life last year."

"Absolutely."

"So I'm in his debt. Forever. Damn it. I hate being in his debt."

"He's that kind of a friend, maddening, but someone you're glad to have around when it counts. Definitely somebody you'd want in the bomb shelter."

"Only if it's well-ventilated. He's got a gas problem. Have you noticed?"

"Riding in that trunk with him nearly killed me."

"In more ways than one. There's something else. Did you win some money betting you could stand on the bottom of a swimming pool longer than Binky?"

"Who told you that?"

"You did."

"What?"

"In the hospital. You were a little loopy from the morphine. You fessed up to all kinds of things, including making that stupid bet."

"It wasn't stupid. I won."

"I'm just quoting you. You're the one who called it stupid."

"You said it yourself. I was on drugs."

"Not when you made the bet."

"Yes, well, there *is* that."

"How much did you bet?"

"I bet a hundred initially."

"You bet a hundred dollars you could hold your breath longer than him? What were you thinking? You told me you were going to try to be more of an adult."

"I walked away with four hundred."

"But you're going to give that money to charity, right?"

"What? Already done. The Children's Christmas fund. Are you mad at me?"

"No. I just thought you were going to make an effort to

grow up."

"I thought I was grown up."

"Sometimes you are. After all that's happened, I'm just glad you're still here with me and not up in the mountains moldering in a national park."

"Not as glad as I am."

"Oh, I think I'm more glad."

"I'm more glad."

"I am."

"Prove it."

"Perhaps I will, if you think you've completely recovered from your head injury."

"I'm plenty healthy."

"Right now?"

"Now would be great. And then maybe again later."

"My," she said, slipping into my arms. "You must be feeling extra healthy."

"I think I am," I said, kissing her. "By the way. . . what other things did I confess to while I was loopy?"

"If you're good, I'll tell you one day."

I made a mental note to contact the Children's Christmas fund so I could make a donation.

Made in the USA
Middletown, DE
13 July 2019